ELEMENT OF LIFE

ORDER OF THE ELEMENTS: BOOK 5

EMMA L. ADAMS

PREFACE

The magically gifted have always lived among us.

After centuries of living in hiding, a group of mages banded together and created their own parallel world to the everyday one, a paradise designed as a home for the magically inclined. Mages, vampires, elves, shapeshifters and many others flocked there, and for centuries, they flourished, ruled over by the Council of the Elements.

Then, several decades ago, the spirit mages turned on their fellow Elements and slaughtered them. The resulting war brought an end to the old Council of the Elements and left the magical world in ruins.

Since then, it has remained fractured. Clans of shapeshifters, vampires, and others rule the cities, while the Court of the Dead dominates the areas even the bravest fear to tread. It may be a paradise no longer, but to many of the magically inclined, it's still home.

Welcome to the Parallel.

If there was one guarantee in my life, it was that the Order of the Elements would always show up in my life whenever I least wanted them to.

I might have been grateful for the mundane intrusion, considering my recent return from within the jaws of death, but that didn't mean I had to look at the two Order members who entered Devon's shop that morning with anything other than wary disdain. Especially when one of them was my former nemesis, Judith French, and the second was a shifter called Femi who'd been her backup when she'd tried to have me arrested.

"You've come to the wrong shop." I reached for the pouch at my waist, prepared to employ a cantrip or two if they refused to leave. "We don't do business with Order lackeys."

"I'm not," she said. "We're not with the Order, I mean. We don't work for them anymore."

I raised a brow. "And I'm in the running to be the next Death King."

"It's true," she said defensively. "I know you and I haven't always got along, but I'm not lying. Both of us decided to leave the Order at the same time."

"What do you want me to say, congratulations?" Did she have nothing better to do than to come into our shop and try to get me to fall for her bullshit? "Sure you weren't fired?"

That was the only reason I could think of for Judith to willingly leave the organisation she'd devoted her entire life to serving. She'd happily let her job become her personality, and I couldn't imagine her throwing it all away of her own accord.

Admittedly, she wasn't dressed in the smart casual office wear she usually wore when the Order sent her to hassle us, while her lank dark hair looked as though she hadn't washed it in days. A far cry from the polished exterior she'd worn the last time I'd seen her in the Order's base, guarding one of their top-secret labs. As for me, I wore my usual jeans and nerdy T-shirt rather than the armoured uniform of one of the Death King's guards, a position I'd never officially given up despite my return to relative normality. I'd prefer for Judith not to upend my fragile new life by bringing the Order's security on her tail.

"I wasn't fired." Judith's face flushed. "I'm telling the truth."

"Right." Why was I wasting my time talking to these people? Judith and her friends had had it out for me since our days at the academy, especially after I'd ended up on trial for learning illegal spirit magic and had lost a huge chunk of my memories as a consequence. She'd seen to it that I made a nice collection of fresh unpleasant memories in the months and years afterwards, and even if she *had* left the Order, I was the last person she'd seek advice from, and the feeling was mutual.

"We oppose Mr Holland's new position in the upper room," said Femi.

Judith nodded. "We want him fired and jailed for breaking the Order's laws."

"Tell that to the upper room, not me." I kept my tone disinterested, though her words made my heart skip a beat. *Did she finally see sense?* "I don't work for the Order anymore."

"Neither do I, for the most part," said Devon from behind me. "They don't listen to me unless they want to buy cantrips from me, and I've never said a word to the upper room in my life. Did you actually hand in your notice and officially quit?"

"Well…" Judith faltered.

I tilted my head. "You didn't. So you're still reporting to the Order."

"We aren't," she insisted. "We're still Order members because otherwise they'd hunt us down and demand an explanation, but we're working against them from within."

Hmm. Perhaps it wasn't surprising that some of the Order's members had begun to question how things were run, given that Mr Holland had seized his position through illegal means, but that didn't mean I could trust any of them as far as I could throw them.

"That's a risky decision to make," I said. "You saw what happens to people who get in Holland's way."

"We saw," said Femi. "In London. We weren't invited to the gathering, but if we had been, we'd both be dead."

Judith's mouth pressed together. "We saw it on the news. It was horrific. But... but the Death King got out, didn't he?"

Hmm. Seeing the carnage of the explosion at the Order's event might have been a wakeup call, if they hadn't believed the public story, but both of them must know they had no way to stand up to the spirit mages now controlling the Order's highest ranks. The one person who might be able to help them was the Death King, which was likely the real reason they'd picked me to come to for advice.

"I was there, too," I said. "I barely escaped with my life, and yet as far as I'm aware, it's the spirit mages who took the blame for the attack, despite the fact that it wasn't them who were responsible."

"I know it wasn't," said Judith. "It was him. Holland."

Not just him. Holland wasn't a spirit mage, and he was merely a figurehead placed in control of Birmingham's Order branch so nobody would unearth the real culprits behind the attacks.

Namely: Hawker, a former lich... and Dirk Alban, my old mentor.

"Look," Devon said. "As thrilled as I am that you've finally realised the obvious, that doesn't mean we need another target painted on our backs. If you want to plot against the Order from the inside, you'll need a lot more allies, and you'll need somewhere to hang out which isn't our house."

"We already have one," said Femi. "We've been meeting up at Carla He's place."

My brows shot up. "Is that why she and Craig have stopped coming to D&D night?"

At least they'd had the sense not to draw more attention to Devon and me, though I didn't appreciate Judith recruiting my friends to risk their necks alongside her when she had about as much experience at espionage as I had at professional skydiving.

Thankfully, at that moment, my phone buzzed in my pocket. "I have to take this call."

I pushed open the door to the back room and walked through, accepting the call as I closed the door behind me.

"Liv?" Mum's voice came from the other end.

"Hey, Mum," I said. "How's Elise?"

"She's great," Mum responded. "She's baby-proofing the house. I haven't had to do that for a long while."

Mum had had me at a young age, before she and Dad had split up, and while she'd met and married Elise when I was a teenager, I hadn't known of their plans to have any more kids until fairly recently. Her wife's upcoming offspring might have been a delightful surprise if it wasn't for my worry that my future sibling might find themselves saddled with the same issues I had. Magic wasn't always genetic, and my spirit magic had been self-taught besides, but I still couldn't guarantee their safety as long as Alban and Hawker were at large. No matter how hard I tried to keep my family away from the weirdness that comprised the majority of my life, it always seemed to find them anyway.

Mum and I chatted for a few minutes about everyday topics of little consequence, then I excused myself once I was sure Judith and her friend had gone. I re-joined Devon in the shop, where she glowered at me. "Thanks for leaving me alone with them. I had to promise to take Judith's phone number down in order to get rid of her."

"What's going on with Judith?" I picked up the paper on which she'd scribbled her number. "I'm not sure even *she* knows what she's getting herself into."

"That's her problem," Devon said. "Never mind her. Let's get on with prepping for D&D night."

"Now we're talking."

———

A few hours later, our game night kicked off. We had a smaller group than usual, with the newer addition of Bria, the Death King's Fire Element and the second of the Elemental Soldiers to join our campaign. Opposite her sat Ryan, the Air Element, next to Trix, my elf friend and the only member of our original group present aside from Devon and me. Meanwhile, Dex, my fire sprite sidekick, flew around playing NPCs and causing sparks to dance across the board whenever we needed to increase the tension.

Bria scowled when she rolled a natural one at a critical moment and face-planted instead of striking the enemy. She'd learned the rules pretty fast, considering she'd been born in the Parallel and had never even picked up a die before Dex had strong-armed her into joining our group. Without three of our other members—two of whom had apparently gone off to join Judith's ill-conceived attempt at a vigilante group working against the Order from the inside—we'd had to adjust our campaign, but Devon was a good improviser and gave everyone a fair shot. It was also a way to exercise my lucky dice—which had earned the nickname because of a particularly fortuitous streak during our first campaign—and to thoroughly forget the Order and its associated bullshit.

After we paused the game for the night, the others travelled through the node on top of our house and back into the Parallel. Devon, meanwhile, started to clear away the discarded takeout cartons around the game board. "Aren't you going back to the castle?"

"In a bit." I helped her tidy up, wondering if it was worth telling the Death King about Judith's visit earlier. I hadn't mentioned it to the others, but maybe he could offer me advice on whether I could make use of having allies within the Order. It wasn't like he'd never done the same himself, after all.

"Thought you were gonna convince the Death King to join our group," Devon said. "Go on, I'll clean up the rest. I know you want to see him."

"Cheers." I grabbed my coat along with my Parallel bag and the pouch containing my cantrips. Then I hopped through the node, passing through the invisible current of light through the middle of our living room and landing in the muddy area near the fence circling the Death King's castle.

Outside the gates, I spotted Bria and Trix talking to one another, but they parted ways before I caught them up. Bria entered the castle's grounds, while the elf remained outside. He gave a smile and wave when he saw me.

"What were you talking to Bria about?" I asked Trix.

He shrugged. "Oh, not much."

"You don't have to keep secrets from me," I said to the elf. "You know you can trust me, right? I don't tell tales."

Trix drew in a breath. "Okay… I'm trying to find the elves."

"The elves?" I blinked. "You mean aside from your friends?"

"There aren't many of us left," he said, "but the Death King thinks they would make good allies."

"He has a point," I said. "You're friendly with the other elves in Arcadia, aren't you?"

"Yes, and Bria is going to help, too," he told me. "It'll be good for her to get in contact with her kin."

"Her…" I trailed off. "She's an elf."

Of course. It'd taken me way too long to realise Bria wasn't fully human, but she had a hell of a lot more secrets than she let on. Not that I was one to talk, but still. *An elf?*

"Yes… half elf and half human," said Trix. "She didn't tell you?"

"Must have missed that one." The clues seemed obvious in retrospect, from her speed and stealth to the fact that she shared so little of her own history. "I'm guessing the Death King knows."

"He knew before I did."

That figured. At least Bria hadn't been recruiting the elf to join some shady scheme, because it wouldn't be a wise idea to attract the annoyance of the Death King's Air Element. Last I'd heard, Ryan had every intention of asking the elf out on a date. "All right. I'll see you in a bit, Trix. Be careful, okay?"

After Trix had departed, I entered the darkened grounds through the gate and approached the castle. I didn't need to knock anymore, so I pushed open the oak doors and stepped into the entrance hall.

The Death King waited for me on the dais at the back. It wasn't immediately obvious he wasn't a lich wearing an illusion of his own face, not when he'd always worn the same outfit which covered him from head to toe even when he'd been dead. Only subtle differences stood out, like the fact that he no longer floated above the ground, and there was a solidness to his presence which hadn't been there before. It was late at night, but he still wore the full armour and long coat of the King of the Dead, but it was Greyson Beaumont who looked back at me from his eyes, and he didn't hesitate for an instant before striding up and taking my hand, pulling me against him.

"Ow," I said, when we broke apart. "I didn't notice how spiky that uniform of yours is before."

"It's protective armour," he said. "It wouldn't do much good if it was made of feathers."

I poked him in the chest. "You didn't even need armour as a lich."

"No, but it looks impressive."

I snorted. "Were you always this conceited?"

"I've been dead a long time." He slid a hand up the side of my face. "Give me the chance to enjoy being alive again."

I knew the feeling. Not only had I recently been dead myself, but everyone had thought the curse on the former House of Spirit had been irreversible, and none more so than their leader. That he'd been granted a second chance at life was a miracle I wouldn't easily forget.

"*Are* you enjoying it?" I asked.

He searched my face. "You sound surprised."

"I thought you were struggling to adjust." As a lich, my emotions had been dampened and I'd felt disconnected from my very self, but I'd only endured that existence for a short time. For the Death King, it'd been years, and after his return to life, he'd spent a week hiding from public view, believing his fellow liches would displace him at the first opportunity. Needless to say, I'd talked some sense into him, but I'd suspected he'd take a while to fully adjust to being human again.

"My other liches have been difficult to deal with, but there are upsides." His fingers brushed behind my ear, causing warmth to pool inside me. At the same time, a question nudged at the back of my mind. Had we done this before? I couldn't remember the details. He'd implied liches could theoretically have sexual relationships with non-liches if they were good enough at conjuring up an illusion of a human form, but I'd lost my memories before he'd become King of the Dead. We hadn't exactly ended our relationship on a good note, considering the secrets we'd been keeping had led to both of our untimely deaths. Really, I should have known from studying Shake-spearean tragedies at the Order's academy that that would end badly.

"What is it?" he asked. "What are you thinking?"

"I'm thinking that there's still a lot I don't remember," I said. "About us, I mean."

Greyson tilted his head. "Have you remembered any more since you came back?"

"No." The occasional glimpses I'd had into my past had stopped after my return to life, and I hadn't had any new recollections about our shared history. We'd been close to one another, I knew, yet it seemed I hadn't told him about my gift for spirit magic, and *he* hadn't told me his days were numbered and always had been. Every spirit mage born into the House of Spirit invariably turned into a lich, but Dirk Alban had learned magic independently and had killed the last Death King in an attempt to return the spirit mages to supremacy. He'd also trained me to be his successor, but I'd turned on him at the last minute, ripping out his soul and nearly dying in the process. In saving my life, Greyson had given up his own and became the new Death King, and he'd believed that change would be permanent.

Ten years later and the miracle that had saved both of us had also returned my dead mentor to life again. Dirk Alban's soul had remained bound to an amulet which the vampires had stolen from the scene of his death, but Hawker had managed to steal it back and resurrect its owner. Now all three of us were locked into the same conflict again, and my lack of insight into my own history made it difficult not to worry that this battle would end the same as the last one.

"Nothing?" he said.

I shook my head. "Maybe I need another near-death experience in order to remember."

His brow crinkled. "I'd rather keep those to a minimum."

"Guess I could always ask Judith," I said. "She showed up at our shop earlier claiming she left the Order and that she believes me. Mad, eh?"

"She's had a change of heart, has she?" he said. "I'm not surprised."

"I am," I said. "I can't believe she expected *me* to help her plot against the Order from the inside."

"Maybe she didn't know who else to ask," he said.

"That's depressing as shit," I told him. "If you ask me,

she's trying to find a way of absolving herself of any blame for all the crap she did to me at the academy. *That,* I wish I could forget."

His expression turned preoccupied. "I can't say I know her reasons, but it might be that knowing what Holland did weighed too heavily on her conscience."

Hmm. "How are the other liches dealing with the situation, then?"

"With great impatience," he said. "Some of them, anyway. The majority had long resigned themselves to living under the curse, but with my return to life coupled with Hawker's attempts to lure them away… they're restless and angry."

"I figured." It wasn't Greyson's fault he'd been hit by a cantrip which would have brought him to a permanent end if I hadn't seen to it that he'd returned to life instead, with the side effect of freeing him from the curse which bound the entire House of Spirit. But the other liches didn't necessarily see it that way. "They're just going to have to wait their turn."

"Yes…" He lifted his head, looking around the hall. Then his gaze sharpened.

"What is it?" I asked.

"Someone's attacking the castle," said Greyson.

2

Greyson and I left the castle at once, descending the stone staircase into the grounds. His long-legged stride overtook me in seconds, while it still sometimes took me off guard to see him walking and not gliding above the ground like a lich. He reached the gates first, where two grisly piles of flesh and bone lay in the place where his security liches had stood.

"Those cantrips again." I swore. "But who—?"

A cold sensation rippled over my skin as a pair of invisible hands reached for my life essence. I spun around, facing the dark form of a lich camouflaged against the gloom.

So there are more traitors in here, are there?

A second lich bore down on Greyson, whose hand thrust deep into the lich's core, ripping out its life force. I did the same to the second lich, and a stream of energy flowed from its shadowy form into my palm. Power flooded my veins, light rippling through my fingertips as the lich evaporated into nothingness.

Greyson headed towards the stone staircase. "Backup will be here in a second. I'm going to the hall of souls."

Another lich tried to follow him, but I barred its path, draining its life essence until its shadowy form evaporated on the spot. As Greyson vanished through the front entrance into the lobby, the Elemental Soldiers sprinted from the direction of the castle's back door, while several Spirit Agents astral projected into the castle grounds. Assuming they were Greyson's backup, I ran to help them fight off the remaining attackers.

Miles reached into another lich and wrenched out its life force. I tracked down another, but in the gloom, the shadowy liches were hard to spot unless they used magic and drew attention to themselves. My less-than-stellar eyesight didn't help, though I found myself glad I'd worn my contacts and not my glasses, because if they'd been knocked off, I'd have a hell of a time tracking them down. Even so, I had to rely on the light of the astral projecting spirit mages to find my targets. When the last lich turned to dust, I headed to the gates to find Ryan, who'd discovered the two heaps of flesh and bone which had once been guarding the castle.

"How'd they get in?" Bria came to join us, wearing a pair of baggy shorts and a T-shirt along with slippers which looked several sizes too big, suggesting she'd been woken from a dead sleep when she'd been called to help defend the castle and had grabbed the first clothes she could reach. "What happened to the liches on security duty?"

"Judge for yourself," said Ryan.

Bria regarded the two piles of rotting flesh, her face paling. "Were those *liches?*"

"You remember I mentioned cantrips which can make the undead fall to pieces?" I said. "The cantrips return them to life, only for their magic to eat them from the inside out."

"Fuck."

Pretty much. It surprised me that she hadn't seen them before, though maybe it shouldn't have, since she hadn't moved to the castle until after the Crow's death and the consequent end of my frequent encounters with disintegrating phantoms which had fallen victim to his cantrips. The Elemental Soldiers launched into a discussion about taking it in turns to guard the castle themselves so the enemy wouldn't be able to try the same trick again, while I crouched beside the piles of rotting flesh and tried not to breathe in the stench while I hunted for the cantrip which had finished them off.

Bria's eyes rounded when I picked up the cantrip and showed it to the others. "I thought all the cantrips with their mark on them were destroyed."

"Whose mark?" I asked her, not recognising the curling lines on its surface.

"Long story." When I shot her a suspicious look, she added, "They're called the Family, and they like to put their signature on things."

"Hawker was using them before," Miles added. "Might be him."

I studied Bria, wondering how much she'd really known about the illegally created cantrips. I'd never had much in the way of conclusive answers about this so-called Family, though I'd heard their title mentioned before, but the consensus was that they were Bria's problem to deal with since we had more than enough enemies of our own. Like Dirk Alban, Hawker, the Order… and whoever had decided to disintegrate the Death King's security liches. As if we'd needed the reminder that even being dead wasn't a guarantee of protection—not to mention that the Death King had nearly perished due to one of those cantrips himself. This was a message, all right, and not a pleasant one.

I went back into the castle, in search of Greyson, and found him standing outside the hall of souls. Dex was there, too, flitting around the ceiling in a trail of fiery light.

"No trouble?" said Greyson. "You dealt with them all?"

"Aside from the person who threw lich-killing cantrips at your security," I said. "Is Hawker under the impression those cantrips can do you any harm?"

"I suspect not," he said. "No… this was most likely a threat to the other liches, and a reminder that they aren't free from the curse yet."

I'd thought as much. If Dirk Alban had shown up, he wouldn't have simply thrown a cantrip and ran off. Maybe Hawker would, but I got the impression the two were working closely together and that Alban wouldn't appreciate him going behind his back. Especially as most of Dirk Alban's former allies had already met unfortunate ends. His other apprentice, Mr Cobb, had died at Hawker's hands after the two had come to blows, while the Crow had escaped Alban's fate by turning into a vampire, only to end up being killed by one of the same cantrips Hawker had eventually used to bring both himself and his former ally back to life. If I were a lich, I'd be reluctant to join them, given their track record, but desperation bred questionable choices.

"Want to search the swamp for the person responsible?" I asked. "Or will they have fled by now?"

"Most likely, but the vampires might appreciate a warning," he said. "Lord Blackbourne hasn't contacted me since he packed up and moved."

"Of course he hasn't," I said. "He only agreed to stay near Arcadia so you wouldn't take his authority away from him. Do you even know his new address?"

The vampires had vacated their headquarters and moved to a different location after several attacks on their council house in the centre of Arcadia. Their choice was somewhat understandable due to their proximity to Arcadia's citadel and its transporter, but Lord Blackbourne's penchant for running away at times of crisis was starting to wear on me.

"I do," he said. "I think it's worth paying him a visit, if just to see where we stand with the vampire lords."

"Sure, why not." It was close to midnight, but the vampires were most active at this hour and I was too wired to go home and sleep after the fight.

Greyson led the way out of the castle grounds, where Ryan had moved the remains of the dead liches out into the swamp to bury them properly.

"We're trading shifts," they said. "Bria will be joining me on security duty in a minute."

"Good," said the Death King. "I'd advise you to work out a rota between yourselves."

"There are only four of them, though," I reminded him as we walked towards the node. "The Elemental Soldiers can't stand guard twenty-four hours a day, not if they want to get anything else done."

"I hoped to convince the Spirit Agents to move here to

the castle, too," he said. "But they have yet to accept my offer."

"Oh, right." The Spirit Agents were the only independent group of spirit mages I knew of here in the Parallel, and Greyson had lived with them before his ascension to the position of the King of the Dead. I still had a fair number of questions about that phase of his life. "Speaking of the Spirit Agents, I wondered why you went to school at the Order's academy, if you grew up in the Parallel. Is that typical?"

"My mum enrolled me at the academy," he answered. "She wanted me to have a life outside of the Parallel, so she paid for me to attend the Order's best school. I kept up my studies out of habit after both my parents were dead, travelling back and forth between Earth and the Parallel."

We stepped through the node and reappeared somewhere on the outskirts of the far side of Arcadia, which I vaguely recognised from when we'd confronted the vampires who'd been involved in the illegal cantrip trade.

"I never asked," I continued. "What happened to them? Your parents, I mean? Did they fall under the curse, too?"

He was silent for a long moment. "My parents were in their late teens at the time of the war. They escaped its effects by a hair's breadth, but they didn't expect to have a child so soon afterwards. My father succumbed to the curse before I was born. I found out later on that he chose to die a permanent death to avoid being chained to the Court of the Dead, and he never knew I existed. My mother, on the other hand, asked to have her magic permanently taken away in order to enable her to raise me without falling prey to the curse herself, but she died when I was thirteen."

Oh, Greyson. My eyes pricked with tears, and I looked away, blinking hard as I squinted at our dark surroundings. The street was far neater than I'd normally expect of the Parallel, more like a middle-class suburb back in England than the battle-scarred streets of central Arcadia. Manor houses stood at intervals, each surrounded by wide lawns and neat gardens. We weren't that far from the Crow's old house, which had been blown to pieces courtesy of the combined magic the Death King and I had unleashed against him. Lord Blackbourne must have concluded there was no remaining threat at his former ally's base, but this part of the city would have made me edgy if not for Greyson's steady presence at my side.

Greyson was in full Death King mode when we reached the doors to a manor house surrounded by hedges carved to resemble various animals. Like all vampires' abodes, dark curtains were pulled across the windows to keep out every speck of daylight. A dazed-looking human stood at the end of the gravel path which led to the door, his eyes shining and bite marks on his pale neck.

"We're here to see Lord Blackboune," said Greyson.

"Is he expecting you?" asked the human.

The Death King gave him a look. The kid's gaze flickered up and down his armoured outfit, comprehension dawning as he realised who he was talking to. "Back in a second."

"I swear they're getting slower," I muttered.

"Being a vampire's subjugate takes its toll, I imagine," said Greyson.

The human returned a few moments later, breathlessly beckoning us into the manor house. "Come in."

We followed him into the hallway. Like all vampires' homes, the decor was sumptuous, all gilt fittings and polished wood. The crimson carpet—which I'd assumed had been artfully chosen to hide bloodstains—led to a room dominated by a long table which might well have been lifted from the old council house. There, the leader of the local vampires waited for us, dressed in his usual smart attire. Lord Blackbourne's elegant features suggested Asian heritage, while his dark hair was as glossy as his polished shoes.

The leader of the vampires smiled at us. "Being human suits you, Greyson. Oh, and you brought Olivia with you, too. Excellent. To what do I owe the pleasure?"

"Someone attacked the castle using one of those cantrips which kills the dead," I said. "I thought you'd want to know they're in circulation again."

"Oh, I'm aware of that," he said. "That's why I moved our council house to a suitable distance from the swamp."

"And you weren't just trying to avoid us?" I raised a brow. "I notice you didn't keep your distance from the Crow's old place."

"I saw no need to avoid it," he said. "The two of you ensured that it will never be used as a laboratory to concoct illegal cantrips again, after all."

"Doesn't mean all your fellow vamps are on the straight and narrow."

Lord Blackbourne eyed the Death King. "Does she speak like this to you, too? I suppose your shared history gives you a reason to dismiss her alarming lack of manners."

"I have no complaints with how Olivia speaks," said the Death King. "I do, however, agree with her statement. A number of your fellow vampires were involved in the Crow's illicit activities, and they might not all have perished alongside him."

"I believe the threat has been taken care of," said Lord Blackbourne. "However, you're right to be concerned about these cantrips."

He reached into a pocket and pulled out a gleaming coin, which was entirely blank except for a pattern of lines etched into the back that didn't look like part of the usual markings on an active cantrip.

"Recognise the mark?" asked the vampire lord.

I glanced at Greyson. "The same mark was on the cantrip someone threw at the Death King's security liches tonight. The attacker ran off without showing their face, leaving their lich allies to attempt to infiltrate the castle, but they failed. Do you know what the mark is?"

Bria had recognised it, too, but I hadn't been able to wrangle any answers out of her yet.

"The mark is a signature which belongs to a group who call themselves the Family," Lord Blackbourne said. "Rather bland, in my opinion. You've met some of their assassins before. They also worked with mages within the Houses of the Elements."

Ah. "So they were with Davies and the others who infiltrated the Death King's trials?"

"Among other things," he said. "The Crow obtained the materials for his cantrips from them. They're a known menace in Elysium, as Greyson is aware."

"Precisely," said the Death King. "Which is why I'd like to ask why you chose now to bring up the subject when you've been aware of the Family's existence for considerably longer than most."

Lord Blackbourne put the cantrip down on the table in front of him. "This so-called Family was one of the major sponsors of the illegal cantrip trade. They still are, and their current location remains unknown. The same with their manufacturers, whoever they may be."

"I have people searching Elysium for the manufacturers and the Family themselves," said the Death King. "I couldn't help but notice that none of your fellow vampires has volunteered to use their extensive connections to track them down, though they're certainly capable of doing so."

"We have been occupied in relocating our base," the vampire lord said. "Including our prisoners, some of whom were involved with the illegal cantrip trade themselves."

Damn. I'd forgotten that moving their base also meant moving their prisoners—including Brant, my ex-boyfriend, who'd been drawn into the illegal cantrip trade when he'd accidentally traded away his own soul to the vampire known as the Crow. His mistake had landed him in the Order's custody, who'd stripped away his fire magic before trading him over to the vampires to serve out the rest of his life sentence. His own choices had cost him dearly, and despite how he'd screwed me over, I couldn't forget that the Order had come close to stripping my magic away, too.

"So you know nothing of the manufacturers of those cantrips?" said the Death King. "Where did you obtain that one?"

"Some delightful person left it on my doorstep the day

after I relocated here," said Lord Blackbourne. "Not the homecoming I'd hoped for."

Oh, hell. "Nobody picked it up, did they?"

"My security human," he said. "Very luckily, the spell has no effect on the living, and we swiftly made use of a neutralising cantrip to dampen its effects before it hurt any of my fellow vampires."

"Where'd you get a neutraliser spell from?" There were only two possible answers, and there was no way Devon had sold one to him. "Did you steal them from the Order?"

"Such accusations, Olivia."

He sure as hell hadn't got them from Devon, and she'd been making neutralisers for us to use on the transporters in the citadels ever since the enemy had opened up a node linking Elysium to London. The route was closed for now, but only as long as we kept reapplying the neutralising cantrips on a daily basis. It wasn't like we could spare people to watch every citadel at once, but it would help if the vampires made the slightest effort to help us.

"I stole one myself, so I can't talk," I added. "Just wondered if you'd heard from the Order lately, since I had a couple of ex-Order members show up on my doorstep asking to make an alliance with me."

"How interesting," he said. "Anyone important?"

"Sadly not." Judith and Femi were low ranked, especially if the former had quit her new security job down in the basement. That had been risky enough on its own, considering defying Holland and his cronies was pretty much career suicide at best. He had the whole of the Order's local branch under his watch, and if we weren't careful, the rest of the country would follow.

Yet it wasn't the Order that had been Dirk Alban's target. He'd wanted the power of the Death King. That had always been his goal, and I had little doubt that had changed during the years since I'd last seen him alive.

"The Order has always fancied itself as the Court of the Dead's equivalent on Earth," said Lord Blackbourne. "They hold the lives of their mages in their hands… not in as literal a sense as yourself, of course, Greyson, though it wouldn't surprise me if they wished for as simple a measure of control."

What in hell was he going on about this time? "I don't follow."

"Come on." The Death King's voice was clipped. "If you have nothing more to share with us, then we're leaving. Do let me know if you find any more of those cantrips, won't you?"

"Naturally," said the vampire lord. "I bid you farewell."

Honestly. I'd hoped for more than cryptic statements that did nothing but fuel my annoyance, but we'd been dismissed, so the Death King and I left the vampire's house and retraced our steps through the suburban area towards the node we'd come in through.

As we walked, the Death King's persona slid away until Greyson walked at my side once again. "That was more instructive than I expected."

"Must have had low expectations, then," I said, with an eye-roll.

"Generally, it's best not to go in with any expectations whatsoever when it comes to the vampires," he said. "Lord Blackbourne is set in his ways. He's never dealt with a crisis like this before."

"Wasn't he alive during the last war, though?" I said. "Unless he hid underground…"

"That's precisely what he did," said Greyson. "He and his fellow vampires took refuge in their bunkers to escape the backlash of the spirit mages' battle. If they hadn't, they'd likely have perished along with most of the others who fought on the front lines."

I dug my hands in my pockets, annoyance prickling at me. "He can hardly blame us for wanting to avoid another war, then. What did he think would happen when he *stole* Dirk Alban's soul amulet and hid it in his house?"

"I imagine he assumed nobody would ever find out he had it."

That figured. "What about this Family, then? Isn't that something we should look into?"

"I put Bria in charge of handling them," said Greyson. "I can't say I know where this latest batch of cantrips came from, though."

Bria's handling them, is she? "Who's looking into the illegal cantrip trade, then?"

"The Spirit Agents," he answered. "We're sure there must be at least one hidden location where the Family's allies are manufacturing the cantrips, but not to the same extent as the Crow was before. They have their sights set on bigger and better things now, after all."

"You mean another war." We'd prevented said war at least twice already, but with Dirk Alban alive and kicking, I had little doubt that this would be his final gambit… and that he'd accounted for me in his plans.

After all, I'd once been primed to be his successor.

3

After we returned to the castle, I went back home to find Devon in case someone had left a warning cantrip for her, too. They hadn't, luckily, but my chat with the vampire lord had made me too uneasy to sleep properly, so I compensated by astral projecting from my bed in the hopes that my body would get sufficient rest while I was absent.

When I astral projected through the node into the castle, I found the Death King pacing outside the hall of souls, and he raised a brow when he saw me floating across the lobby. "You might as well have stayed in the castle."

"I didn't want the Order to ambush Devon while I wasn't around," I said. "Or whoever threw that cantrip at your security."

"Speaking of the Order," he said, "they sent a messenger here about half an hour ago."

"They did?" I said. "Who the hell sends messages at this time of night?"

Hawker. The night was his domain, whether he was human or lich. What was he doing now, using the Order as a mouthpiece?

"The messenger was human," he said. "And terrified, I might add."

"Speaking on behalf of whom?" I asked. "Not Mr Holland? Or whoever is calling the shots?"

"The very same," he said. "It seems he wishes to finish our conversation from the event in London."

"Conversation?" I echoed. "You mean the event where his allies used inferno cantrips to slaughter a few hundred people?"

"Yes, and where Holland offered to undo the curse on the Court of the Dead."

"Before the aforementioned cantrip incident," I added. "Yeah, no thanks."

"I got the distinct impression it wasn't the kind of invitation that one ought to decline," said Greyson.

"You're seriously thinking of going to meet with the Order?" I asked. "They tried to have us killed."

"Technically, they tried to frame us as murderers by causing a mass slaughter," he said. "They left us alive."

"Hell of a technicality."

The Spirit Agents had taken the blame, in fact, but it wasn't like they could defend themselves from the Order's slandering when they weren't even allowed to leave the Parallel without breaking the law. Yet the Order thought *Greyson* would agree to speak to them in person? Yeah, right.

"I want to know how many of them are reporting to our enemies," he said. "And how many might be convinced to join our side."

"Even if there were any remaining potential allies in the Order's ranks, they wouldn't announce themselves in front of Holland, would they?" I pointed out. "This couldn't be more of a trap if Devon was sitting in front of it wearing her 'this is a trap' DM face. If this is some master plan of yours, then please enlighten me."

Greyson studied my transparent form. "I have an inkling that our enemy is communicating via the Order."

"You mean Dirk Alban."

It made sense. He'd been in the Order's employment himself when he'd illegally taught me to use spirit magic during my time at the academy. Now his allies had completed his plan of infiltrating the Order's upper ranks, why wouldn't he return to the place which had inadvertently given him the means of attempting to help the spirit mages rise to power again? As a bonus, Mr Holland's predecessor had been the one who'd signed an agreement with the former Death King to place a curse upon the entire House of Spirit, so it added a nice sense of irony that he might end up being the one to remove said curse. If I believed a word any of them said, anyway, which I didn't. The curse was their leverage over the other liches, and I didn't see them relinquishing it anytime soon, whatever they claimed.

"It was me they invited," said Greyson. "But I thought you should know."

I studied his face, pale under the dim lighting of the hall. "You mean I don't have to come with you."

Tension crackled in the air as he waited for my answer. That he'd told me of the Order's message pointed to the shifting ground between us, given the number of times he'd exasperated me to no end by paying the Order secret visits even when they'd gladly have had him killed.

This time? He was leaving the offer open for me to walk in there with him at his side.

"It's your choice," Greyson said.

"Not really a choice, if Alban's there." I looked him in the eyes. "I'm coming with you."

———

The meeting was set for later that morning, so I returned to the castle in person after attempting to snatch a little more sleep in my own bed. When we were due to leave for the Order, Greyson left the castle in the care of the Elemental Soldiers, while Dex took charge of guarding the hall of souls.

"Personally, I think you're out of your minds," the fire sprite said. "Going back to that hellhole, I mean."

"Not sure I disagree." I looked sideways at Greyson, who wore his usual Death King armour, minus the mask which had once concealed his face. I wasn't sure he'd even slept the previous night, but his eyes were sharp, his mouth pulled into a serious line.

"Let's get this over with," Greyson said.

We made for the node without further delay. It was technically a violation of the Order's rules for me to keep crossing back and forth between Earth and the Parallel, but I'd long since stopped caring about that kind of crap. Hopping over to the city centre via a node instead of taking the bus was so much of an improvement that it'd take more than a threat of discipline from the Order to convince me to give it up.

The Death King seemed oblivious to the occasional stare we attracted from the ordinary people we passed on our way to the Order's headquarters, though even the Order didn't care too much about what the public thought their offices were actually used for. Their go-to method for maintaining magical secrecy was to let people draw their own conclusions whenever they saw something odd, and in an era where the internet was rife with conspiracy theories and rumours, even video evidence of magic would be dismissed as false by most people. Unless a full-on war erupted on their doorstep, they'd remain oblivious.

My heartbeat quickened as we neared the doors, and to no surprise whatsoever, one of the two shifters on security duty barred my path. "State your name."

I flashed my Order ID. "Liv Cartwright, here to accompany the King of the Dead."

For one glorious moment, the blood drained from the guards' faces as they took in my companion. Then they both stepped aside, leaving us a free route through the doors. "Go in."

"They didn't even ask what we were here for," I murmured to the Death King as we walked into the lobby. "Standards are slipping, aren't they?"

Granted, few would refuse entry to the King of the Dead, even under their new leadership. My nerves spiked again as we neared the corridor where Mr Holland's office, formerly Mr Cobb's, was located. Holland had recently been promoted to the upper room, but it seemed he'd kept his old office, because the Death King headed that way without slowing down.

The door opened before we could knock, and Mr Holland beckoned us into the room. "Do come in, both of you."

If I could describe Mr Holland using one word, it'd be 'bland'. He had plain grey hair, sideburns, and glasses perched on the end of his nose like an ageing professor. Not threatening in the slightest. Yet my shoulders tensed when he surveyed the pair of us, his gaze lingering on the Death King's all-too-human face. "I'm glad you took me up on my offer. And you brought Olivia with you, too."

I gave him a hard stare. "Thought you worked for the upper room now. Why are you still down here?"

"I prefer the view from this level," he said. "Besides, the upper room is soon to be obsolete. Changes are sweeping through the Order, the same as the Houses of the Elements, and your own House, too, Greyson."

My heart gave an uneasy flip, but the Death King's expression remained impassive. "What is it you want from me, Alexander Holland?"

"An agreement," he said. "I recently reminded you that my predecessor and yours worked together to place a curse upon your people. You've broken the curse on yourself, and I'm sure your liches will want you to do the same for them. I can help you with that."

"You want to offer to break the curse on the other liches?" said the Death King. "In exchange for me pledging my undying loyalty to you, perhaps? Or would you like to throw in a promise to cancel the war your allies intend to unleash in the Parallel?"

"There will be no need for a war, if we encounter no opposition to our goals," said Holland. "The Order was created to prevent another spirit war, in fact, so it seems remiss of us not to adapt our methods with the times."

"Where's Alban, then?" I asked. "Not like him to hide and let others do his dirty work. Especially the man who once had his apprentice's memories stripped out."

I had to admit, I was kind of curious how much Alban knew of Mr Holland's involvement in my punishment. Holland had once been the Order's chief interrogator, before his hunger for power had seen him throw his lot in with the very spirit mages he'd once despised. Admittedly, it'd been Hawker who'd initially struck a deal with the Order, not Alban, but as far as Alban was concerned, I was still that teenager he'd manipulated into learning spirit magic in the hope of one day succeeding him. I hadn't known at the time that his plan was to take over the Order, bringing the spirit mages back into a position of authority across both realms, but I'd bet he hadn't planned for the Order to slam me with a memory spell and wipe out all recollection of our lessons.

"Alban has his own goals to deal with," Mr Holland said stiffly. "I am in charge of supervising this branch of the Order, that is all."

"Did you tell him what you did to the Crow?" I went on. "And Cobb? Does he know that the reason Cobb cracked and tried to murder Hawker was because he lost his magic at the Order's hands? What would Alban say to that, I wonder?"

Mr Holland barely blinked. "Barrett Cobb was little more than a follower. I, however, have aspirations."

"Which involves betraying your principles, right?" I said. "Was it worth it to you, gaining the favour of the upper room in exchange for turning your back on everything you ever supported?"

"Yes," said Holland. "It was."

Well. At least he was being honest about his corruption, but it didn't make me less inclined to want to punch his lights out.

"You would do the same," he added. "By all accounts, you did exactly that when you chose to take on Alban's apprenticeship."

"Okay, first off, I was fifteen," I said. "I also wasn't in possession of all the facts. Namely, that my master was secretly a power-hungry despot-in-the-making. What's your excuse?"

He was silent for a moment. "You didn't grow up in the paranormal community before spirit magic was banned. It's a shame, really, that you were raised in ignorance the way you were. You might have made better choices."

I looked him in the eyes, icy hatred flooding me. "You were the weapon of that authority when it suited your goals. You're nothing more than an opportunistic bastard. Don't try to paint me as the only one of the pair of us who made poor choices."

Mr Holland's jaw tightened. He was in the wrong, though, and he knew it. He didn't even have any magic of his own, for all the authority he wielded. I'd bet that was precisely why he'd taken up Alban on his offer. Why would he resist, when Alban could easily rip out his soul if he refused? He'd never stood a chance.

"So I take it you decline my offer?" he said to the Death King. "You wish to let your fellow spirit mages remain cursed?"

"Forgive me if I don't hold you to your word," the Death King responded. "My people trust me to find a solution for them. They would not believe the same of you."

"You think them loyal?" said Mr Holland. "I remember your predecessor, too. I witnessed the initial signing of the contract, did you know? The former Death King was all too eager to sign away his people's freedom in order for him to gain total domination over them. If you refuse this offer, your people will believe the same of you."

"I wouldn't be so sure."

Mr Holland turned to me instead. "And you, Olivia? You were cursed to an existence as a lich not so long ago yourself. You have an open offer on the table to stand at Alban's side, for reasons I frankly cannot fathom. Perhaps he'd rather not see all the work he put into training you go to waste."

"I thought we cut ties when he tried to take the former Death King's power for his own," I said. "In the process, he wanted to gain domination over the liches, and I didn't see him falling over himself to undo their curse then. I don't trust *any* of you to do a damn thing to help them."

"Are you certain you can survive in defiance of us?" he said. "You might have the gift of spirit magic, but your soul is as fragile as it ever was, and as valuable."

His stare bored into mine, and unwittingly, a memory rose at the back of my mind, of his grim expression looking down at me as he sentenced me to be stripped of my memories.

I gritted my teeth and managed to hold his gaze. I wasn't alone this time, and I would not be afraid of him.

"Is that all?" said the Death King. "If I refuse your offer,

I take it you're not going to keep sending your messengers into the castle?"

"I confess myself disappointed," said Mr Holland. "You hold the lives of your people in your hands, and it would be in their best interests to accept my offer. If we resolve this without any need for bloodshed, then it'll be worth it, will it not?"

There doesn't need to be bloodshed for a spirit mage to kill another. I held my tongue, tasting bile at the back of my throat at the memory of how I'd taken Dirk Alban's soul in my hands and unleashed the former Death King's overwhelming power from my palms like bolts of jagged lightning, impaling everyone who got too close until their blood painted the walls of the citadel.

I shook off the memory as I left the office along with the Death King. Everyone gave us a wide berth when we crossed the lobby, even the guards by the front doors. I shot them both a stony look as we passed by, not afraid of them in the slightest. I wasn't even afraid of Mr Holland, despite my knowledge that he'd been the one who'd ordered my memories to be taken away.

No... it was the spectre of Dirk Alban who hovered at the back of my thoughts, threatening everyone I cared about. It had always been him.

The Death King and I didn't speak a word until after we'd crossed over into the Parallel again, landing outside the castle's grounds.

"It's pretty much a given that Alban is coming for your liches, and soon," I finally said. "Should we warn them?"

"They already know," he replied. "I've made no secret of the fact that the enemy views them as pieces on a game board."

"You don't think any of the others will turn against you?"

"I've made it clear that they will have to be patient if they wish for me to remove the curse on them," he said. "Perhaps some would choose the easy way out, but they also know of the fate of those two guards last night."

"The lich-killing cantrips are still in circulation." A shiver sprang to my skin. "No need for bloodshed indeed. I wonder if he'd say the same if Lord Blackbourne confronted him about the cantrip someone left on his doorstep."

"Lord Blackbourne had a neutraliser spell."

Which he probably swiped from the Order himself. "Come to think of it, Lord Blackbourne implied that the Order saw themselves as like the Court of the Dead, in that they control the fates of their mages. You don't think they're planning on forcing obedience by turning everyone into liches or something, do you?"

"I doubt it," he said. "Most liches can't survive on Earth for long. Besides, being bound to that many souls... it's not something most spirit mages can handle."

"How does it work, then?" I asked. "I mean, you didn't bind the souls of every lich here to their amulets, right? Some of them were here long before you were."

"I didn't bind them all, but when a lich surrenders their soul amulet to me, there's a power transfer involved," he said. "There's also a transfer of trust. After all, I have access to their souls, which means I could theoretically end their afterlives whenever I wished to."

"Have you..." I was sure I already knew the answer, but I ploughed on. "Have you ever done that?"

"Yes," he said. "Many times. If I strip a soul from an

amulet, then it cannot be reversed. Either the soul disappears, or, on occasion, it becomes a phantom. Usually the former."

"No wonder phantoms are so pissed off." I suppressed a shiver. "So… do you want to go back to Lord Blackbourne and ask if he has an insider within the Order? You're certain he's not allying with them?"

"I'm certain he isn't," he said, "but it's true that he hid underground during the last war and is likely to be making arrangements to do the same again. He has no desire to get involved in spirit mage warfare."

"He's the one who wanted me to give *him* information on Dirk Alban's plans," I said. "Too bad I still don't remember most of it, and what I do remember is pretty much common knowledge now."

To the vampires, certainly. Yet they were content to sit this one out despite knowing the devastation which had struck the rest of the Parallel during the last war.

"True," he said. "I'm inclined to believe he's playing a guessing game. He doesn't have insiders in the Order, not after what happened to the last ones."

"Or perhaps Brant told him." *He'd* been in the Order's jail. Had he overheard some of the enemy's plans, or were there more details he hadn't shared with me?

Greyson's frown deepened at the sound of my ex-boyfriend's name. "Are you sure he knew anything of import?"

"No." I touched a fingertip to the corner of his mouth. "Jealous?"

"Not in the slightest." His hand slid around my back. "I have nothing to fear from him."

"Uh-huh." His touch brought a frisson of heat to my skin, and I leaned in to kiss him lightly, then deeper.

"Get a room!" said Dex's voice from above. "Elements above, there are dozens of empty rooms in the castle and yet you choose to inflict this public display on me."

"Not sure you count as 'public'," I said to the fire sprite, releasing Greyson.

"You wound me." The fire sprite sniffed. "Are you going to give me something useful to do, or am I to stay here until you two finish attacking one another's faces?"

"There's no need to be so dramatic," I told him. "Really, it's lucky for you that the liches who tried to break in here didn't get closer to the hall of souls."

"At least then there'd be some excitement," he said.

Three more sprites flew over our heads to join him. Aria, Dex's girlfriend and air sprite; Mav, the water mage who'd belonged to one of the contenders for the Death King's Fire Element; and Terren, the earth mage who we'd saved from a cage where Hawker had trapped him in order to use the life force of countless sprites to power the machinery in the citadel.

Greyson watched the four of them circle the hall. "We have one of each sprite now."

"Not sure I'd say that," I said. "They do whatever they like, even Dex."

The fire sprite pouted. "I'm getting tired of playing security guard. Nobody ever goes in the hall of souls anyway."

"I'd like to." I turned to Greyson. "Dex can go outside, right?"

"Sure," he said. "The other sprites can watch the door instead."

I could hear an unspoken question in his voice, but I couldn't explain the instinct that drew me to the place where my own severed soul had once resided, and the place which I hadn't revisited since my return to life.

At Greyson's touch, the door swung inward, and we walked into the hall of souls.

4

The hall of souls stretched out before us, its high ceiling supported by pillars and its shelves lined with disc-shaped amulets, each one etched with the skull symbol of the Death King. I halted before the shelf which contained my own soul amulet and carefully picked it up.

While I no longer felt the presence of life brimming inside the amulet, the faintest trace of energy hummed below the surface. A fragment of my own life essence, but no longer the only force which anchored me to an earthly form. A memory flickered behind my eyes, of holding a similar amulet in my hands as I stood at Dirk Alban's side.

Greyson gave me a quizzical look. "Do you remember something?"

"Nothing concrete." I placed the amulet back on the shelf, eyeing its neighbour. Greyson's soul amulet, which he'd placed in peril on more than one occasion, hummed with the faintest trace of spirit energy despite its dormant state. "I don't know, I was just thinking about what Holland said, about my soul being fragile. And valuable, too. What do you think he meant by that?"

"Alexander Holland is nothing more than a puppet," said Greyson. "No doubt he's parroting Alban or Hawker."

I pulled a face. "Look at what Hawker did in the citadel, though. He used the sprites as a battery, but it was human souls which he sacrificed in order to create a node linking the citadel to Earth."

Greyson's gaze lingered on the shelf before us. "I would like to hope Alban knows better than to repeat the mistakes of his predecessors. I suspect the reason so many spirit mages lost their lives in the last war was through their view of each other's souls as nothing more than currency."

Souls were also sacrificed to create the nodes. People died for it. Nausea rose in the back of my throat at Hawker's hints that the creation of the very Parallel itself was steeped in the blood of spirit mages. "Pretty sure Alban thinks he's immune to the mistakes of his predecessors. Besides, there's one factor that wasn't there last time."

His head tilted. "Which is...?"

"This place." I drew in a breath. "I think we need to consider the possibility of him trying to use the very souls in this room as bargaining chips, not just those of the liches he's lured over to his side."

His followers had also bargained with human lives, like the Crow. A memory stirred of my own voice, speaking what felt like a lifetime ago. *"Why does this soul thief need the souls of elemental mages, then?"*

"To use in a spell, I think," Brant replied. "The rumours say

that if one gains possession of a mage's soul and conducts a certain ritual, they can take our magic for their own."

In the end, Cobb had wanted the Death King's soul, not just any old mage's, but the Crow had made a habit of tricking other mages into signing over their souls to him, which had made Brant sell me out and ruin his own life in the process. Souls were valuable, all right, whether in a soul amulet or otherwise.

"Perhaps," Greyson said, "but I won't use my people as bargaining chips myself. Not even as a last resort."

"I know." I also knew how deeply he cared for his fellow liches. Far more than most of them would ever know. "I think I'm done in here. Let's go."

We walked out into the main hall, where we found Felicity and Cal waiting for us. The Water Element, a curvy black woman with a friendly smile, addressed Greyson first. "Our shift's over, so Ryan and Bria are guarding the gates now. Anything you want us to do?"

"Yes," he said. "Since Bria has been neglecting my request for her to talk to the Houses of the Elements, I would like the pair of you to go to Elysium instead."

A scowl appeared on Cal's face. The slight Asian guy was the least friendly of the Elemental Soldiers, due in no small part to the former Fire Element's betrayal, and he hadn't warmed to me like the others had. "Fine, but I don't expect them to be welcoming."

"Which House do you want us to speak to?" asked Felicity.

"Whichever you believe is most likely to listen to you," came Greyson's response.

"Not Earth or Fire, then," Cal said. "I doubt the Houses

will be much help either way. They're too close to the Order."

"They aren't in direct contact any longer," said Greyson. "This is an opportunity for you to ensure they don't make an alliance with the Order's new management. Sell the benefits of forming an agreement with me instead."

Hmm. While I didn't know the Houses personally and had no experience with them, an idea had begun to take shape in my mind. While the two Elemental Soldiers left the castle, I turned to Greyson. "You aren't going in person?"

"No." His brow pinched. "I've had quite enough of tedious negotiations for one morning."

"Did you even sleep last night?" Not that I was one to talk, but I'd at least laid down while I'd been astral projecting. Greyson seemed as prone to wandering around the castle at all hours of the night as he'd been as a lich.

"I find it hard to rest. Too many people need me."

"They need you functioning," I said. "You're not dead anymore."

"I'm aware of that." His fingers moved up the sleeve of his armoured coat, an almost self-conscious movement. "There never seems to be enough time."

"Welcome to how life works for us mere mortals." I closed the distance between us. "Would you go take a nap if I asked you to?"

His mouth tilted into a smile. "For you, I'll make the effort."

"All right, then." I kissed him lightly. "I'm going for a walk."

I left the castle and made my way through the swampy grounds, past where Ryan and Bria stood guarding the gates. On the other side, I spotted Trix near Neddie the zombie horse.

"Hey," I said to the elf. "What're you doing here?"

"I'm going to Arcadia," he responded. "I need to find out if there are any elven artefacts in circulation."

"Someone didn't steal one of your heirlooms again, did they?" I asked.

Early in my employment for the Order and at the start of our friendship, I'd offered to steal Trix's heirloom back from an earth mage who'd intended to put it up for auction in Arcadia. Incidentally, the same mission had led me to find Dex, trapped in a cage in said earth mage's lair.

"No," said Trix, "but Bria wants to find one and she's stuck guarding the castle."

I glanced over at her and Ryan. "Then I'll go with you. I heard a certain illegal cantrip trade might be in business again, and I want to ask some questions at the warehouse."

If this so-called Family was behind the cantrips' resurgence, it might be out of my area, but I couldn't forget that the Collective of Spells had been the Order's prime cantrip supplier. Had they noticed the Order's change of leadership, or did they not care as long as they got paid?

Trix and I walked to the warehouses on the edge of Arcadia, where the city bordered the swampland, and past a tree where I'd once hidden my weapons stash. Nowadays I kept all my spare gear in the castle instead, though I carried a pouch of cantrips at my waist.

"You think someone is smuggling cantrips out of the warehouses again?" Trix asked.

I shook my head. "Someone did use a reusable cantrip to attack the Death King's guards last night, but I think they're widespread enough at this point that the people running the COS probably aren't involved."

"Oh, Ryan told me about the attack," said Trix, worry clouding his eyes. "It's dangerous at the moment, isn't it?"

"Honestly, I'm used to it by now." I cast a glance over the ramshackle warehouses in front of us. "Meet you back here in half an hour."

"Sure." Trix bounded over to join the queue leading into the warehouse which housed the main market in Arcadia, selling everything from cantrips to other magical items with varying effects. In the queue outside, practitioners mingled with elves and even a few vampires who wore their hoods up during the day. I knew better than to bother asking the people inside the warehouse itself if they had any involvement with the illegal cantrip trade, so I headed for the storeroom adjacent to another warehouse where desperate practitioners carved cantrips for a pittance.

The stocky guy at the door frowned at me. "I know you."

"We've met," I said. "I tipped you off about the cantrip smuggling scheme, back when I worked for the Order."

"You're still with the Order?" He glanced behind him, fumbling for another cigarette.

"Not anymore," I said. "I found better employment. More ethical."

It was hard to tell from his expression how much he knew about the Order's change of leadership or its current involvement with the spirit mages. It wasn't like I particularly cared about drawing their attention, not after the events of that morning, but I'd rather they didn't hurt any more innocent people.

"Good for you," the man said, in notably careful tones. "Stay away from magic, is my advice."

I stifled a laugh. He didn't know I was a spirit mage? Admittedly, working as a low-ranked retriever had once been as good a cover story as it was possible to have. Nobody in the Parallel had known how I'd wound up working for the Order's lowest ranks and had assumed I was a lowly practitioner, which was partly why Brant had tried so hard to convince me to move here with him. He might have been right in that it'd have been a quieter existence, but the shit show he'd made of his own life made me infinitely glad I hadn't accepted his offer.

"What kind of cantrips are the Order asking for these days?" I asked. "Are you selling only to the local branch, or have you moved to selling to the other branches as well?"

Suspicion sparked in his eyes. "Why the interest?"

In answer, I adjusted my cloak, displaying the Death King's emblem and hoping that its owner wouldn't be *too* mad at me for what I was about to do.

The man's cigarette fell from his lips as he recognised the skull symbol. "You're with *him?*"

"The King of the Dead is my new employer," I said. "As it happens, he's interested in finding a new cantrip supplier of his own. Your reusable cantrips would be incredibly useful to him."

"The Death King wants to buy from us?" Nervousness strained his voice. "Are you sure?"

"Positive," I lied. "I reckon he can offer a better price than the Order, between you and me."

"I…" He paused. "I'll have to check with the boss, of course… but I'm sure he'd be delighted to serve the King of the Dead."

Uh-huh. More like scared of losing his soul. The Death King's reputation remained intact, after all, and few outside his Court knew of his return to life.

"Do that," I said. "Send a messenger to the castle, and we'd be happy to work out the details between ourselves."

Assuming His Deathly Highness didn't raise hell with me for forming allegiances behind his back. But if I wanted to stop the Order's supply chain, I could think of no better way than to put a Death King-shaped barrier in their way. As a bonus, I might as well take out the remainder of the Crow's illegal cantrip trade while I was at it. Unless Alban was buying the lich-killing cantrips directly from a private manufacturer, which he might be. Cutting out the middleman.

Still, I was pretty damn proud of myself when I returned to the market to wait for Trix near the warehouse. The elf slipped out of the crowd, his expression pensive.

"Got what you were looking for?" I asked.

"No, but there's an auction tonight," he said. "There are rumours an elven artefact will be up for grabs."

Oh, boy. "You don't want me to sit in on it again, do you?"

"No, Bria is the one who wants the artefact."

Interesting. "Is this to do with her secret mission?"

"Are you on a secret mission of your own?" he said. "Why did you want to talk to the owner of the factory?"

"Because they're the Order's main suppliers," I said,

"and I thought I might convince them to take on a new major client instead. Namely, the Death King."

His brows shot up. "Have you told him?"

"Not yet." He usually bought his own cantrips from a private supplier, but I hadn't seen any deliveries in a long while and we relied on Devon for certain cantrips, like the neutralisers. Besides, my main objective here was to slow down the Order and take away one of their advantages.

If His Deathly Highness said yes, of course.

———

"What did you do?" Greyson answered as soon as I knocked on the door to his suite, which suggested he'd at least tried to grab some sleep, but hadn't got very far. His coat and shoes were off, but his eyes were wide awake.

"Well," I began. "I hope you don't mind, but I may have implied to the Collective of Spells that you could give them a better deal on their cantrips than the Order."

His brows rose. "You laid out an open challenge?"

"The Order is one of their biggest clients," I said. "They can't stop selling to them or they'd go bust, but you have the cash to make up for it, don't you?"

"Yes," he said, "I do, but this strikes me as a move which will severely anger the Order."

"The Order already threw the first blow when they tried to manipulate us into letting them take the other liches' lives into their hands," I said. "Think about it. With Devon no longer making cantrips for them and the COS sending most of their supplies to you instead, they'll lose a huge chunk of their magical prowess. Don't forget Cobb already ran off with a bunch of their best cantrips, too.

Each base only has so many, and I have an inkling that the COS is supplying their London branches, too."

"Yes, they are," he said. "I looked into it."

"There you have it," I said. "I don't know if this will work, but it doesn't look like Alban is keeping a close watch on the Order. Some of their staff are rebelling, too. And the guy he has acting as his mouthpiece isn't even a spirit mage."

He tilted his head on one side. "Are you saying that you want to take the Order back?"

"Not yet," I said. "I think it's a weak link, though. Alban isn't paying them close attention, and it might be possible to win them over to our side without the need for an open conflict."

Okay, Judith and her friend weren't exactly the highest rank in the Order, but they'd convinced a few people to join them, and more might follow if they didn't screw up and expose themselves.

Greyson studied me. "I hope you know what you're doing, Liv."

My heart skipped a beat or two at the sound of my name in his low voice, and before I could say another word, he brushed his mouth over mine.

"Does that mean yes?" I murmured against his lips.

"It means I'll think about it." He released me, leaving a frisson of warmth behind. "Deal?"

"Deal." I left his suite, hoping he'd give me a definite 'yes' before the COS sent their messenger to the castle to negotiate with him.

As I climbed down the steps at the front of the castle, the shadowy form of a lich crossed my path. "I want to talk to you, Olivia."

The lich's cold unfamiliar voice brought a chill to my skin, and I suppressed the urge to back out of range. All the liches sounded the same, but that wasn't really their fault, after all.

"What about?" I asked.

"You're no longer a lich," he said. "How?"

"It wasn't deliberate." I should have guessed they'd have questions as to my miraculous return to life. "The enemy threw a cantrip at me which would have killed me if I hadn't found a way around it."

"The same cantrip killed two of us last night."

So it had. "It's a double-edged sword. I'm sorry you're still cursed, but we don't have any more of those cantrips, nor the means to use them to cure everyone."

"That friend of yours carves cantrips."

I bristled. *Keep Devon out of this.* "She's never created one of those before. Besides, I don't think you want to offer yourselves up as lab rats for a cantrip which will inflict a fate worse than death on you if it goes wrong."

Another lich joined the first. "I think you're hiding something, Olivia. We both do."

"Like what?" I said. "I don't have any of those cantrips with me."

Besides, even if I had, I'd need a serious boost of magical energy in order for them to properly work, which I'd only seen in the citadel before, while the only source I knew of which generated enough energy to bring someone permanently back to life was the life force of a spirit mage. In other words, to undo the curse on everyone in the Court of the Dead, an equal number of mages would have to offer up their own lives. That was, in a roundabout way, what the Order was offering when they promised to break the curse. I sure as hell wouldn't be sharing the details throughout the entire Court of the Dead. After all, the only living spirit mages on the property were the Death King himself and yours truly.

The two liches moved closer, emanating a chilling aura. I tensed, prepared to draw on the strength of the nearest node to fight back, but they turned away without another word and drifted across the grounds.

Dex flew to my side, his hands flaming. "Want me to slap some sense into them?"

"Nah, it's not worth it." I shook my head. "I have a feeling we'll see more of that the longer this goes on."

Mr Holland had offered to free them from the curse, and if they found out about his offer, I wasn't convinced all of them would say no. Whatever the sacrifice.

"Where have you been, anyway?" Dex asked. "You left me behind."

"You never asked to come with me," I said. "I didn't think you were interested in the markets."

"You went to the market?" he said. "To ask about those illegal cantrips?"

"I didn't learn anything new," I said. "Not about the illegal cantrips, anyway. Instead, I decided to see if I can snatch away the Order's cantrip supply. I think the Order itself is a weak point with Hawker and his allies. They don't care enough about Earth to focus all their attention there, so I figured we could try to take away some of their resources."

"The Order," he said. "Didn't you and His Deathly Highness go to visit them yourselves this morning?"

"Yeah, we did," I said. "Holland tried to recruit us. We said no."

"Good," he said. "Don't give them the time of day."

Just as long as they don't find out about the Order's offer. I looked at the retreating liches, unease slithering over my skin. They might do a lot worse than threaten me if they learned the Order had offered to solve all their problems... if they paid the price with their souls.

5

————————

That evening, Devon and I were kicking off a gaming session on the Xbox when Bria appeared in the middle of the living room in a flash of light. Dex zipped into view, too, not looking contrite in the slightest when Bria flashed an alarmed look at him. "Dex, you should have mentioned you were taking us into Liv's house."

"I thought it was implied," said the fire sprite.

At least they didn't land on the gaming table this time.

"Dammit, Dex," said Devon.

"I forgot the node comes out directly into your house," Bria admitted. "Sorry. Dex said you'd be willing to help us."

"What is it?" Devon sounded as suspicious as I felt. What was with people using our house as a revolving door between Earth and the Parallel?

"There's a magical object I need," said Bria. "An elven artefact which was sold at an auction in Arcadia. A vampire ran off with it and escaped to Earth."

"You went to one of those auctions?" I asked.

Devon shot me a grin. "Didn't you set an auction hall on fire once?"

Thanks for that one, Devon.

"It wasn't me, it was Dex," I protested, referencing the incident when I'd gone to retrieve Trix's elven artefact from an auction and ended up regretting bringing my new fire sprite sidekick along with me. "I was trying to stop a rogue earth mage from making a quick getaway, and Dex got a bit overexcited."

"Bet the vampires loved that," Bria remarked. "Anyway, as I was about to say, the vampire took the object, came to Earth, and then ran into the Order's headquarters of all places."

"The *Order?*" Oh, no. "You're joking, right?"

"Nope," said Bria. "I couldn't follow him inside, and he never came back out. I don't know if he was going to give it to them to look after, or if he was just waiting for the coast to be clear before running."

"Either way, he must have allies in there," said Devon. "Otherwise the Order would have kicked him out."

"Yeah," I said. "They don't take kindly to being fucked around with. They won't be happy with any break-in attempts, either. If you get caught, you won't get any mercy."

"If I do, the best I can hope is that they hand me back to the Houses," said Bria. "If I wind up back in the Family's home, then I'd be better off being caught by the Order instead."

I sincerely doubted that was the case. "Does the Family's home contain a dungeon equipped with anti-magical shielding and hundreds of guards, not to mention cantrips which can destroy even a lich?"

"Not that I recall, but the Family have a vendetta," Bria responded. "The Order… whatever dickheads are running the show in there, they don't know me. There's no personal stake in this for them. The worst they can do is lock me up."

"If you get caught, they'll strip the magic out of you the way they do to other mages who break the law." Did she seriously not know how much of a bad idea it was to tick off the Order? "Trust me, it's worse than death for most people."

"I doubt they *can* strip out my magic," she said. "I'm designed to be more resilient than most humans. The Family saw to that."

Devon and I both stared at her. I'd never heard of her openly admitting to the extent of her magical talents, but what kind of mage couldn't be stripped of their magic? She sure as hell wasn't a spirit mage. I'd have blamed it on being half-elf, but the word *designed* painted a different picture entirely.

"What in hell did they do to you?" Devon asked.

"Tested experimental cantrips on me, mostly," Bria said. "Hard to remember most of it. I was too young."

"They did that to you when you were a kid?" I said. "Damn."

"Nobody ever said they were model parents," Bria said. "To top it off, I'm half-elf, so that alone might grant me immunity to half the spells they might use on me."

Is that true? She was the one taking the risk, but breaking into the Order's base was one hell of a gamble to make. While it sounded like the vampire had taken shelter in there to avoid being followed, when Devon mentioned the illegal cantrip trade, Bria didn't seem to know about the former link between them and the Order. The vampire might have taken his contraband into the Order's base simply because he knew he wouldn't be followed, but we couldn't count on her plan not backfiring horribly.

"I left Miles watching the Order," said Bria, "but they might catch him if he stays out there too long. We have to get in there before they realise we're spying on them."

"If that's the case, take Dex with you," I told them. "Dex? You still here?"

The fire sprite flew into view. "What is it?"

"You know the way around the Order," I said. "Bria and Miles are planning on breaking in, so I'm sure you can show them around."

"Another stealth mission?" he said. "Fine, but I expect compensation."

"You'll get some new dice later if you're good." Devon jumped to her feet and went into the shop to grab some cantrips for Bria to take with her. As for me, I warned Bria to avoid the basement, especially if she was taking Miles with her. As a spirit mage, he'd be far more vulnerable to the Order's tricks, and so would Dex, for that matter. Still, he'd wanted some action, and chasing a lone vampire around carried a lower risk than most of the alternatives.

If they didn't get caught, that is.

When they'd gone, Devon and I exchanged raised eyebrows.

"She has a death wish," I said.

"Her choice," said Devon. "This Family sounds like a piece of work. Heard of them before?"

"Through the Death King," I responded. "Sounds like they were involved in illegal cantrip experimentation."

On *people,* if Bria's story was any indication. Even the Order's hidden lab where they'd experimented on ways to kill liches without access to their soul amulets didn't come close to that level of depravity.

Devon's brow wrinkled. "With the Crow and the others?"

"Pretty sure they were allies," I said. "Except the Crow was more concerned with stealing mages' souls and turning liches into rotting piles of flesh than experimenting on humans."

"Lovely," said Devon. "Why would the Order let a vampire hide in their headquarters? I wonder what he stole from Bria?"

"I'll ask Dex later," I said.

"That's why you sent him with them?"

"That, and he's bored," I said. "He got jealous of me for going to the market earlier. I thought I'd give him something to do. Also… I didn't get the chance to look around the Order when the Death King and I went there."

"I can't believe you went back at all."

"Holland didn't make it an optional invitation, and I refused to let the Death King go alone," I said. "Besides, Holland doesn't scare me. Is that weird?"

"Yes," she informed me. "Seriously, what are you thinking? First you piss off the Order *again,* and then you make the Death King so annoyed with you that he declines to let you spend the night in his castle."

"Excuse me?" I said. "I'm here because it's the weekend and I wanted to take the night off and play video games. What makes you think I annoyed him?"

"Because I saw him when I popped into the castle earlier," she said. "He had that look he always wears when he's annoyed because of something you did."

"I didn't know he had a specific look." I filed that information away for later. "Okay, what I did was tell the COS's representative at the market that the Death King was interested in taking the Order's place as their main cantrip buyer."

Devon broke into laughter. "You didn't, Liv."

"It was an impulse decision."

"So Grey got mad."

"Actually, he just said he hoped I knew what I was doing."

"Well, duh," she said. "What you're doing is playing the exact same game he does, except he's on the receiving end of it now."

"He isn't mad at me," I said. "He just needs space to think through his options."

"Said that, did he?"

"No, he didn't, but he's adjusting to being human after a ten-year gap and half his liches are mad at him for not curing them of the curse, too," I said. "I thought I'd give him the night to think about it. I'll check back with him about the cantrips tomorrow when the COS sends their messenger to the castle. If they come to an agreement, then you won't have to worry about not making enough cantrips to supply an entire army."

"Like that's why you did it." She rolled her eyes. "Seriously, Liv, why cantrips?"

"Because they're the Order's main source of magical power, and I think they're connected to Alban's plan," I said. "Not just in the obvious ways, either. Holland offered to undo the curse on the liches, and you know what the price is for that spell."

Her expression shadowed. "A life."

"Exactly," I said. "A life for *every* lich. I doubt those illegal cantrips are being manufactured at the COS's warehouse, mind you, but it's not a bad idea to bring them under close watch."

I doubted Hawker and Alban were carving the cantrips themselves. Most likely, they had some practitioners doing it for them… under duress.

"Then you'd better hope the Death King says yes," said Devon. "Dealing with those illegal cantrip traders is like cutting the head off a hydra. Stamp one out and another shows up to take their place."

"I know," I said. "Brant implied a while ago that the enemy's end goal was to steal mages' souls to use in some kind of ritual. I know what he ended up doing was taking the Death King's soul instead, but it's been on my mind lately. Maybe the Crow had other reasons for forcing mages to pledge their lives to him."

"Why not talk to Brant yourself if you think he's involved?" she queried.

"I don't think he is," I responded. "The Crow never told him anything. Besides, he's not worth the effort."

"You aren't wrong there."

Devon and I returned to our video game while we waited for the others to return from their trip to the Order. Dex came back first, flitting out of the node in the middle of the room.

"How'd it go?" I asked him.

"The Order's security is as inept as ever."

"They got caught?" said Devon.

"No, they got away," he said. "Not without exposing themselves to everyone on security duty, though. Oh, and that delightful leader of theirs."

"What… not Holland?" Bria had run into *him?*

"She stole that elven artefact literally from under his nose." He hooted with laughter. "It was priceless. On top of that, she set half the back yard ablaze."

Bria didn't do things by halves. "You didn't see any illegal cantrips, did you? Like those inferno cantrips, or worse?"

"Nothing of the sort," he said. "I *did* see a certain acquaintance of yours hanging around the lobby despite claiming to have turned her back on the Order."

"Who, Judith?" She'd returned to the Order's base after she'd openly admitted she intended to betray them? Granted, she might have chickened out, but she wasn't being nearly careful enough.

"Craig and Carla, too," said Dex. "They're *awful* at trying to recruit people using stealth, by the way. If I'd been a security guard, I'd have caught them red-handed."

I groaned. "I can't babysit Judith on top of the shit I already have to deal with."

"It might interest you to know they're holding a meeting tomorrow morning," he added. "With the others who want to resist the Order's current leadership."

Dammit, Judith. If I didn't intervene somehow, she'd get herself killed.

Before I could reply, Bria hopped through the node and landed in the living room underneath Dex.

"Well done," I said. "You're officially ahead of me on the Order's most wanted list. And trust me, that's saying a lot."

"I'm honoured," Bria responded.

Dex zipped overhead. "Hey, you should take it as a challenge."

"I'm sure I'll piss them off again at some point soon enough," I allowed. "It's pretty much a hobby of mine. Anyway, you had a legitimate reason to break into their headquarters."

I hope so, anyway. That she'd ticked off Holland hadn't been on my list of predictions, but she'd probably run circles around him in a literal sense. Why anyone would entrust him with a valuable artefact was as much of a mystery as to how he could possibly remove the curse from the entire Court of the Dead at once.

Unless… did he have the means of doing so right there in the Order's base?

Dex stayed behind to drift around the living room after Bria left, at which point I asked him, "Are you positive you didn't see anything else which looked dodgy? None of those cantrips which can kill liches?"

"No, I didn't," he said. "Why would they keep *those* in their base?"

"What about neutraliser cantrips, then?"

"Neutralisers?" he said. "Pretty sure I saw some of those, but if you want me to steal from them, you're out of luck." He waggled his transparent hands.

"You aren't going to steal them." I reached for the piece of paper with the scribbled phone number on it. "Judith is."

Devon lifted her head. "This I'd like to see."

6

Later that night, I astral projected through the node and into the castle grounds. The Death King waited on the other side, hovering on the spot. While astral projecting, he looked so much like his lich self that it was easy to forget he was alive now when he hadn't been beforehand.

His gaze landed on me. "More night-time wandering?"

"Have you decided whether to take the trade deal from the COS or not?" I asked.

"I already gave you my answer," he said. "If it means that much to you. I think the entire operation is rotten to the core, personally."

"Exactly," I said. "Cobb was involved in its creation, which pretty much says it all. They treat their employees like shit, and they willingly ignore the illegal crap happening behind the scenes."

"And you want me to openly support them anyway?" he said.

"No, I want to change it from the inside," I said. "You're the Death King. Just mentioning your name will give me the clout I need to get them to agree to change the rules. Taking away the Order's supplies is just one perk."

He shook his head. "We're supposed to be preparing for a war."

"And we'll need weapons to do it, right?" I said. "The whole point of this is to divert the Order's chain of supplies to the castle. To us. We'll have more firepower, and we'll also have eyes all over Arcadia without the need to rely on the vampires. Especially as they aren't central in the city any longer."

Surprise flickered through his features. "Did Lord Blackbourne bring this on?"

"I know he's your ally, but he's looking out for himself alone," I said. "He hid underground during the last war. You only convinced him to stay in the city by threatening to take his place. Why not try the same strategy at the markets?"

"Because I never wanted to work in the cantrip trade, for a start."

"You never wanted to rule the Court of the Dead either."

"Olivia." He shook his head at me. "I do hope you plan on taking on the burden of overseeing any negotiations or else delegating to someone else, because I have other matters to attend to. Like preventing a mutiny among my liches."

"I thought you said they were mostly under control."

"I didn't say that," he said. "They're restless. Whispers are going around the castle that the two of us are hoarding knowledge of how to break the curse. If they find out about the Order's offer..."

I know. "They won't. Holland was lying through his teeth, anyway. There's no way for the Order to break the curse themselves. They'd need help."

Namely, from the spirit mages.

"I know that," he said. "But I doubt the Order is sitting back and taking our refusal lying down."

"I'm planning on attending a meeting with Judith French and some other Order employees tomorrow morning, so I'll see what they have to say."

"You're doing *what?*" he said. "Olivia, what are you thinking this time?"

"I'm thinking that the Order is the enemy's weak spot," I said. "They think they've already won, but it's an Earth-based institution which happens to have countless other branches which *aren't* under the enemy's control. If we take away their resources, then either the enemy will have to step in directly or give up and cede control."

I knew this could go wrong in a hundred possible ways, but it wasn't like I had no experience with cantrip regulations due to the years I'd spent helping Devon fill out paperwork for her business. Besides, the Death King didn't have to be openly involved for his name to give me enough leverage for them to agree to my terms... which Devon and I had spent several hours working on last night. I had a draft already written, in fact.

"You've certainly thought this one over," said the Death King. "Do I get to meet the employees at my brand-new warehouse, or do you plan to do that yourself?"

"You've heard of outsourcing, haven't you?" I said. "How much of your fortune do you actually spend on the castle, anyway? I know for a fact that your heating bills are zero."

"It's not the money that bothers me," he said. "The game you're playing… if you anger every other authority in the Parallel, you'll find yourself with a lot of enemies."

"I'm already the Order's number one enemy," I said. "Besides, there's one major authority in the Parallel who I'd like to think would have my back."

"I do." A shiver danced over my arm as he ran his hand from my shoulder to my fingertips before he disappeared. "I always do."

When morning came, I showered and dressed before going downstairs to give Judith a call. Devon wasn't yet awake, so I grabbed the scrap of paper and my phone before inputting Judith's number.

Judith answered after the third ring. "Hello? Who is this?"

"Hey, there."

"Liv?" Suspicion laced her voice. "What is it?"

"I'd like to take you up on your offer," I said. "And join your cause."

"What's the catch?"

Sensible of her not to take my word for it. "The catch is that if I hear you're reporting to the Order, I'll 'volunteer' you to join the Death King's army of the dead."

"That won't be necessary." The merest tremor underlaid her voice. "I'm on your side."

"Uh-huh," I said. "So, about this meeting this morning…"

"How do you know there's a meeting?"

"You need to work on your stealth skills," I said. "Whereabouts and what time?"

"I'll text you the details," she said. "You'd better not tell the Order. I heard you were at headquarters yourself the other day. With the Death King... and Mr Holland."

"It wasn't a friendly conversation, don't you worry about that," I said. "We'll talk more in person."

I hung up, hearing Devon come downstairs. When she entered the living room, she looked at the phone in my hand along with the scrap of paper. "You're really going to meet with her."

"Guess so." I heaved a sigh. "It couldn't have been anyone else, could it?"

"Better her than Gap-Toothed Dave."

"Or all those guys who tried to pretend we were dating after I lost my memories."

"Them too." She pulled a face. "Seriously, what brought this on? What was the final straw which made her turn her back on the Order? I mean, if you forget that she's still spending her nights hanging around their lobby, that is."

"I'll ask her," I said. "As for why she's kept her job, I can't begrudge her for wanting to pay rent."

"Guess not, considering I did the same," she said. "For too long. I don't know what the alternative is, to be honest."

"The Death King," I said. "I spoke to him via astral projection and he said yes to becoming the COS's main customer. That's one step from taking over them himself."

Devon blinked. "That's your plan? Or his?"

"Why not?" I said. "The Death King is probably the richest guy in the Parallel."

"And also your boyfriend," she said. "If you can use that word about an immortal lich… or a former immortal lich lord, rather. Elements, this whole situation is confusing."

"Tell me about it," I said. "I'm the one living it."

"Does he make you happy, though?"

I blinked at her. "What does that have to do with anything?"

"Um, a lot?" she said. "You're about to rope the poor guy into becoming a factory owner in Arcadia of all places, and the fact that he's willing to go along with that says it all, but still."

"He watched me lose my memories of our entire relationship and he waited for me all this time," I said. "I think that says more than him deciding to go along with my bizarre schemes, to be honest."

A grin broke out on her mouth. "I should have seen it coming. I mean, he did meet your mum. Brant never did."

"*Devon.*"

She laughed, while I shook my head at her. Still, hope buoyed me as I went to finish getting ready for my meeting with Judith and the others.

***

At eleven, I walked into the pub Judith had directed me to and ordered a coke before joining Judith and three other Order members at a table. One was Femi, her part shifter friend, while the other two looked to be plain old practitioners. Not exactly an elite fighting force.

"Is this it?" I asked.

"No, there are two others coming," said one of the practitioners.

"Oh, Liv," said Judith. "Have... er, have you told your new boss about this? Does he know you're here?"

"The Death King?" It gave me some satisfaction to see the others flinch at the mention of his name. "I mentioned our meeting, yes. He says he won't get in your way."

"He's... he's not working with the Order at all?"

"No," I said. "They invited him to speak to them because they wanted to make him an offer, which he turned down. There is no agreement between us and the Order."

"Good," she said, shifting position on her bar stool. "We'll just wait for the others..."

"I have a question," I said. "What was the tipping point? What made you turn on them?"

Judith's mouth parted. "I..."

"Was it what you saw in the basement?"

Her face paled. "I... you don't know what was down there."

"You're forgetting I was a lich at the time," I said. "Believe me, I saw it for myself."

"You were a *lich?*" said one of the others. "How'd you come back from that?"

I sipped my coke. "Long story, and not one I'm inclined to share with people I don't fully trust."

"Do you trust *them?*" Judith pointed to the doors. Two more people had walked in: Craig and Carla He, from our D&D group. The siblings, both of Chinese descent and academy graduates like me, both worked for the Order's admin side. While they'd never quit the Order, they'd never worked against me, either. I waved them over, and Craig gave me a sheepish look. "Hey, Liv."

I arched a brow at both of them. "Is this why you skipped out on our last gaming session?"

"Sorry," said Craig, sitting down opposite me. "We had some shit to deal with."

"Didn't mean to blow you off," added Carla. "Turns out the Order was getting suspicious with us for spending too much time with you. So we did some digging around and didn't like what we found."

"Yeah, Judith was about to tell us what led to her turning her back on them," I added. "Go on, tell us."

Judith scowled, fiddling with a napkin. "When I was working for their security team down in the basement, I heard… things."

"Like what?" I said. "Aside from their plan to manufacture cantrips to kill liches?"

"They weren't manufacturing them," she said. "It was a lab, of sorts, where they were testing cantrips. On… on souls."

I stiffened. "Souls?"

She gave a shudder. "They had… they had soul amulets. Active ones, I think. They were using cantrips on them. Not sure what they were trying to do."

My stomach lurched. "Where in hell did they get those from?"

Not the Court of the Dead. The Death King had kept his soul amulets under close watch ever since his own amulet had been stolen. No… they must have belonged to the enemy's own people, who'd surrendered their souls to Hawker and Alban only for their allies to use them for their own purposes.

"Are they still doing that?" asked Craig, looking just as horrified as I felt.

"I don't know," she said. "I asked to be transferred to another department afterwards, and then... and then I started planning to leave."

I swallowed hard. "If that's the case, then we can't delay any longer. Luckily, I have a plan."

"Like what?" asked Judith.

"We should target the Order's cantrip supplies," I said. "They're the main source of power for everyone at the base, including Holland. He has no magic of his own. If all their cantrips were either diverted or rendered useless, they'll have little means of defending themselves if, say, the Death King's Elemental Soldiers stormed the place."

"We can't steal every cantrip in the entire building," she said. "Not without being caught."

"You don't have to," I said. "You know those neutraliser cantrips? They can instantly snuff out any magic, including other cantrips."

"You want to steal them yourself?" she asked.

"You'd have an easier job than me," I said. "I'm not on the Order's rota any longer and plenty of them saw me walk in with the Death King a couple of days ago. Oh, and there was another break-in last night, which they'll probably find a way to blame on me as well."

"You knew the people who broke in and started a fire in the back yard?" Judith asked. "I should have guessed you were involved."

"I wasn't, not directly," I said. "The good news is that I know where their neutraliser cantrips are. In the retrieval unit. That's basically the easiest part of the Order to steal from."

"We can't steal them without being noticed," she protested.

"There's such a thing as an invisibility cantrip."

"But..." She trailed off. "Even if we weren't seen, everyone would know they were missing as soon as they checked the record book."

I looked her in the eyes. "I remember an incident a while ago about a cantrip delivery which mysteriously wasn't logged in at the Order's base. Could the same thing happen again, on a bigger scale?"

Her face flushed like a traffic light. "Um. That's not... it wasn't..."

"Spare me the excuses." I rolled my eyes. "Anything you might have done to sabotage Devon, do it a hundred times over and you might stand a chance of stopping them."

"It's not a bad shout," said Carla. "Take away their defensive cantrips and they'll be open to attack from both sides. Not everyone in there is happy to let the rogue spirit mages run the show. They just know what'll happen if they speak out of line."

"Yeah, well," I said. "This won't stop them altogether, and as for what they're doing in the basement... is that still going on, do you know?"

"I don't think it is," said Judith. "I haven't seen Holland in there for a while. He's too busy with his new position in the upper room."

Good to know. "All right. Focus on the cantrips for now and smuggle out as many neutralisers as possible. They won't be expecting another theft, especially so soon after the last one. I'd say we should do this right away, within the hour. Who's in?"

"I'm in," said Craig.

"Same," added Carla.

Judith gave a reluctant nod. "I guess…"

"You can put together a plan," I told them. "Meanwhile, I'll send someone to keep an eye on you. You'll know him when you see him."

Judith gave me a quizzical look, but I said nothing more. Instead, I rose to my feet, waving goodbye to Craig and Carla as I left the pub.

After I hopped through the nearest node back to the swamp, I made my way to the castle and found Dex outside the door to the hall of souls. "Good news. In an hour or so, you can have fun going back to the Order to supervise Judith and some others while they sneak around and steal all the neutraliser cantrips from the retrieval unit. How does that sound?"

"You're sending me to babysit *her?*" he said. "No thanks."

"You're the one who wanted to get in on the action," I said. "You know Craig and Carla, right? I trust them, but I'd prefer someone to watch Judith and cause a diversion if she draws attention or otherwise gives the game away."

"I'm not convinced," he said. "I'd rather start a few fires instead."

"You can if you like." I grinned. "You know what the other part of our plan is? Drive Holland out of his office. With violence, if necessary. Make him feel unsafe in that upper room seat he gave up so much for."

For now? It was time for me to do some business at the market.

7

As it turned out, I didn't need to worry about the Death King digging his heels in. When I left the castle, it was to find him prepared to head off to Arcadia's market himself.

"The ambassador and I came to an understanding," he said. "I'm going to speak to his supervisor in person."

"You spoke to him?" I must have missed the ambassador's visit while I'd been on Earth. "Why do you feel the need to go in person, then?"

"I think it's necessary to make an impression," he said.

"You know, wandering around on your own kind of defeats the purpose of having any security at the castle."

"I wouldn't say that." He leaned forward and brushed his lips over mine. "I'll see you in a bit."

And without another word, he disappeared in a flash of light.

"He... seriously..." I spluttered, staring at the spot where he'd vanished. "He's just trying to get back at me for my own scheming, isn't he?"

Nobody answered, of course, because the only people within hearing distance were the skulls in the pillars at the top of the stairs. I peered out of the gates and saw Felicity and Cal were currently on guard duty, talking to a group of people outside. I recognised a couple of them as Miles's Spirit Agent friends. The Death King hadn't called them here, had he?

"Hey, Liv." Shelley, Miles's second-in-command, gave me a wave as I walked over. She was a tall black woman with a streak of pink in her curly hair, who carried a suitcase and a large backpack as though she was on her way to the airport. "Sorry to drop in like this, but our base was attacked, and we don't have anywhere else to go. The Death King always said we could come and stay here if we needed to."

He'd said as much to me, too, but part of me hesitated to let a bunch of people I didn't know well into the castle. "Where's Miles?"

"He and Bria had to go do something urgent," she said. "It's to do with that illegal cantrip trade. Anyway, is the Death King in?"

"Not at the moment, but he'll be back soon," I said. "Come on in."

"Are you sure?" said Felicity. "I know he did say the Spirit Agents could come here, but still."

"They might as well come into the grounds, right?" I said. "It's not like they haven't been here before."

"Nobody's coming in without being checked for disguise cantrips," Cal said. "We're not falling for any tricks."

"Honestly." Felicity rolled her eyes at him. "All right, if

it makes you feel better. Everyone show me your cantrips as you come in, okay?"

I helped them watch the newcomers walk into the castle grounds, wondering what Bria and Miles were doing and if it had to do with their thieving mission at the Order. Why had the Death King decided *now* was the best time to leave his castle to go to the markets in person? It was bad enough that the Spirit Agents had been targeted by the enemy, but the Death King's habit of acting like he was still invincible was starting to get a little concerning, to say the least.

"Who attacked you?" I approached Shelley, who was in the process of returning her cantrips to her backpack after showing them to the Elemental Soldiers for inspection.

"Assassins," she answered. "Bria says they worked for the Family and the rogues within the Houses."

Hmm. "Where are Bria and Miles, then? Seems a weird time for them to run off."

"Elysium's main supplier turned out to be smuggling cantrips to the enemy a while ago," she said. "They've gone to see if he's up to his old tricks again. Personally, I'd say not. He probably fled when the city was under attack a few weeks ago."

Is that our missed connection? I knew virtually nothing about Elysium's cantrip suppliers, but it wouldn't surprise me if they'd been connected to Arcadia's black markets as well.

At that moment, the Death King reappeared on the castle's steps in a flash of light. Addressing the Elemental Soldiers, he said, "What's going on?"

"Good, you're back." I strode over to him. "The Spirit

Agents' base was attacked by assassins, so they had to come here. That's not a problem, isn't it?"

"No, but they'll have to deal with being up to their necks in boxes of cantrips," he said. "I just bought the COS's entire supply to be delivered as soon as they can manage. I'm now their primary client."

"Excellent."

His jaw twitched at my reaction, his gaze roving among the newcomers. "I don't remember offering to turn my castle into a shelter for displaced mages."

"Be nice," I told him. "You hardly need the entire castle all to yourself. The other liches spend most of their time outside anyway."

Before he could voice an objection, Dex zipped over the fence, glowing the colour of flames. "Liv, get over here."

"What's going on?" I asked.

"We need help," he said. "Your friend Judith got herself caught by one of the Order's vampire allies."

"Oh, for the Elements' sakes." I glanced at Greyson. "Really sorry, but I have to run."

"Be quick, and don't get caught." His disapproving stare followed me as I ran after Dex, out of the gate and towards the node.

"Since when did the Order have security vampires?" I asked the fire sprite.

"I think it's the same one who was hiding from Bria and her friend yesterday," he responded. "He must have been helping the Order keep an eye out for more potential break-ins."

"Great." I reached into the pouch at my waist for an invisibility cantrip before I hopped through the node, landing on the high street. Roaring traffic replaced the swampland, and once I'd turned invisible, I made for the Order's headquarters.

It immediately became apparent that a scuffle had broken out inside the lobby. A box of cantrips sat half-open on the floor, while several guards lay sprawled near the doors, and a wiry vampire had Judith in a headlock. She flailed and struggled to break free, but the vamp's grip was iron, and her face turned bluer with each passing second.

Dex zoomed overhead, dropping sparks onto the vampire's head, but he dodged them without losing his grip on Judith. She might not be my favourite person, but that didn't mean I wanted to watch her get strangled by an enraged vampire.

I approached, unseen, and slammed a handful of spirit magic into the vampire's chest. He keeled over backwards, dropping Judith in the process, and she rolled to the side, gasping for breath. The others who were supposed to have gone in with her were nowhere in sight. Had she tried to smuggle the cantrips out alone and got herself caught?

"Come on." When she lay on the ground instead of getting up, I grabbed her arm, pulling her to her feet. "Grab that box and run."

"Stop them!" shouted one of the guards who lay prone near the doors.

I raised a hand, blasting him in the chest with spirit magic and sending him sprawling head over heels. Judith lurched to her feet and scrambled to grab the discarded box of cantrips. "Liv... Craig and Carla are around the back somewhere."

"I'll get them," said Dex.

The vampire I'd knocked out had already begun to stir, so I left Judith to deal with the cantrips and ran back to the vampire's side. "You, mate, are coming on a one-way trip to the Death King's castle."

The vamp looked pretty lightweight, so I slung his limp body over my shoulder and ran towards the node, trusting Dex to guide the others after me.

As soon as the two of us landed in the swampland, the vamp woke up and started struggling and kicking. My grip broke on his flailing arms, but before he could slide out of my grip, I punched him in the temple, knocking him out cold. Not as effective as wielding my D20, but it got the job done.

Judith and Femi appeared from the node behind me, clutching the box of neutraliser cantrips between them.

"Care to help out?" I called over to the mages by the gates. "We need as many hands as possible over here. Can someone help me get this vamp in jail before he wakes up again?"

A group of perplexed spirit mages took the cantrips from the equally bewildered Order members, which caused further confusion when Dex reappeared with Carla and Craig in tow, carrying another box of cantrips between them. Since nobody offered to help me with the vampire, I carried him through the gates myself and dropped him at the foot of the stairs, a moment before Greyson emerged from the castle to see what the hell was going on this time.

"What is that?" He climbed down the stairs to join me.

"An unconscious vampire." I prodded the vamp with

my foot. Still out cold. "Want to lock him in your jail, or should we take him to Lord Blackbourne?"

He gave me a long-suffering look. "We'll keep him here."

While the Death King took the vampire to the jail across the grounds, I supervised the others while they carried the pilfered cantrips into the castle. We'd successfully swiped the Order's entire neutraliser cantrip supply, though with a tad more of a disturbance than I'd planned for. Coupled with the Death King's new agreement with the COS, though, we'd cut off the Order's supplies on two levels.

After the other ex-Order members left for the node, I found Judith had stayed behind, warily eyeing the skull-lined pillars outside the castle.

"I can't go back home," she said. "The guards saw my face."

"Not every person at the Order will have seen you," I said. "Besides, you must have known there was a chance you'd be spotted."

I tried to feel sympathy for her. I really did. She'd had her world upended, after all, yet so many people were suffering as a direct result of what the Order had done, including everything she'd enabled while she'd worked for them. She'd even got *me* arrested, which she seemed to have conveniently forgotten. Besides, the castle was crowded enough without adding my once-enemy on top of all the spirit mages.

Her expression crumpled. "If they send people after me…"

"They won't have enough guards to spare," I told her.

"Besides, if they haven't sent anyone after *me* yet, you're probably fine."

Neddie the zombie horse came wandering over, and Judith jumped violently. "Oh. God. Is that horse dead?"

"Trust me, you wouldn't like staying here in the castle." I petted Neddie on the head. "Tell you what, if you ask nicely, Devon might give you some cantrips to give you a fighting chance of escaping if the Order does show up at your house. That's all I can do for you."

Her shoulders slumped. "Okay. Thanks."

While she reluctantly sloped away, I spotted Miles approaching the gates, along with Ryan, and I ran over to meet them. "There you are. What's going on?"

"Bria's missing," said Miles.

"What do you mean, missing?"

"She disappeared when we were looking for the elves," he said. "We shut down a warehouse out in the wasteland where the Family had set up another illegal cantrip operation."

So that's where they came from. It was understandable that Bria and Miles had wanted to put a stop to it, but this wasn't a great time for one of the Death King's Elemental Soldiers to go missing.

"The rest of the Spirit Agents are in the castle," I said. "I think the Death King wants you to help him with security duty, but he's dealing with a vampire we caught near the Order while we were 'liberating' several boxes of cantrips from them."

"Never a dull moment with you, is there?" said Miles.

Ryan eyed the box of cantrips Judith had left behind. "What's in there?"

"Neutraliser cantrips. We can stash them in the back room."

I spent the next few minutes carrying the Order's cantrips into the break room while the spirit mages settled into the dormitories which had last been used during the Fire Element contest. There weren't enough spare rooms for everyone, so it was their only option. The upside to the Spirit Agents' presence was that we had more people to share security duty and give the Elemental Soldiers a break. Bria remained absent, though, and I found myself wondering what had been important enough for her to run off at a critical time like this. At least she and Miles had taken out the last of the illegal cantrip manufacturers, though we had a fairly extensive collection of our own.

Once the cantrips were securely put away, I went looking for Greyson and found him outside the jail. "Has the vampire woken up yet?"

"I intended to question him about his relationship to the Order, but he's refusing to tell me much," he said. "I wanted to confirm whether or not they're making a common habit of hiring vampires, which might add more difficulty to our plan to obtain control over their base."

"Is the dude working for the Order, then?" I tried to keep the surprise from my voice at the notion that Greyson had finally warmed to my idea about taking the Order's branch from Hawker while his back was turned.

"Not directly," he said. "He said he was delivering an artefact to a trader, but Bria attacked him, so he was forced to seek shelter within the Order's headquarters."

I made a sceptical noise. "Since when was the Order ever a place of shelter for runaway vampires?"

"Believe it or not, it was originally designated as a safe place for paranormal beings on the other side of the nodes," he said.

"Before they started hunting down people for using illegal spirit magic and kicking up a fuss every time anyone used the nodes without their permission," I added. "Which probably lasted about five minutes, because the first thing they did when they opened their doors was make spirit magic illegal."

"The original Order worked in close cooperation with the Parallel's Council of the Elements," he said. "I'm told almost all their mages were present in the Parallel during the massacre. That likely explains why there are so few of them left."

"Maybe, but that doesn't mean they needed to take the coward's way out and cave into the spirit mages' demands," I said. "Especially when the spirit mages put Holland in charge of their base instead."

"I don't disagree," he said. "I just wanted to remind you that the Order was created as a direct result of the last war, and Alban is reacting to that. He won't find himself without sympathisers in their ranks even if Holland is removed from his position."

"Maybe not, but it can't hurt to take away some of his influence," I said. "I forgot to mention—when I met with Judith earlier, she told me they were experimenting on soul amulets in their basement as well as killing liches. They can't have got those amulets from you."

His expression shadowed. "Hawker traded the lives of his own people to them."

"Not really surprising, given that he did the same to the liches who he thought weren't loyal enough."

I'd have met a similar fate myself if Dex hadn't helped me escape, but it sounded like the enemy had moved their experiments to the Parallel now. The Order, meanwhile, had gone back to being utterly inept at keeping their headquarters adequately defended.

"So," said Greyson. "When do you want to go back to the Order and claim leadership over their base?"

"We'll give them a bit of time to stop freaking out first," I said, hiding a smile. "And see if Hawker retaliates when he figures out that we've taken away their supplies."

"Fair enough," he said. "And then?"

"I'll need to borrow one of your Elemental Soldiers." I turned back towards the castle. "Also, I think you should establish some house rules for your new guests before they take all your weapons and cantrips."

I'd already seen some of them hanging around the weapons room and peering into my newly acquired cantrip boxes when I'd been carrying them into the castle. We'd soon have more than enough cantrips for an army when the massive order from the COS showed up, but I'd rather not lose all the neutralisers before we needed them.

Greyson pinched the bridge of his nose. "Right. I'll have a word with them. I don't typically have the same difficulties with sprites."

I shot him a grin and headed back to the castle myself to check up on my cantrip boxes in the break room. There, I found Ryan had taken it upon themself to guard the room from any curious spirit mages.

"What're you going to do with those?" The Air Element indicated the boxes. "Don't you think the Order is going to be pissed off with you?"

"Yes," I said. "That's why Devon and I going to set up

an ambush for when they inevitably send someone after me. Want to come and help us out?"

———

"We're doing *what*?" said Devon.

"I didn't think you'd object," I said. "You've been waiting for the Order to mount a direct attack on the shop for weeks. Might as well get it over with."

Ryan had agreed to come and help out, and Dex insisted on joining us as well. The hyperactive fire sprite zoomed around the shop, while Devon let out an exasperated sigh. "I already gave Judith a whole box of free cantrips to stop her from crying all over me. I don't need to waste any more on a false alarm."

"She thinks the Order's going to lock her up," I said. "I think they're far more likely to come here instead, so we need to give them a good scare."

She pursed her lips. "I do have a couple of new cantrips I'd like to test out. All right, then."

We set up Devon's new cantrips beside the shop's entrance, fixed with tripwires so they'd go off as soon as someone opened the door. We'd opted to go without the neutralising cantrips because they came with the unfortunate side effect of turning off the node, a mistake I'd made once before. That meant we'd have to use another means of overcoming our intruders. Luckily, Devon was more than prepared.

"Sure they're coming?" said Ryan, after we'd finished setting up the last cantrip. "Because this might get awkward if any customers showed up in the morning."

"Pretty sure the Death King's my only regular

customer now." Devon surveyed the cantrips with an expression of satisfaction. "Give it an hour, tops. They'll come."

Sure enough, as we were in the middle of a mild debate over the direction of our D&D campaign, the door snapped open and several people ran into the shop. I rose to my feet, my hands alighting with spirit magic straight from the heart of the node. Meanwhile, Dex zipped at them, showering sparks from his hands.

As the intruders grabbed for their cantrips, Devon's trap sprung, blasting them off their feet and shooting a spiderweb-like substance at them. Sticky webs covered all three Order guards, pinning them to the shop floor.

"Let us out of here!" one of them yelled from beneath the sticky web.

"Tell the Order that this shop is under the protection of the Court of the Dead," said Ryan. "And if any of you come here again, then you'll face the might of all the Elemental Soldiers."

Hands raised, Ryan blasted air magic into the Order members, sending them flying through the doors and into the street. The three of them landed in a pile of webbing, and I stifled a laugh when one of them tried to stand up and found his legs were stuck to another guard's head.

"Good luck with that." I shut the door, and then I high-fived Devon and Ryan. "Nicely done."

8

Triumphant, I returned to the Death King's castle with Ryan to report on our victory over the Order's guards once they'd finally hobbled away from the shop, covered in the remnants of Devon's webbing spell. When we reached the castle, we found Lord Blackbourne waiting outside the gates while two of the Spirit Agents looked on suspiciously.

"Olivia," he said. "I hear you brought one of my kin to the castle earlier today."

"You mean one of the Order's allies," I corrected. "Do you want to take him into custody?"

"Yes, I would," said the vampire lord. "I'm sure the Death King would prefer to have the individual taken off his hands."

"I'll ask," I said. "I was on my way to talk to him anyway."

I didn't expect Greyson to kick up a fuss about getting rid of our uncooperative prisoner, considering he'd refused to answer any questions thus far and was a potential security risk. Sure enough, when I found Greyson in the lobby and explained, he said, "Lord Blackboune is welcome to take his fellow vampire into custody. That's one fewer nuisance for me to deal with."

"The spirit mages are that bad?"

"Two of their teenage members have spent all evening playing frisbee in the corridor with the sprites."

I grinned. "That's one way to bring some more excitement into your castle. Anyway, I'll go with Lord Black-bourne to make sure his prisoner doesn't give him the slip."

His brows rose. "Are you sure?"

"Yeah. I won't be long."

He didn't offer to come with me, though I wouldn't have objected despite the fact that I also needed to talk to Brant. If anyone might know about the enemy's most recent cantrip-related schemes, it was him, and I'd rather be forewarned.

Lord Blackbourne didn't seem to be particularly surprised that I wanted to accompany him back to the vampires' jail. He simply glided into the Death King's prison and returned within a minute with the limp body of his fellow vampire slung over his shoulder. The intruder's hands were cuffed and his head lolling as though the vampire lord had knocked him out cold. He wasn't having the best day, that was for sure.

"Didn't you want to bring someone else to help you restrain him if necessary?" I asked. "I'd volunteer, but I'd figure you'd rather have another vampire help out."

"No," the vampire lord said shortly. "I'm capable of handling a simple rogue myself."

Someone was in a snippy mood. "Do you know him?"

"I recognise his face," said Lord Blackbourne. "He's a known troublemaker in Arcadia for borrowing large sums of money and using them to procure artefacts he can't otherwise afford, before selling said artefacts to traders for profit and then wriggling out of repaying the original loans."

"Bria said he stole some kind of elf artefact from an auction, so that makes sense," I said. "He took shelter inside the Order's base to escape the people trying to get it back."

Together with his unconscious passenger, Lord Blackbourne and I walked through the node and emerged into the suburbs of Arcadia where the vampires had relocated their base. He tilted his head at me as we neared their headquarters. "Remembered anything else about your history with Dirk Alban?"

"Nope," I said. "Haven't heard from the man himself either, before you ask. Has he come to thank you for looking after his soul amulet?"

The vampire looked at me askance. "You're very lucky that Greyson has taken a liking to you."

"Believe me, I know."

When we reached the door to the council house, he called two other vampires over to help carry their prisoner to their jail. Meanwhile, I went looking for Brant. Few of the other cells in the vampires' prison were occupied, so it was easy enough to track down the ex-fire mage in a cell at the far end of the corridor. He rose to his feet the instant he set eyes on me.

"Liv..." He cleared his throat. "What are you doing here?"

"Helping Lord Blackbourne bring in a new prisoner," I

said. "He attacked my allies at the Order's base and the Death King wanted to get him off his hands."

"The Order?" he echoed. "Are they hiring vampires as their security guards now?"

"The Order used to hire vampires as ambassadors before the last ones met an unfortunate end, if you haven't forgotten." I referenced the night I'd been asked to help the Order escort him to the vampires' jail, only for assassins to kill our vampire escorts en route. Brant, meanwhile, had made a run for it and left me to take the blame.

"They don't hire ambassadors anymore, though, right?" He clearly remembered as well as I did, because he wouldn't meet my eyes. "Because that would mean they're working with Lord Blackbourne as well as Hawker and his allies."

"No, the guy who attacked us wasn't any kind of ambassador, just a rogue," I said. "I take it you didn't see any vampires while you were in the Order's custody?"

"Of course I didn't," he said. "Why? What brought this on?"

I glanced over my shoulder to make sure nobody was listening in. "Did you know the Order was also conducting experiments involving soul amulets?"

"What?" His eyes widened. "Of course not. You know I didn't see a bloody thing when I was stuck in their jail. They certainly wouldn't have told me anything about their secret plans."

"You're the one who told me about Cobb's plan to steal the soul of a mage to begin with," I reminded him. "Okay, I know it was the Death King's soul he was after, but you said yourself that you were supposed to trade over your soul to the Crow when the war was won. Did you know what he planned to do with it?"

"Of course not." His brow pinched. "He never specified, but I didn't hear anyone mention soul amulets. Why do you want to know, anyway? The Crow died ages ago."

He doesn't know. Guess I shouldn't be surprised. "Just trying to stamp out the last of the illegal cantrip trade. Know of any more of their safe houses?"

"No," he said. "I told them everything I knew, anyway."

"By 'them', do you mean the Order?" I said suspiciously.

"And the vampires," he said. "Why?"

I narrowed my eyes. "Because the Order is now answering to Alban and Hawker, of course."

At the sound of Alban's name, he sank backwards onto a bench. "He—*he* can't be back. They're lying, right?"

"Oh, he is." My last shreds of sympathy fled. "I'm the one who has a good reason to fear him. Not you."

Brant's face was pale in the darkness. "Liv, you can't stay there in the castle. If you get any closer to the House of Spirit, the curse will take you, too."

"I already died once," I said. "I came back, and I fully intend on curing the other liches, too, without relying on the Order to do it for me."

"The Order offered to undo the curse?" he said disbelievingly.

"It's the second time they've made that offer. Last time they blew up a bunch of innocent people when we said no, so I'm not holding out much hope that it'll end well."

He rose to his feet again. "You were lucky to escape alive, Liv. Don't stay involved. It'll kill you."

"Tell me something I don't know," I said. "I have to stay

involved because I'm a spirit mage, Brant. I won't turn my back on the others."

Hearing movement nearby, I turned away. Brant didn't say a word while I retraced my steps down the corridor, where I found Lord Blackbourne near the newcomer's cell.

"You might want to ask our vampire guest about his involvement in a scheme to take the soul amulets of liches and use them to experiment on," I said to him. "That seems to be Hawker's plan for his allies."

"Is it?" The vampire lord's mouth twisted with distaste. "I suppose it prevents them from fighting back."

I don't think that's all there is to it. But I needed more clues before I could figure out the rest. Brant didn't know. He hadn't been given access to that information.

Souls contained power and spirit mages' souls most of all—enough to act as batteries for the machines in the citadels, and even to create nodes. Look at what Hawker had achieved in London with one mass sacrifice. With the souls of his allies in his hands, I had my doubts that he had benign intentions for them.

"You had a thought, didn't you?" said the vampire lord.

"Not a complete one," I said. "I don't know if Greyson told you or not, but the Order is trying to bribe us into cooperating with them with the promise of lifting the curse on the rest of the liches. Might they have the cure for the curse at their headquarters?"

"You're the one who seems to be in the habit of breaking into the Order's property," he said. "I can't say I know what they're hiding inside their base."

"I didn't exactly have the chance to explore when I was subduing that guy." I glanced at the vampire's unconscious form inside his cell. "Anyway, it seems a pertinent question to ask. If the Order *does* have the means of undoing the curse, it'll be tough to talk the other liches out of listening to them."

"Then you'll have to get the answer from the Order yourself," he said. "Are you finished with the fire mage?"

"Yes, I am," I said. "If he gave you the addresses of any safe houses, it might be worth checking to make sure Hawker's people haven't moved in there. He gave the same addresses to the Order as well."

"I'll take care of it."

Brant called down the corridor to me as I approached the stairs. "Liv, please don't stay with the Death King."

I cast a look in the direction of his cell. "Brant, you're facing a lifetime of incarceration. Focus on your own shit."

I climbed the stairs and left him behind, part of me knowing that this would be my last visit. I had nothing more to say to him, and if I wanted the truth, I'd find the answers elsewhere.

I walked back to the node alone, halting for a brief moment to peer over the fence into the ruins of the Crow's estate. I didn't expect to see anything inside, and since any cantrips which might have been there had long since been removed, there was no point in sticking around.

Upon my return to the swamp, I heard a commotion on the other side of the fence. In the castle grounds, Greyson stood surrounded by a group of liches. When I walked in, they turned in my direction, and then in a tide of shadow, they swarmed around me as well as him.

"What's going on?" I reached Greyson's side, noting his

grim expression and the hostility emanating from all directions. Oh, boy.

"You were supposed to set us free," said the nearest lich. "Instead, you refused the Order's offer to undo the curse on us."

Oh, shit. I should have known the other liches would figure it out sooner or later. "The Order is full of liars who are out for their own gain and nothing else. If we accepted their offer, they'd either refuse to undo the curse without forcing you to swear allegiance to Hawker or Alban, or else turn you into their lab rats. It wouldn't be the first time."

"What proof do you have?" said another lich. "None of us have left the castle in years, nor have we been allowed to talk to the Order ourselves. You expect us to follow your lead, yet you conceal the truth whenever is convenient."

Damn. There was no arguing with that one, but that didn't mean the Order would solve all their problems rather than creating a shit-ton of new ones.

"I don't deny you've had a rough deal," I said. "I was a lich myself until recently. I know how it feels to be cut off from your former life, and if I knew a way to break the curse without risking the Order turning you into lab rats, I'd have told you."

"Precisely," said Greyson. "If the Order had their way, you'd die permanently... or worse."

"Says who?" said the lich. "We've nothing but your word to go on."

"Trust me, it won't end well if you believe the Order instead," I said. "When I was a lich, they tried to use a cantrip on me which would have blasted me out of existence without the need for my soul amulet. They were using Hawker's liches' soul amulets as experimental tools until recently, too, suggesting that even his allies were nothing more than conveniences to him. Also, I might add that most of you can't survive on Earth without access to the nodes, which means entering the Order's base will be doubly risky for you."

"If that's what you want, though," added Greyson, "by all means, feel free to go and join them."

Nobody spoke a word for a long moment. Then one of the liches addressed Greyson. "It's *her* fault. Before she showed up, you treated us all equally. Now she always comes first, and the pair of you broke the curse on yourselves without telling the rest of us how to do it."

"If Olivia hadn't come here, then we wouldn't have any hope of removing the curse from anyone at all," Greyson told them. "She believed it was possible to bring me back from death even before I thought so myself. And *I* believe she can do the same for you."

My face flushed at his praise, but I kept my attention on the liches. "Just give me a little time and I'll figure it out."

"Be patient," said Greyson. "You've waited this long. You can wait a little longer. Now, go, and stop bothering my Spirit Element."

Nobody argued any further, and the liches began to disperse. I shot him a smile—then a lich spun and stabbed his hand into my chest.

I reeled back, coldness flooding me from head to toe. Greyson's eyes widened and he moved to intervene, but there came a flash of orange-red light as a transparent figure shot overhead. *Dex.* I drew his offered power into me, and flames blasted from my hands, breaking the lich's grip. The shadowy figure turned into ashes on the spot, while I caught my balance, breathless and shivering. "Dammit. Greyson, he'll come back… we need to find his soul amulet first."

The other liches had backed away from the flames, sensibly, and Greyson strode towards them, emanating menace. "The next person to attack Olivia or myself will find themselves suffering a fate that will leave them wishing for a permanent end. Leave. *Now.*"

The other liches fled in all directions, while I sank to my knees, cursing the weakness that the chilling touch of the disintegrated lich had left behind. "I think he was a spirit mage."

I heard Greyson start to reply, but all faded to blackness.

———

Dirk Alban stood at the front of a classroom, which was empty aside from the two of us, and he held a soul amulet in his hand.

"This is a vessel for a soul," he said to me. "If a spirit mage binds a soul to an amulet like this one, the soul's owner turns into a lich, bound to the spirit mage's will."

"Why would I want a lich following me around?" I asked. "I thought they fell to pieces here on Earth, anyway."

"They do," he said. "It's also considerably difficult, though not impossible, to use such magic without access to a strong source of energy, like a node. Ideally, you'd need to be in the Parallel."

"I don't understand why anyone would want that, though." The idea of binding another person to myself was unappealing, even if Dirk Alban usually had good reason for the topics he chose for our private lessons together. He always knew which subjects I'd find most useful.

"You never know what knowledge you might need, Olivia," he said. "People like us… we're misunderstood by the world at large. Many will want us dead, but others will trust us with their lives and souls."

The amulet glowed in his hand, and I recoiled. "There's a person's soul in there? *Now?*"

"Yes," said Dirk Alban.

I didn't hear what else he said, because the world faded out, and my vision flickered back into focus to find Greyson leaning over me. Softness cushioned my back, telling me I lay on the sofa in his private suite. "Ow."

"The lich's touch damaged your soul," said Greyson. "I fixed it, then I figured I'd let you sleep it off. You needed the rest."

"Cheers." I sat up, noting the shadows under his eyes which indicated he was nowhere near as well rested. "I let my guard down. I shouldn't have."

"Don't blame yourself," he said. "I'm the one who let the liches discuss mutiny inside my own territory."

"You couldn't have known," I said. "I assumed they wouldn't guess the Order's plan. I wonder how they found out?"

"People talk," he said.

"I'm starting to regret telling Lord Blackbourne." I shook my head. "He's refusing to get involved, but it would help if we knew if the Order was bluffing or not. If they *do* have the cantrips to restore the liches to life on their property, then we might be able to steal them back like we did with the neutraliser cantrips."

"I doubt they do," he said. "Besides, according to Miles, they were likely manufactured at the warehouse he and Bria disrupted."

"Or one of the safe houses Brant told the Order about," I added.

His brows shot up. "Did he now?"

"I passed on word to Lord Blackbourne, so it's up to him if he wants to pursue that line of inquiry," I said. "I take it Bria set the warehouse she found on fire?"

"She and Miles shut the place down," said Greyson. "Then she went after the Family in person to ensure they don't try the same again."

"So that's where she disappeared to," I said. "I thought you didn't like people going behind your back."

"You helped me see the hypocrisy of that outlook."

Warmth filled my chest at his words. "I did?"

"Yes." He leaned closer, his lips brushing mine. "I'm going to give orders to the other liches. Please try not to get attacked again."

"I'll try not to." I watched him leave, then slumped against the cushions for a moment to get my breath back. I was drained and tired but also starving, so I pushed to my feet and headed for the break room to find the others. It was morning by now, and faint sunlight streamed in through the window and the smell of frying breakfast came from the kitchen area. On the sofa, Ryan sat polishing their sword next to Cal, who was playing a video game on the console which was hooked up to the flat-screen TV at the front. Felicity glanced over at me from where she stood buttering toast and gave me a smile. "Help yourself to breakfast, if you like. I know you didn't get to go home last night."

"Yeah, I need to change my contacts too." Breakfast sounded good, though, considering I'd skipped a few meals lately, so I grabbed some toast and went to join the others.

"What the hell happened last night?" Ryan put their sword down. "The Death King said you were attacked."

"Attempted mutiny," I said. "Supposedly, I'm a terrible influence on the Death King and the other liches wanted to take me out of the picture. One ex-spirit mage gave it a good shot, too."

"Seriously?" said Ryan. "That's utter bullshit."

"You thought that at first yourself, Ryan," Felicity reminded them. "You too, Cal."

I raised my brows at both of them, and Cal shrugged and stood up from the sofa, offering me his seat. "Nah, you're all right."

"I'll take that as a compliment." I sat down, while Cal turned off the games console and went to nose through the boxes of cantrips I'd pilfered from the Order. "Ryan?"

"What?" they said. "I joined your D&D group. Clearly, I don't hate spending time around you."

I grinned, wondering when and how I'd grown so comfortable around the Elemental Soldiers. The idea of joining their ranks was nowhere near as unappealing as it had once been, that was for sure.

"No news on Bria?" I asked Ryan. "The Death King said she was dealing with the Family in person."

"Miles mentioned the elves," said Ryan. "I'm not sure anyone knows *what* she's doing."

"Speaking of elves, how's it going with Trix?" I asked.

Their expression closed off somewhat. "I don't know what you mean."

"I'm not making fun," I reassured them. "I know it's none of my business, but Trix and I were friends from my first visit to the Parallel, pretty much. We go back a long way."

"I know," said Ryan. "Look... I came to live in the castle to get away from other people's expectations. Even in the Parallel, it felt like I could never be what anyone wanted me to be, so I stopped bothering to make an effort to be anything other than myself. Now Trix shows up and doesn't expect me to change, and it feels like a trick on behalf of the universe."

"It's really not." I understood what they meant, though. Ryan had come a long way from the prickly Air Element who'd once blasted me in the face with magic rather than accept that I might not be the enemy. "Believe me, you shouldn't give up on a good thing, even if it seems too good to be true. I should know."

Ryan lifted their head. "You mean the Death King."

"Greyson," I said. "Yeah. I do. He's calling me his Spirit Element now."

"Damn, I should have known," said Ryan. "I owe Felicity, then."

"What, you made bets against me accepting a job as his Spirit Element?" I said indignantly, looking around at the others.

"Yes," said Felicity, shooting me a wink. "I bet on you staying here."

"Glad one of you has faith in me." I bit into my toast. "Did Greyson join in?"

"No," said Ryan. "He said there was no need because he'd win in the end."

I choked on my mouthful. "That figures. Why'd you bet against me?"

"I thought you'd have more sense. Now you're stuck here with us."

"Watch it, you." I settled back in my seat, grinning around at my friends. "Or I might change my mind."

I wouldn't, though. Greyson had me, and he knew it.

After a quick trip home to change and shower, I returned to the castle's entrance hall, only to find no signs of Greyson anywhere.

"Looking for His Deathly Highness?" Dex flew down from the ceiling. "He was in the hall of souls the last I checked, waiting for that lich who attacked you to return to an incorporeal form."

"He's still not back?" I made for the door to the hall of souls, which opened the instant I touched it. "Whoa. Did he leave it unlocked?"

"You're the Spirit Element," Dex reminded me. "I bet he changed the settings to make it open for you."

Voices sounded from within the room, and my shoulders stiffened when I made out the shape of Greyson, in full Death King mode, facing the lich who'd attacked me. I trod closer, ready to use my magic if necessary, but the lich made no move to strike either of us. Then I saw the Death King held his soul amulet in his hand.

"Why did you attack my Spirit Element?" The Death King's voice echoed in the wide hall, sounding almost as creepy as it had as a lich.

"Because she's a spirit mage," said the lich. "You're taking sides with the people who saw to it that we were cursed to begin with."

"Are you forgetting *I* am a spirit mage?" said the Death King. "So were you, in fact, when you lived."

"Also, you might have forgotten only a spirit mage can bring you back from death," I added. "Kill all the living spirit mages and you'll only doom yourself. If you wanted to join Hawker, then you should have just gone with him rather than staying here."

"I don't want to join Hawker," said the lich. "I want my life back."

"Then you shouldn't have tried to take mine." I glanced at the Death King, wondering what his plan was for the lich who'd betrayed him.

The Death King lifted the soul amulet in answer. A glow suffused the edges, and the lich let out a sound halfway between a gasp and a cry. His shadowy form began to fade around the edges as the glow transferred from the soul amulet to the Death King himself. Chills raced through my entire body as I realised he was drawing out the lich's life force from his soul amulet, inch by inch. The shadowy form of the lich grew fainter by the second, until it evaporated into nothing more than dust.

The Death King placed the vacant soul amulet on the nearest shelf. "He won't bother us again."

"Can I keep that?" I asked.

He frowned at me, now looking more like Greyson than the fearsome Death King who'd just obliterated someone's soul. "What in the world do you want a soul amulet for?"

"I have a feeling I might need it." When he didn't object, I stepped over to the shelf and scooped up the amulet in my hand.

"I hope *not*," he said. "I wouldn't recommend making anyone dependent on you for their survival. Even the dead can disappoint you."

"Believe me, I know that," I said. "How did he and the others find out about the Order's offer, anyway? Did he ever tell you?"

"He said that someone from the Order told him that they bargained with me for the cure and I turned them down," said the Death King.

My brows shot up. "Ah, so that's how they decided to get us back for stealing their cantrips. They told the liches the truth."

The details of our meeting with the Order had been bound to come to light eventually, but I wished the liches would have a little more faith in us. It wasn't like the Order had actually proved that they had the means of undoing the curse on their property or otherwise. Besides, if the other liches had seen the cantrips they'd been making in their basement, they might have had second thoughts about believing a word they said.

When we left the hall of souls, I heard shouting coming from down the corridor which led to the Elemental Soldiers' quarters.

"What is it this time?" I left the lobby and walked down the corridor, where I found Miles and several spirit mages standing off against a group of shadowy liches.

The Death King strode ahead of me, smoothly placing himself between me and the liches. "Is there a problem?"

"Your liches seem to have an issue with you letting us stay here in the castle," said Miles. "Not all of them are fans of spirit mages."

The Death King's jaw tightened. "I gathered as much from the lich who just paid the price for mutiny with his soul. If anyone shares his opinion, then feel free to direct your grievances at me rather than at my guests."

I waved the vacant soul amulet at the liches, to be rewarded when they flinched away. "Have some goddamn patience. We're working on finding your bloody cure, but if you're going to insist on starting petty arguments every time our backs are turned, don't blame me if it takes longer than you'd like."

At a further glare from the Death King, the liches drifted out of the corridor without another word of argument. After a moment, the spirit mages left, too, and then the Death King and I were alone.

At once, he became Greyson again, exhaling in the faintest sigh. "I generally prefer not to resort to threats, but they're testing my patience."

"Why have the liches suddenly turned anti-spirit mage?" I slipped the soul amulet into my cantrip pouch. "Was that the Order's intention when they spread word among the liches about their offer of curing them? They wanted the liches to turn on the mages who are the reason they survived death to begin with?"

"It's beneficial for them to turn us against one another," he said. "Both for the purposes of creating discord and distracting us from finding the cure ourselves."

"Which means either taking over the Order's base or tracking down Hawker," I said. "Unless… did Miles and Bria find any of those cantrips at the warehouse they shut down? The ones which can bring liches back to life, I mean?"

"Good thinking," said Greyson. "I'll ask."

At the end of the corridor, we found our new guests congregating inside their new common room, which had once been occupied by the contestants during the trials for the Death King's new Fire Element. Wooden tables and chairs filled most of the space, while they'd set up a small kitchen area at the back complete with a microwave and toaster. I assumed the spirit mages had divided up their chores the same way they had at their old base before they'd been turfed out, because the room was pretty clean considering the number of people crowding inside. When they spotted us, a hush spread throughout the room and all eyes turned in our direction.

"No need to stare," I said. "Is Miles around?"

"Sure." The straw-haired spirit mage approached the pair of us, chewing on a piece of burnt toast he'd acquired from the stack of plates in the kitchen area. "What's up?"

Greyson waited for the others to return to their conversations before speaking. "Did you and Bria find any illegal cantrips in that warehouse?"

Miles stopped chewing. "I never thought to check. I mean, most of the cantrips we found weren't completed, and once we got the practitioners out of there, nobody was left to finish the job."

"Who were the practitioners?" I asked curiously.

"Elves." Miles grimaced. "The Family captured them

and forced them to work in that warehouse to make cantrips for their own use. We set them free, but I didn't think to go back and check on the cantrips they might have left behind."

"I'd advise you to send someone to check," said Greyson. "We're intending to strip away as many of the enemy's cantrips as possible. Where are the elves now?"

"In hiding," said Miles. "I helped them escape while Bria diverted the Family's attention."

Elves. Nausea flooded me at the very thought of someone forcing the elves—who were generally the most mild-mannered beings I'd ever met in the Parallel—to carve deadly cantrips against their will.

"As long as they're safe, I'd keep your attention on the warehouse and make sure the enemy doesn't come back," said Greyson.

"Hey, no need to boss me around," Miles said. "I'm not one of your Elemental Soldiers."

"You grew up together, right?" I looked between them, wondering how long Miles had known Greyson. Perhaps longer than I had, even if I discounted my years of missing memories.

"Sort of," said Miles. "Greyson and I met when he first came into the Parallel, a newbie spirit mage with no clue what he was doing."

I stifled a smile. "So you taught him everything he knows?"

"Yes, I did." Miles reached out and poked Greyson in the arm. "He might want to pretend he's always been the badass King of the Dead, but some of us remember otherwise."

"I knew him before, too," I said. "Back on Earth, I mean."

"Right, because of his double life." Miles tried to poke him again, but Greyson smoothly stepped out of the way. "Took forever to pry the details out of him. I never asked, Grey… how's being alive again treating you?"

"Fine," said Greyson.

Miles grinned. "Let me guess, you're struggling with human limitations. Not getting enough sleep? Forgetting to eat? Thinking you can walk through walls?"

"I'm handling it," said Greyson. "I might remind you that during your first attempt at astral projection, you never left your body at all and ended up walking into a river."

"Ha." I looked between them, warmed by their easy banter. I was glad Greyson had begun to relax into being human again, even if most of his Court remained deceased. "I haven't seen him walk into any walls yet, but there's still time."

"Wait and see," said Miles. "You know, you might want to hire some cleaning staff if you're planning for the castle to be inhabited by living people again. There was a spider the size of my fist in the dorm the last time I went in there."

"It *is* an ancient castle," I reminded him. "Complete with ghosts."

"I believe the dead still outnumber the living, in any case," said Greyson. "I would, however, appreciate it if you checked to make sure there aren't any more of those cantrips lying around where anyone can pick them up."

Miles's expression sobered. "I'm not on guard duty this

morning, so I can grab a couple of people and take them with me to the warehouse. If we find anything illegal, we'll let you know."

"Good," I said. "Is there a reason the Family picked elves in particular to carve their cantrips for them? I know they have strong magic, but so do mages."

"Yeah, and the mages have an unpleasant history with the elves," Miles said. "Bria can tell you more, but it's not the only time they've tried to take credit for someone else's creations. The elves actually built the citadels, did you know?"

My mouth parted. "I thought the spirit mages built them."

"I thought so, too, but the elves have lived in the Parallel from the start," Miles said. "It's their tools which were eventually adapted to make cantrips."

Damn. That brought a whole new dimension to the dilemma of how to rebuild the Parallel once Alban's plan for domination had been brought crashing to the ground. While I had no desire for the spirit mages to gain supremacy in the magical realm like they'd had before the war, I didn't think it was a good idea to outright ban the use of spirit magic all over again either. There had to be a way to strike the right balance, and whatever replaced the current system would have to be different enough to avoid repeating the same mistakes all over again.

It wasn't up to me to decide, of course, and it wasn't as though I hadn't made some fairly monumental mistakes myself. Like trusting Dirk Alban, for instance, and not telling the other liches about the Order's offer to cure them of their curse.

Speaking of which...

As Greyson and I left Miles to grab some allies to take with him to the warehouse, I said, "I think it's safe to say the Order have already made their next move against us. That means it's our turn."

"To do what?" Greyson said. "What are you scheming?"

"To take back the Order's base," I said. "It's the only way we can expose whether or not they're hiding a cure. I'll give Judith a call."

———

An hour later, I hopped through the node on top of our living room and landed on the road adjacent to the pub Judith had picked as our meeting place.

Judith, who happened to be walking past at that moment, jumped a foot in the air. "What the hell are you doing? We're in public!"

"Calm down. It's not like the Order is watching." It was a miracle I'd convinced her to leave her house, much less come to another meeting, given her paranoia following her botched attempt at smuggling cantrips out of the Order's base. "We're nowhere near their headquarters."

"Still." She gave a nervous glance at the node. "Good job they don't watch all the nodes."

"They don't watch all their enemies either," I said. "Look, they won't waste their time sending anyone after you if they haven't already. They only lift a finger when it's really worth it to them, and they know I won't rush to rescue you if they take you hostage."

She made a disbelieving noise. "Why should I trust a word you say, then?"

"Because the Death King and I are your last hope to

survive this mess with your job intact," I said. "Maybe your life, too. Besides, you agreed to this meeting."

We entered the pub and found a table in the corner to wait for the others. While Judith was even twitchier than normal, she wasn't the only one. Even Craig, ever the joker, had an uncharacteristically serious demeanour today, while Carla had forsaken her usual bright clothing in favour of dark and subdued tones.

"What's up, Liv?" she said. "You want to take back the Order... now? We don't have anywhere near enough allies."

"We also don't have much time," I said. "Do any of you have a copy of the rota? When we go in, we'll need to know who's at headquarters and whether they're likely to stand in our way. Including the upper room."

"We can't attack the upper room!" Judith squeaked.

"That's not the plan," I said. "I wouldn't mind berating them for letting Holland have his way, but if we knock out everyone in power, we'll look less legitimate. Unless they aren't around, of course."

"The last takeover happened when they were gone, didn't it?" said Craig. "They don't stay at the base all day and night. They go home late in the evening, and then they come back first thing in the morning. Except Holland, I think, but that guy is unpredictable."

"Then it'll have to be at night." I drummed my fingers on the table. "Tonight, in fact."

"*Tonight?*" said Judith. "No way. Their security is still on high alert after the last couple of attacks on their base."

"They have no neutraliser cantrips," I said. "No defence against magical attacks, and no opportunity to order replacements. If we take enough allies with us, then we should be able to overwhelm them. Especially if our allies include the Death King's Elemental Soldiers."

"Is that even allowed?" Judith said. "Isn't this exactly the same as what Holland and the spirit mages did?"

"With less bloodshed," I said. "And with the intention of handing control back over to the Order members who are actually supposed to be running the place once they've proven they won't give into the enemy's demands again."

"That's still... illegal," she said uncertainly. "We're staging a coup, aren't we? Like Holland?"

I almost felt sorry for her for stubbornly clinging to her black-and-white worldview despite everything she'd seen to the contrary. "Look, if we don't step in and turf Holland out, nobody else is going to. There's no legal way to do it short of involving the other Order branches, and we don't know if any of them are working with Hawker and his allies, too."

"But..." Carla hesitated. "Aren't we outnumbered? Even if we go in at night, there's usually plenty of Order staff wandering around."

"Not necessarily," I said. "Once we take out Holland and his defenders, we can ask the others who they'd rather work for. Him or us. Holland is a power-grabbing hypocrite. Doubt he has many fans, except those who want to ride on his coattails to power."

"Not a bad shout," said Craig. "It's a mad idea, but what isn't?"

"As for the rest of the upper room," I went on, "I'd rather they didn't get away with granting Holland the power they gave him, but that doesn't mean it's feasible to replace them all just yet. It's also possible the extent of Hawker's influence was hidden from them. Anyway, the Death King doesn't want to run the Order, but he's willing to take control for as long as necessary. So am I."

"You're really not coming back to the Order even if things go back to normal, then?" Judith said. "Why do you prefer the Court of the Dead? It's an awful place."

"Because I'm a spirit mage, and I have no faith in the Order to ever truly accept that," I said. "Besides, the Court of the Dead grows on you, if you give it enough time."

She gave me a look as though she thought I was seriously unhinged, but I didn't particularly care. The others broke into a discussion of how to obtain a copy of the rota for tonight and see who might be convinced to join us against Holland, while I mentally ran through the Order's defences and what kind of retaliation we might expect to face. They'd be on the lookout for trouble, but that was fine by me.

Today would be Holland's last day as part of the upper room.

———

After the others dispersed following our meeting, I returned to the Parallel to discuss our plan with the Death King and the Elemental Soldiers. While His Deathly Highness himself agreed more readily than I might have expected, Ryan was sceptical. "You think it'll work? Storming in there with all guns blazing?"

"Better than how Holland did it," I said. "Coercing the upper room into making decisions by slaughtering the Order's staff in coordinated terrorist attacks, I mean. If we time this right, nobody has to die at all. Granted, I wouldn't mind punching Holland in the face."

"Who even is Holland, anyway?" said Ryan.

"The same dude who sentenced me to have two years of my memories stripped out," I said. "Now he's working directly for the man who was the reason I got caught. Yeah, I know."

Ryan scowled. "Then I'd be more than happy to let you use him as a punching bag."

"I'll see to it that he loses his seat with the upper room first," I said. "The goal is to get him to surrender, take all of Hawker's and Alban's allies in the Order's base into custody, and then make sure the people who are left won't let them take control again."

"You don't think they'll fight back in the process?" said Felicity.

"I do," I said. "But let's be realistic, this is our best shot. If we wait any longer, we run the risk of them obtaining enough cantrips to make up for the ones we stole from them. This way, we get to help the Order's innocent employees escape without losing their jobs or their lives, *and* we find out if they really are hiding the means of undoing the liches' curse at their base."

Whether they were or not, I had an inkling we were running on borrowed time. Alban and Hawker would attack the Court of the Dead directly sooner or later, and the fewer allies they had to call on for backup, the better.

When night fell, I armed myself with as many cantrips as I could carry, neutralisers included, as well as the soul amulet from the unfortunate lich who'd attacked me the previous day. Just in case I needed it.

The Elemental Soldiers and I gathered outside the

castle, along with a few spirit mages who'd volunteered to come with us. The Death King was the last to join our group, clad in his usual armoured gear with an honest-to-god sword strapped to his waist. My heartbeat quickened, and I fervently hoped he wouldn't have to *use* the sword.

Time to storm the Order of the Elements.

10

Once our group had travelled through the node to the high street, we made straight for the Order's headquarters. With five of us clad in armour leading the way, we probably looked like a lost cosplay group to anyone who glanced in our direction, accompanied by the Spirit Agents in their battered, ragged Parallel-style clothing. Not to mention Dex, who flew amid our group, his fiery form practically vibrating with excitement.

At the Order's doors, the two security guards exchanged glances when they saw our group approaching them. "I didn't know you were coming here today, Death King. And… Olivia."

"Holland is expecting us." Not exactly a lie, given his open challenge. "Both of us."

To my immense surprise, the guards parted to allow us to enter the lobby. Nobody tried to stop us, at least until they saw the Elemental Soldiers and Spirit Agents attempting to enter, too.

"What are you doing?" asked one of the guards. "You can't be in here."

Everyone ignored his protests, while the Death King and I kept walking without pause, cutting through the centre of the lobby with our allies at our back. More guards congregated around our group as though wondering whether they were supposed to attack us or not. That played into our hands, since the rest of our group occupied the guards' attention while I yanked open Mr Holland's office door without knocking and flung a neutralising cantrip into the room.

A fizzling sound like the electricity short-circuiting came from within, while Mr Holland leapt to his feet when I kicked the door fully open. "What are you doing, Olivia?"

"Taking you up on your offer," I said.

The Death King entered the room behind me. "I would be delighted to cooperate with the Order, but not as long as you remain in control of this branch. *Or* your spirit mage allies, for that matter."

Mr Holland's gaze darted between the pair of us. "What? You can't come in here and depose me. You don't have the authority."

"Don't I?" The Death King's voice lowered menacingly. "I happen to have a working contract with the Order which decrees that I may step in to assist if they're under attack from hostile forces. I would say the fact that Hawker is manipulating the Order by using you as his puppet certainly qualifies."

"Yeah, so hand over the cure for the liches and get the hell out," I added.

"That is enough!" Mr Holland's face flushed bright red.

"First you refused my offer, then you sent your people to steal from us, and now you have the audacity to come back and threaten me directly even after everything I've done for you."

"Your predecessor turned an entire group of mages into liches and cursed them to stay that way forever," I said. "You persecuted spirit mages for years, jailed innocent people, conspired with the Houses of the Elements to make life a living hell for all mages in the Parallel—and most recently, you sat back and let one of the very mages you claim to despise take power over this Order branch due to your own ambitions. You've done nothing for any of us except ruin our lives."

His mouth dropped open. "*You* are nothing more than a criminal who never should have been allowed to walk free. I wish I'd seen to your execution."

"Would you have done the same to Dirk Alban, if you'd known he lived?" I queried. "I think we both know the answer."

He lunged at me. I saw the attack coming, and my hand shot out and grabbed his life essence. In my other hand, I revealed the soul amulet I'd taken from the lich the Death King had killed, while Holland remained frozen mid-motion, his eyes bulging at the sight of my hand clenched around the bright essence I'd pulled from him.

His Deathly Highness himself blinked a couple of times as he realised what I was doing, but he didn't intervene. Not yet, anyway.

"If you resist, I can bind you to me for the rest of your life," I warned Holland. "And as a lich, that might be for a very long time."

I let go of his life essence, and Mr Holland sagged

against the desk. "What do you want me to do? I have no magic of my own. They do. Hawker... Alban... they have the world at their feet. Both worlds. They're winning."

"Not yet," I said. "We have no intention of letting them win this, but you risked the lives of everyone in this building when you surrendered and let him gain control over this base. For that reason alone, you can expect a lifelong jail sentence at the very least."

"The others won't stand for it," he insisted. "Why is nobody coming to defend me?"

"Because we did this the diplomatic way," I said. "More than a few members of this branch are willing to resist your control. Others might have been too afraid to run because their livelihoods depended on their employment here, but that didn't mean they supported Hawker or Alban."

"As for those who did?" said the Death King. "My Elemental Soldiers are rounding them up as we speak. They should be ready by the time we're done in here."

I pushed the door open and revealed the others herding the bewildered Order staff members into the corner of the lobby. At a gesture from the Death King, Ryan walked over with a pair of handcuffs and snapped them on Mr Holland's wrists. With him and his allies restrained, we'd have free rein to search the place for any hidden cantrips, including those intended to remove the curse from the liches. If they existed, of course.

"I'm going to search the basement," I said to the Death King. "Want to stay here, or would you prefer to come with me?"

In truth, I didn't know what I'd find in their old labs, nor was I keen to return to the place where I'd almost met a grim death, but if the Order had a cure hidden on the property, it would be down in the lower levels.

"I'll escort Mr Holland to his cell while you search the basement," said the Death King.

"Good call." I beckoned Dex to join us as the Death King and I took our captive into the elevator, riding it down to the lower floor.

As we walked out into the metal-walled, draughty corridor, Dex scared a couple of guards away by throwing fireballs at them until they ran for the stairs or elevators. Meanwhile, I parted ways with the Death King at the cells comprising the Order's prison.

"I never liked this place." Dex shuddered theatrically, flitting alongside me down the corridor. "What're you looking for in here?"

"Any illegal cantrips," I said. "If anyone sneaks up on us, feel free to torch them. I'm not taking any chances down here."

Judith's tales about what she'd seen in her time guarding the lab lurked in the back of my mind, and while I doubted that I'd find any experiments in progress here, that didn't mean there wasn't any evidence left behind. The usual stifling sensation intensified the further we walked, as though an invisible force pushed against me from all angles. Despite my best efforts, my steps slowed, and I rested a hand on the wall for balance.

"What's up with you?" said Dex.

My head throbbed. "This place always does weird shit to my magic. And my memories, too."

"Your memories," said Dex. "This whole thing wasn't a scheme for you to get your memories back, was it?"

"Of course not," I said. "I've never had a useful,

coherent memory come back when I've been in this place. Anyway, we need to see what the Order has been hiding."

This part of the Order's base seemed mostly abandoned, though, which fit with my theory that they'd moved their labs elsewhere. There was only so much they could do from Earth, besides. In the Parallel, their magic was stronger, their resources more numerous and the nodes easier to reach.

I turned a corner, realising I was retracing the steps I'd taken as a lich, towards the lab where I'd almost been vaporised by a deadly cantrip. As I passed through a doorway I recognised, a cold sensation pierced my skin, and a faint mist hung in the air. The chill grew worse when I approached the lab at the end, the place where I'd nearly met a permanent end. Lives had been lost in this very room, leaving the taint of the dead behind.

Dex made a small noise. "I don't like it in here."

"You and me both," I murmured. "This is where the liches died."

"I'm aware of that." Dex cringed behind my back when movement stirred ahead of us. A chill raced through my nerves as a cloud of darkness turned into a humanoid form. Not a living person, but a phantom.

When a second phantom appeared beside the first one, I took a step back. I'd always wondered if phantoms were actual ghosts of real people, and I suspected these had once been the victims of the lich-destroying spell. Did they recognise me now I was human?

I faced the two floating forms. "I'm not here to threaten you. I'm here to stop the people who did this to you."

"Why are you talking to them?" Dex wanted to know.

"Because I think they used to be liches."

Liches, whose souls had been severed from their amulets and left adrift. When neither phantom answered my comments, I scanned the room behind them. Nothing magical remained, not even the abandoned soul amulets of the unbound, half-dead liches, nor any obvious way to free them. Conscious or not, it didn't seem right to leave them in here alone.

"Come on, Liv," said Dex. "This is creeping me out. There's nothing here."

"I'm aware of that," I said. "They must have moved all their cantrips into the Parallel."

I couldn't say I was surprised, but it meant the Order was effectively a dead end. We'd still claimed a victory over Holland, but whether it'd be worth it remained to be seen. As I turned away, the phantoms moved closer to me, and I suppressed a shiver.

"You want to leave?" I gestured to the door. "Feel free. We've taken over the whole building. Also, it might interest you to know that Holland's in one of the cells down here, and he's the reason you ended up in that state. Feel free to torment him a bit before you escape, if you like."

I left the door to the lab open when I walked out, and the phantoms floated past me in a cloud of nebulous shadows. Dex shuddered, clinging to my shoulder. "Come on, let's get out of here."

After leaving the nightmare room behind, Dex and I found the Death King near the cells at the opposite end of the lower floor, where Mr Holland sat in a slumped position on a bench behind a barred door.

"Has he admitted where the cure is yet?" I asked.

"He said it isn't here," said the Death King. "He claims the Order never had one."

"Thought so." I stepped closer to the barred door and addressed Holland. "What about those dead phantoms, then? The ones you killed with experimental cantrips?"

His face turned the colour of the pale grey walls. "Phantoms?"

"You haven't seen them?" I let a smile steal onto my face. "They're on their way here, and they're *very* excited to meet you."

"Hawker and Alban will be here soon," Mr Holland insisted, a tremor in his voice. "They won't stand for this. You're a fool. We might have come to an agreement without the need for strife and bloodshed."

I gave him a sharp look. "How do you know when he and Alban will be back? They're in the Parallel."

"They have people watching this place, you fool," he said. "A messenger will have gone to tip them off the instant you showed up."

"Come on," I said to the Death King. "Let's leave him to the phantoms."

Hoping Mr Holland was bluffing, I let Dex take the lead as the three of us made our way back to the elevator and returned to the lobby. The elevator halted and the doors slid open, revealing the Elemental Soldiers guarding several handcuffed staff members.

"Death King." Ryan beckoned us over. "We have Holland's allies secured, but they're saying Hawker will know the base has been taken by now."

"Holland claimed the same." A shiver raced through my blood when the automatic doors slid open at the front.

Then, as if conjured up by our words, Hawker himself walked into the Order's base, a scowl on his face. His hair was shorter than before, but he had the same deep-set eyes, the same pale face with a hint of wrinkles. Four men surrounded him, all spirit mages, judging by the chill they brought in their wake. Ah, hell. He'd come armed for a fight to the death.

"I have to admit, I didn't expect this move from you." Hawker's gaze went to the Death King first. "I thought you had better things to do than to take command of the Order."

"Did I say I wanted to take command of the entire Order of the Elements?" asked the Death King. "This branch had inadequate leadership and security, so I saw fit to step in and help them out, at least until the former upper room can be restored to their former positions."

"I never thought you cared if the Order stood or fell," said Hawker. "Either of you."

"I'd rather you and your scumbag allies didn't have any more power than you already do," I said. "Besides, you killed innocent people on your route to taking over this base, and the survivors of the massacre you unleashed deserve better than being forced to do your bidding."

The Death King studied Hawker, his expression as impassive as a lich's. "Is Alban with you, or did he send you alone?"

"Alban can fight his own battles, and I can fight mine." Hawker's gaze slid to my face. "If you've forgotten, I killed you once already."

"Care to tell me what you did with the cure to the curse?" I said. "Or was Holland lying through his teeth when he told us one existed at all?"

"It doesn't matter," he said, "because you'll never see it."

The four spirit mages closed in around him in formation, and the air vibrated with magic, stark and threatening.

My breath caught in my throat. Our reckoning had been a long time coming. He'd won our first battle, but our last had ended inconclusively when Dirk Alban had ordered him not to kill me. This time, though? He was prepared to go all-out and disregard the consequences.

Bring it, then.

11

The spirit mages closed in around Hawker, who raised his hand. Energy coalesced in his palm, pulled directly from his allies. Or rather, willing sacrifices.

As for me? Nobody was getting sacrificed on my watch, but the Death King's strength bolstered mine, and we sent a coordinated blast of spirit magic at Hawker. One of the other spirit mages took the hit, swaying but managing to stay on his feet. A shield spread around all five of them, semi-transparent and humming around the edges.

The Death King and I conjured up a similar shield between us, giving the Elemental Soldiers the chance to herd the Order members out of the line of fire. With one hand, I held the shield in place, a rippling current of energy which repelled any attacks Hawker sent our way.

With the other, I struck back. Bolts of magic shot from my palm, while the remaining Order employees ran from the building or barricaded themselves in offices. With the coast clear, the Death King added his attacks to mine, while I looked for a weak spot in Hawker's shield. Their formation was flawless, of course, but so was ours. The Death King and I stood side by side, while Hawker's attempts to strike us down simply bounced off our shield. Unfortunately, our magical attacks had the exact same effect on him—or lack thereof.

"You know, I didn't have to offer to help you." Hawker addressed the Death King, the merest hint of breathlessness in his voice. "I could simply have obliterated all the liches in the House of Spirit rather than letting them continue to suffer under the curse. Olivia, you'll know how easy it would have been for me to do so, I'm sure."

"That's what you did to the liches whose soul amulets you took downstairs, isn't it?" I said. "You destroyed them, turning them into phantoms and trapping them in here forever."

The Death King moved slightly at my words, but I couldn't spare him a glance with Hawker bearing down on the pair of us.

"When a lich is obliterated without their soul amulet present, they usually disappear," said Hawker. "For some, it'd be a welcome end to their suffering."

"They shouldn't have been cursed to begin with." With his eyes on my face, I slipped a neutralising cantrip into my hand. "And I'll give you a welcome end."

I flung the cantrip at Hawker. As I'd predicted, one of his fellow spirit mages moved in to take the hit, but in the same instant, the Death King threw a second neutralising cantrip into their midst.

Hawker's eyes widened as half his shield vanished with two of his mages out of action. A second cantrip slid into my palm, and the Death King made an identical motion on my other side. In a flash, Hawker's last two lines of defence fell, their magic snuffed out, and the man himself let out a bellow of rage. Magic blasted from his palms, only to slam headlong into our shield—which, unlike his, remained intact.

I reached for my last neutralising cantrip, and a knife flew at me from the side, slamming into my arm. Pain splintered my wrist, and my hand fell limp at my side, dropping the cantrip. I crouched to retrieve it, but one of Hawker's spirit mages got there first, kicking viciously at my injured arm.

Shit!

I bit back a scream of pain and rolled to my feet, but it seemed his allies had broken formation in favour of good old-fashioned brawling. The Death King fought two of them off, while Hawker himself took aim at him.

No, you don't. I ran at Hawker and snapped on my last neutralising cantrip as I tackled him head-on. Another bolt of agony shot up my arm, almost numbing the sensation of my magic being snuffed out. Hawker yelled in rage, his own attack fizzling out before it could hit the Death King. As he shoved me off him, a torrent of air magic shot through the room, catching Hawker in its grip and slamming him against the wall.

Ryan strode towards Hawker, blasting the other spirit mages out of his way in the process. I, meanwhile, scrambled through my pouch for a healing cantrip with my good hand. Blood soaked through my sleeve, and I sighed in relief when I found the right cantrip and healed the wound on my arm. With the pain gone, I ran to join the Death King. He advanced on Hawker, and a halo of white light surrounded him as he took hold of Hawker's life force.

A shiver rose to my arms when another wave of coldness swept through the room. Spirit magic. Hawker couldn't have got his magic back that fast.

"Greyson!" I warned. "Someone else is coming."

I spun to face the doors as a torrent of darkness entered the lobby. *Liches.* Damn, this was bad timing. Without my spirit magic, I had no way to kill them, and if they ripped out my soul, there'd be no reversing it.

As the shadows moved closer, Dex descended from the ceiling in a violent shower of flaming sparks. "Go to hell!"

Flames spread among the liches as Dex unleashed his magic, and I grabbed a cantrip, paralysing one of them. That was all I could do, since I felt nothing but an empty chill when I tried to grasp their spirit energy in my hands. I used my cantrips to fend them off instead, moving to Ryan's side. "Where the hell did they come from?"

"The node, I bet," Ryan said. "Should have shut the damn thing down."

"Looks like he left some of them alive, then."

A burst of light momentarily filled the lobby, obscuring my vision. Before I could do more than blink, Dirk Alban's voice whispered in my ear. "Come with me, Olivia."

A solid hand closed on my arm, and the brightness smothered the lobby and the Order vanished from sight.

When my feet touched on solid ground a moment later, I broke away from the phantom grip, reeling with shock. Blood soaked my arm, even with my wound healed, and it looked even worse in the fluorescent lights. Yet it was Alban who held my gaze, his features surprisingly young to my eyes. Of course, he should be ten years older than he was, since he'd been frozen in time during the years he'd spent trapped inside a soul amulet, but we were much closer in age than we'd been as master and apprentice. His hair was neatly combed, his suit impeccable, his pale hands faintly stained with the blood from where he'd grabbed my arm. We stood in a room I didn't recognise, bereft of furniture or other markings of human habitation. He must have used his spirit magic to transport both of us to some kind of safe house. Too bad my own magic remained nothing more than a mute buzz. *Shit. Shit.*

"What did you do to yourself?" he said. "Where's your magic?"

"I used a neutralising cantrip on your dickhead friend Hawker," I replied. "Why the hell did you grab me?"

"So you wouldn't be killed, of course," he said. "I might not have your trust, but I do not want to see you die."

"You let Hawker and the liches march into the Order to commit murder," I pointed out.

"That wouldn't have been necessary if you hadn't decided to storm into the Order yourself," he said. "You've been busy causing trouble, haven't you, Olivia?"

"Your underling tried to kill me," I retaliated. "Or should that be partner-in-crime? I'm not sure on how your dynamic with Hawker is supposed to work, considering you're both power-hungry maniacs who don't play well with others."

"There's no need for rudeness." He spoke in the same

soft tone he always used, like he was imparting great wisdom to me and that I should be grateful for the honour of hearing him speak. He probably believed it, too, even now. "You were my best hope, Olivia, and I remain convinced that you'll see things my way again."

"You're kidding me, right?" I said. "I bet you said the same to all your apprentices, even Cobb."

"Not true," he said. "Many of the mages I trained had potential, but you? You were unique."

I snorted. "You can't ply me with compliments. That won't work on me."

"I admire that quality in you," he went on. "You set a goal and see it through. What you did to take back the Order would have been admirable if you'd been working for the right person."

"You mean you," I said. "Despite the way you deceived me about your real motives and used me as a pawn. I won't be beholden to you any longer, Alban."

"You might not remember our discussions, but I do," he said. "Our goals were once in alignment."

"Until you killed the former Death King and tried to take his power."

"It's a shame, what the Order did to you," he said. "You'd be more likely to trust me if you remembered more of our history together."

"I highly doubt that," I said. "Nothing that can justify what you did."

"What if I told you it was the former Death King who struck a deal with the Order, cursing every spirit mage with the faintest connection with the House of Spirit?" he said.

"Tell me something I don't already know," I said. "You

didn't want to protect other spirit mages from the same fate, did you? All you wanted was every lich in the Court of the Dead to be under your control instead of his."

"Is that what Greyson Beaumont told you?" he asked. "I understand that I overlooked the extent of your attachment to him at first. If you believe I am out to destroy him, then it's no wonder you tell yourself you hate me."

"I don't need convincing you're a piece of shit, Alban," I said. "And there's nothing you've ever said to imply you don't intend to do the same as before and steal the Death King's power for your own."

"I have no intention of taking Greyson's power."

I raised a brow. "Sure."

"I don't need to," he went on. "Any lich in possession of enough sense is ready to flee his side to join mine. If I want an army of them, it's not beyond my means to create one myself."

He's lying. "Maybe not, but you've always wanted to rule the Court of the Dead. That's why you stole their leader's soul amulet."

"Not at all," he said. "I killed the last Death King because he doomed our fellow spirit mages and would have had us all condemned to the same fate. I had every intention of undoing the curse myself."

"Liar." My voice was flat. "You want his soul amulet, like every one of your allies I've met. Cobb, the Crow... even Hawker."

"Oh, is that the issue?" he said. "I heard of Cobb's tragic fate. The poor man was desperate for his magic back, desperate enough to steal from the King of the Dead. As for the Crow, he too was looking for a way back to life again. Hawker, on the other hand, is rather attached to his quest for revenge on Greyson for the former Death King's crimes and the curse he fell under, while I have different aims."

"But it was you who killed the last Death King," I pointed out. "You never told Hawker that, did you? You never had any intention of letting him claim the former Death King's power the way you promised."

"None of that matters now," said Alban. "What's done is done, and Hawker is welcome to do whatever he likes with his second chance at life. As for me, I have my own goals. The only significant disagreement we have is that Hawker would gladly kill you while I would rather not."

"Really," I said. "Well, I'd rather die than work with you."

"I can make you obey me," he said, reaching into his pocket and pulling out a disc-shaped object. "It would give me no pleasure, but I can do it."

He held up a soul amulet. *My* soul amulet, which he must have swiped when he'd grabbed my arm to transport me here. Tricky bastard.

"You want to bind my soul to you?"

"I never said I wanted to," said Alban. "I said I'd do it if necessary."

A chill swept over me. Reluctant or not, if *he* turned me into a lich, my soul would be directly bound to him, and I'd prefer not to find out how much control that would give him. The Death King had never exerted any control over me, not even when I'd gone against his orders. I was willing to bet he rarely did, yet the other liches had repaid him by turning against him.

I did my best to suppress the flutter of panic in my chest. I had little doubt that we were in one of the former safe houses whose locations were known to Lord Black-bourne, and if that was the case, Greyson would have no trouble figuring out where we were. It was only a matter of time before backup arrived.

I looked Alban in the eyes. "Go on. I dare you."

"Taunting doesn't become you, Olivia."

"Too bad you don't own me, Alban."

A crash came from above our heads and his gaze flickered up. Then Dex flew into the room, showering sparks above Alban's head. In his moment of startled pause, I snatched the soul amulet from his hand. Then I shoved it into my pouch and retrieved a cantrip in its place.

"You bonded with a sprite?" Alban said incredulously. "Do you not know what he used to be?"

At that moment, the door burst open and the rest of my allies ran in. The Elemental Soldiers entered with Ryan in the lead, blasting Alban with air magic. Irritation crossed Alban's face and the attack dissipated before making contact with him. He must be protecting himself in some way, perhaps using his fellow spirit mages as shields the way Hawker had, because Cal and Felicity's magic had the same lack of effect. Water, earth and air magic simply bounced off him, while I set off a paralysing cantrip which fizzled out on contact with its target.

When the Death King entered the room with his hands shimmering with magic, I gave him a cheery wave. "Knew you'd find me."

Alban gave him a steady glare before turning on me, a cantrip flicking between his fingertips. "You might not remember, but I do, Olivia. You'll come back to me in the end."

"No chance."

I moved over to the Death King, who caught my arm. Alban's cantrip arced through the air as we both vanished, and when my feet touched the ground, the world turned fuzzy around the edges. *Not again,* I thought, before darkness filtered in.

12

My vision came back into focus. Dirk Alban faced me across a classroom, the same one as before. A different day, because he wasn't holding a soul amulet this time around.

"The most important skill you can learn as a spirit mage is how to take magic from another mage and use it yourself," he said. "When you draw from a spirit mage, though, they can also do the same to you, creating a bond between you."

"Really?" I said. "What about other mages? Like, fire and water mages?"

"You can draw from any kind of mage, but the connection is one-way, unless the other mage is also a spirit mage," said Alban. "It requires an element of trust, however, because borrowing a spirit mage's magic also enables access to their life energy. The two are one and the same, after all. We just have a little more than most people do."

I stared at him with wide eyes. "Is that why they fight in formations? Like the pictures you showed me?"

"Yes," he said. "Five mages is the perfect setup: one fighter, four defenders who maintain a shield around their fighter. However, in order to attain the highest rank of power, a spirit mage must combine forces with one of each of the other four Elements."

My brow crinkled. "What does that mean? The highest rank of power?"

"The ability to do extraordinary things," he responded. "Like the creation of the Parallel itself."

My mouth parted. "Is that how they did it? They... combined their strengths?"

"The original spirit mages who founded the Parallel made the ultimate sacrifice," he said. "The only way to create a node is with a living soul, so the spirit mages gave their life force to power the nodes and open a way across to the other realm."

"But... didn't that kill them?" I said.

"It didn't need to," he said. "Because each mage combined their strength by bonding with four other mages. That created a loop which gave each mage infinite strength. It's a complex type of magic, and one break in the spell can result in tragedy for everyone involved."

"But it didn't?" I asked. "I mean... it worked?"

"It did," he said. "But sacrifices were made all the same. To create the Parallel, the mages ripped a part of the very fabric of the world away, pushing Earth's magic in that direction. That meant most magic on Earth was pushed into the Parallel, where it remains."

"I don't understand why they wanted to do that," I said.

"Mages have always been misunderstood by those who do not share our gifts, but it became clear as the world modernised that there was no place for us in this realm," he said. "We created the Parallel in order to have somewhere we could openly live as ourselves without fear or strife."

"You weren't alive back then, were you?" I said. "I thought the Parallel was hundreds of years old."

"Of course not." He gave a soft laugh. "No, but my family has a history of studying spirit magic, and I took it upon myself to find out as much as I could. Not easy, with the Order becoming stricter with allowing access to information, but it used to be far easier to find information on spirit magic. Before the war, of course."

"Were you involved in the spirit war, then?" I twisted my hands together under the desk, sweat gathering on my palms. No, he wasn't old enough, surely. Right?

"Of course not," he said. "It's tragic, really. The spirit mages on the Council of the Elements never wanted a war. They were backed into a corner."

I shifted in my seat, unease trickling down my spine for reasons I couldn't quite articulate. "How do you know?"

"My family were deeply involved with the Council of the Elements," he said. "They told me the truth long before the Order's lies became widespread. The truth is that nobody should have died. The Council of the Elements were simply trying to solidify their strengths by combining their power in a similar manner to the spell which created the Parallel. However, the spell backfired, and all those involved died in the process."

I didn't know what to say. "That's... awful."

"Tell me, Olivia," he said. "Do you know what a sprite is?"

I blinked. "An elemental spirit?"

"And do you know why there are fire sprites, and water sprites, earth and air... but no sprites comprised of spirit magic?"

"No," I said. "I know spirit magic is different than the others... but I don't understand what this has to do with anything. Sprites aren't anything like mages, are they?"

"They used to be," he said. "Elemental sprites are the lost souls of the mages who gave their lives during the war. And the spirit mages? They became liches, bound to death. Every last one of them."

I didn't hear my reply, because the world faded out again...

———

I woke with a gasp and jerked upright. I expected to see the Death King looking back at me in his own quarters, but instead, I found myself on the sofa at home. From the light streaming through the curtains and illuminating the gaming table across from me, it was dawn.

Devon walked in and startled when she saw I was awake. "Elements, the Death King wasn't kidding. You were miles away."

"Where is he?"

"I have no idea," she said. "He said you were fine when he took you out of Alban's safe house and brought you here."

"I *am* fine." I rubbed my forehead. "I think Alban threw

a memory spell at me again. I need to get back to the castle."

"Not while you're bleeding."

"The wound healed. I used a cantrip."

"You're covered in blood and you look like hell. Also, I want you to eat something before you go gallivanting off again."

"Okay, mother." I grimaced at the reminder of my all-too human family, who had no idea any of this was happening. "What's going on with the Order? Is Hawker still in their base?"

"You think I know?" she said. "The Death King didn't explain a thing. I'm guessing your plan to take over the Order went sideways?"

"It started fine," I said. "We displaced Holland and locked him in jail, and I slammed Hawker with a neutraliser cantrip when he showed up with some other spirit mages. Unfortunately, I turned off my own magic in the process, and then Alban decided to drag me off before I could find out if the others managed to lock Hawker in a cell."

"Yes, the Death King did say Alban grabbed you." Devon shook her head. "He, of course, ran straight after you, so he didn't see where Hawker ended up, but I can't imagine he'd have been able to do much to resist without any magic. Holland, even less so."

"Last I saw of Holland, he was in a cell, surrounded by phantoms," I said. "Meaning, the ghosts of the liches he had killed. I hope they're still tormenting him."

"He deserves it," said Devon. "So you turned off your magic to stop Hawker?"

"Didn't have much choice." I crossed the room,

grimacing at the blood sticking my sleeve to my arm. "I'm going to wash off this crap."

I went upstairs to shower and change, still feeling out of sorts. The lack of my magic didn't help, though it gave me some satisfaction to know that Hawker was in the same position. Once I'd restored myself to a presentable state, I went downstairs to grab breakfast and joined Devon in the living room.

"You didn't see any of the other Order members, did you?" I asked. "Like Judith? I think most of them fled the base when our spirit mage battle broke out, but I worry that they might have run into trouble. Our plan was only half successful."

We were supposed to keep Hawker from coming back into the building at the very least, but I hadn't counted on him getting there so damn fast.

"No, I didn't," said Devon. "If I were them, I'd have run as far away as possible."

I rubbed my temples. "If Hawker's at large, I need to know in case he comes back to make trouble."

"Would he want to risk it without his magic?"

"I have no idea." I reached out, feeling for the node. While I didn't sense its humming presence, I pictured the swamp in my mind's eye all the same.

"Chill. I'll give you a lift." Devon dumped her cereal bowl in the sink and then took my arm. In a flash, the room disappeared, and we landed in the swamp. Before she hopped through the node again, she said, "Don't get into any more fights. Or at least wait for your magic to come back first."

"I'll do my best." I headed for the castle, not quite able to place my lingering sense of disquiet until I entered the lobby and saw two of the resident sprites flitting around the ceiling.

At once, Dirk Alban's words from the past came flooding back. Sprites had once been *mages*, apparently, but how much of what Alban had told me was the truth? I glanced up at Dex, wondering if I should tell him, but the Death King walked in before I could figure out what to say.

"Olivia." He approached me, relief stark on his features. "I hoped it wouldn't be long before you recovered."

"I'm good." I watched the sprites chase one another for a moment. "Please tell me the Order isn't back under Hawker's command."

His silence went on for a heartbeat too long. "It's not all bad news."

"That's pretty damn bad." I rubbed my forehead. "Let me guess, Hawker's allies already took command of the upper room."

"The upper room never made it back to their base," he said. "Because I called them last night and left a message advising them to stay away until we assembled a team to drive out the interlopers. They were receptive to that advice."

"They were?" I said. "That means all Hawker has on his team is whoever was left in the base when we got out of there, right?"

"Precisely," he said. "Most of the staff weren't present at the time and the rest fled during the battle. All he has, effectively, is an empty building."

"Which is full of phantoms," I added. "Oh, and Holland."

"Exactly," he said. "The Order's remaining staff have temporarily relocated to other bases, or so the upper room promised. Hawker, meanwhile, has access to the limited resources of that base, which won't be enough for him to win another conflict unless his magic comes back."

"Pity we took his cantrips," I said. "Those neutralisers won us the fight."

"Yes, they did," he said. "Also, our first delivery from the COS arrived this morning. It took ten people to carry all the boxes here and they had to employ some of my zombie horses to help them out."

I burst into laughter, imagining Neddie the zombie horse carrying boxes of cantrips which were originally supposed to be the Order's. "Brilliant. Where are they?"

"Piled in the break room, much to the annoyance of my Elemental Soldiers," he said. "If this carries on, we'll run out of space."

"Keep your hair on," I told him. "I'll tell the Order they can have the cantrips back if they agree not to give them back to Hawker or Holland."

"Or Alban," he added. "I didn't see any at that base of his, but I suspect it was a temporary hideout that he planned to abandon."

"The cure wasn't there either." Which meant we were no closer to finding a way to free the other liches.

"No," said the Death King. "I knew better than to believe we'd find it in the Order's building, but it seems Alban and his allies intend to keep it far out of reach."

"So they can continue to hold it over us," I said. "Did the rest of the Order's staff definitely make it out?"

"As far as I know," said the Death King. "If not, then

they volunteered to help Hawker and the consequences will be on them."

"Yes, they will," I said. "Because I'm not holding back next time. How long should we wait before going to challenge him?"

"Preferably long enough for your magic to come back and the upper room to get in touch with me again," he said. "What did you see, anyway? In the memory spell Alban threw at you?"

"I saw another one of his lessons." I racked my brains. "He was telling me how the Parallel was created by mages combining their skills with one another... not just spirit mages, either. He mentioned some kind of formation involving one mage of each type adding their strength to a spirit mage to form some kind of power loop."

His brows crept higher. "Like the spirit mage battle formation?"

"Similar," I said. "He implied that's what backfired and killed the spirit mages during the war, and... and as a result, it created the sprites. They were *mages*. I assume they lost their memories of their human lives, but the backlash of the spirit mages' magic must have ripped them from their bodies."

He stiffened. "And... spirit mages?"

"They became liches, which I'm guessing you knew," I said. "Or phantoms, if they weren't bound to a soul amulet. How did Alban know all this, anyway? He never gave me a definite answer, I don't think."

"I wondered the same," said Greyson. "A spirit mage, well connected, rising within the Order while concealing his magic... and yet with no connection to the House of Spirit? It's no surprise I failed to guess what he was. At the time, I didn't think it was even possible to learn spirit magic without succumbing to the curse."

My heart gave an uneasy flip. "I tried to ask Alban about his family, but he didn't tell me much. He mentioned that he used to research spirit magic before it became hard to access that information."

Yet that didn't explain his skill level. Who had taught *him* to use spirit magic? His family's involvement in the war, whatever that might be, explained some of his interest, but not whatever had set him on course to become a notorious spirit mage.

Greyson studied me. "Don't let him tempt you to come back to him in order to learn the truth. It's what he wants."

"I know better," I said. "Besides, I need my magic back before I challenge anyone, including Hawker."

"It won't take long," he said. "Alban showed no interest in helping Hawker, so I expect we'll find him alone."

"Alban gives zero shits about anyone except for himself," I said. "The only reason he and Hawker are still allies is because Hawker didn't believe me when I told him that Alban tried to take the former Death King's power for himself. He'd promised to give it to Hawker instead. Someday he'll get the message."

Dex flew into the hall again, interrupting us. "There's someone at the gates. Several smartly dressed someones."

I raised a brow. "Vampires?"

"No. Humans."

The Death King straightened upright. "The upper room's members are here. They want to meet us both."

13

I stared at him for an instant. "They came to the swampland? Seriously?"

"It's not like we could meet them at the Order's own base, is it?" he said.

Damn. I was not prepared for this. I'd been dragged through hell more than once in the past twenty-four hours, my magic was cut off, and besides, *nobody* saw the upper room face to face except for the other high-ranked Order members unless they were in deep trouble. Some of them had been at my trial, of course, but most people rarely set eyes on any of their members even while working in the same building.

"You sure none of them are in league with Holland?" I asked. "Because you're inviting them into your home, which has the potential to backfire in your face."

"They have no magic of their own," he said. "That's one of the conditions of joining the upper room, I believe."

"Explains why they trusted Holland," I muttered. "Let

me know which room you want to use, and I'll wait in there. See if I can surprise them a little."

"That one will do." He pointed out one of the rooms which branched off the hall. "I'll bring them in."

The Death King left the castle, while Dex flew to my side. "You're freaking out. I can tell."

"The *upper room* is here," I said. "I bloody well hope they aren't plotting our demise."

"They won't get into the hall of souls," said the fire sprite.

"That's not what I'm concerned about."

There was no name for the deep-seated dread coiling within me at the very thought of the faceless people who'd condemned me to lose my memories, who'd banned spirit magic altogether, who'd cursed the House of Spirit.

Who'd taken away Greyson's freedom.

When the group of six smartly dressed men and women entered the hall, I fought the instinct to back away. Instead, I looked directly at the people who'd conspired to condemn every single lich to suffer for a lifetime, and anger surged within me, unexpectedly potent.

"This way," I said, loud and clear, beckoning them into the side room. "We'll talk in there."

"And who are you?" asked a man with grey hair and glasses who wore a dark suit. He couldn't be more generic if he tried.

"Olivia Cartwright," I said. "Spirit Element."

A murmur travelled through their group as they filed into the room and we all took seats in the Death King's fancy armchairs. Their introductions washed over me, their pointless chatter grated on my nerves, and I held my tongue to keep from telling them exactly what I thought of their actions so far. The recriminations could wait until later.

The first speaker, a man called Mr Strong, began by addressing the Death King. "I hear you successfully trapped the lich known as Hawker inside the Order's headquarters."

"For now," said the Death King. "He's currently stripped of his magic due to a neutralising cantrip, but that won't last forever. If you wish to take back Birmingham's Order branch from him, then you'll have to prepare for the possibility of Alban and his spirit mage allies fighting back. Have you made adequate preparations?"

"We have a team of volunteers prepared to step in and aid us in taking back our headquarters," said Mr Oliver, a stocky balding man in his forties. "More than enough to fight back against the intruders currently occupying the base."

"I hope you're right," I said. "Because we did our best to minimise casualties while we removed Holland from his position, but Hawker brought backup with him. If you fail to bring them to justice before he's able to use his magic, it might cause devastation for the ordinary humans in the area."

"We won't fail," said Mr Choudhary, a heavyset Indian man with the same generic fashion sense as the others.

I wonder if you said the same about losing the Order's base to begin with. I bit back the comment, wondering if any of these people knew half the Order's cantrip stash was currently here in this very castle. None of them had ever fought a battle in their lives, yet we had to depend on people *they* trusted to get Hawker subdued, and I couldn't say I had any faith in them in the slightest.

"I have a question," I said to the room in general. "Why did you let Holland shove his way into your ranks?"

"We did not," Mr Strong insisted. "We obstructed him at every turn, using every advantage the official channels gave us in order to prevent his decisions from influencing the Order's actions."

Except when it came to the lives he took in London, and the experiments he conducted in your base. Not that the upper room ever left their meeting room for long enough to go down to the basement. This was probably the first time they'd set foot in the Court of the Dead, for that matter, but that didn't absolve them of any blame.

"Going through the official channels is too slow in a situation like this," I said. "You must have known Hawker was pulling the strings when Holland gained his position."

"There was no evidence against him," insisted Mrs Bell, a woman in her mid-forties with a pair of silver spectacles perched on her nose. "Alexander Holland was a reliable and loyal Order employee until very recently, and he did have the relevant qualifications for the job."

"But you knew better, didn't you?" I looked around their group. "Just like you knew better than to believe cursing the Court of the Dead, or the former House of Spirit, would do anything other than backfire on you."

"What of it?" said Mr Oliver. "Our actions saved lives."

My fury peaked. "You didn't think there might be downsides to turning an entire group of people into zombies? You ruined more lives than you saved, I guarantee it."

"Our decision was made for the good of both Earth and the Parallel," said Mr Strong. "Spirit magic is too powerful, too difficult to control, and these recent events prove we were right. If it cannot be snuffed out, what else can be done?"

"People are still born with access to that magic and with no way to control it," I said. "No legal way, of course, and even in the Parallel, most spirit mages born since the war have ended up disowned or orphaned."

The Death King left a short pause for my words to sink in before addressing the council. "We have discussed the matter beforehand, but are you certain you have no means of undoing the curse?"

"We are not the ones who enacted the curse on the House of Spirit," said Mrs Bell. "If the spell was so easily removed, it would defeat the purpose, would it not?"

"You seriously cursed every single lich without any way of undoing the spell at all?" I said disbelievingly.

"There are some types of magic which cannot be reversed," said Mr Strong.

No kidding. Like the spells which stripped out a mage's powers, or their memories, with no reversal.

I shot him a blistering glare. "Then I hope you're planning on removing Hawker's magic as soon as possible. I assume you won't delay."

"Of course not," he said. "He will be brought to trial as soon as we have him in our custody."

"He's a slippery one," I said. "I'd advise you to watch your backs. Don't forget Alban and his allies have access to resources within the Order itself, and there may still be insiders among your number."

Only Mrs Bell had the audacity to meet my eyes. "We are all loyal to the Order."

"If that's all," said the Death King, "then we'll prepare

to meet your team on the other side of the nodes when they're ready to take Hawker into custody."

Mr Strong rose to his feet. "We will leave the Parallel and check in with our team. Thank you for agreeing to speak with us."

My rage continued to simmer while they said their farewells and left the room. If one thing had become abundantly clear from our meeting, it was that Alban remained the only person who might have the means of removing the curse from the Court of the Dead after all.

Greyson put a hand on my arm, which somewhat soothed my raging temper. "We'll make sure Hawker gets what he deserves."

I blew out a breath. "I hope so, because the odds are pretty high that Hawker's magic will come back before their team is ready, especially if they insist on doing everything by the book. With him at full strength, they'll have a hard time subduing him."

"I doubt they'll want to delay for long." Greyson walked across the hall. "I'll make sure they get to the node without running into any trouble in the swamp."

"Good call." While he left the castle, I approached Dex, who hovered near the door to the hall of souls.

"What a bunch of spineless twats," he said. "They looked ready to run for the hills the instant they walked in here. How'd they get into positions of power at the Order?"

"The usual way," I said. "Via money and family connec-tions. And now we have to depend on their reserve team to get that maniac Hawker subdued without him unleashing another massacre, since he's locked himself inside the Order's building and won't surrender."

"So you're taking those Order wimps with you to finish him off?" he concluded. "Want a hand?"

"Sure." Unbidden, Dirk Alban's words flitted back into my thoughts. Did Dex remember his life as a mage at all? No, I didn't think he did. He'd told me he knew his name, but whatever spell had ripped away his old life had taken his memories, too.

My chest tightened at the thought. No wonder we'd bonded so easily.

Shaking off my unease, I went looking for more allies and found Trix standing near the gates, talking to Ryan. One side of the elf's face was splattered with blood and his sleeve was rolled up to expose several shallow cuts on his arm.

"Trix, are you all right?" I strode over to join him. "Did someone attack you?"

"Assassins showed up at my house," he said. "I chased them off, no problem."

"Shit." This was not the time for more enemies to target my friends. "Are you sure you're okay?"

"Don't worry, I'll be fine," he said. "Ryan said I could stay at the castle until the coast is clear."

I glanced at the Air Element, whose expression dared me to disagree, and shrugged. "Sure, why not join the party."

"I saw the Spirit Agents are here, too," said Trix. "It won't be a problem if I stay here as well, will it?"

"I'm sure the Death King is resigned to his castle turning into a guest house at this point," I said. "Half the rooms are full of cantrips from the market, too, but I need to make sure Hawker gets arrested without hurting anyone before I handle anything else."

"What, you caught him?" said Trix.

"I *hope* we caught him." I glanced over at the gates, fighting the urge to lie down for a nap. My last night of restful sleep felt like it'd been forever ago. "He locked himself into the Order's base to resist arrest."

"Oh," he said. "Do you need my help to chase him out?"

"Nah, I think we're good," I said. "Greyson… there he is."

Greyson walked in through the front gates. "The Order's team was more efficient than I expected. They're ready now."

"Good." I beckoned to Dex, while Ryan waylaid Greyson to ask his permission for Trix to stay in the castle. As I'd expected, Greyson answered with an exasperated 'Fine', and then accompanied me to the node.

Upon walking into the flare of light, we landed on the high street in the city centre once again. The Order's street had been cordoned off, presumably to prevent ordinary people from wandering into the midst of a potential battleground. Not that the Order's base *looked* any different, except for the notable absence of any guards on duty by the automatic doors.

Dex perched on my shoulder, while Greyson nodded to a group of nearby mages as they walked into view, all dressed in durable gear which was the usual uniform of the Order's best-paid staff. *This must be the Order's backup team.*

I moved closer to the Order's doors, peering through the glass, but I didn't see Hawker inside the lobby. That suggested he'd locked himself in a room, no doubt with a trap or three in the way. Greyson halted at my side. "Has he barred the doors?"

"Barricaded himself in, it looks like," said one of the armoured mages.

I reached for an unlocking spell. "Let me handle this."

Sure enough, when I tilted my head, the glimmer of a warding spell caught my vision. A good one, but Devon's spells were second to none. I set off my cantrip, hearing a fizzling noise as the glimmering shield dissipated. As the doors flew open, a tingle of static rippled over my skin.

"Watch out," I warned.

Magic rippled through the air, and four spirit mages converged on us, surrounded by a fresh shield. Hawker stepped into formation with them, his eyes alight with malice.

Damn. They'd all got their magic back... and mine had yet to return.

At once, the Order's mage squad ran into the lobby, meeting the spirit mages head on without hesitation. A fire mage shot a flaming attack into the spirit mages' formation and one of Hawker's allies fell down, screaming, as his skin caught aflame. Greyson blasted spirit magic from his palm, knocking a second mage sideways. They were going down easier than last time, despite having their magic back, but I wasn't about to complain at our unexpected advantage. An earth mage fighting for the Order took down the third member of the formation, leaving Hawker with only one defender.

Comprehension dawned on me. Hawker and the other spirit mages must have been storing energy from the nodes ready for their attack on the Order, but he and his allies had been bounced back to square one when their magic had been cut off. Add in the fact that they'd been stuck in the Order's building for hours, which was far enough from the nodes and surrounded by enough protective shields to make it hard to access their power, and no wonder they had trouble maintaining their defensives.

As Hawker backed away, my own magic returned with a triumphant buzzing sensation. Energy shot from my palm, taking down the fourth and final defensive mage. That was more like it.

Now Hawker stood alone, panic flaring in his eyes. "You're dooming yourself if you side with them. They hate our kind, Olivia."

"Not as much as I hate you." I reached forwards and grabbed his life force in my hand, and he sagged to his knees as my grip tightened on his soul.

"Enough." The Order's guards all but shoved me away, to my indignation, but I obligingly let go of Hawker as they closed in around him. "We will take him down to the cells to prepare for an immediate trial."

Two of the squad grabbed Hawker's arms and dragged him to the elevator, while the rest of the team spread throughout the building to search for any interlopers. I'd hoped to slip away once they had the building secure, but they insisted on dragging Greyson and me to the court-room to witness Hawker's trial and my general distrust of the Order wouldn't let me decline until I saw him locked up.

The courtroom was not my favourite place, for obvious reasons. Most recently, I'd watched Cobb's trial in this very room, and the Death King had got me off the hook before the Order had found a way to blame me for the situation. This time, they hardly needed my input to know Hawker was a murdering dickhead and to sentence him to lifetime imprisonment and being stripped of his magic.

All the fight had gone out of Hawker by the time they hauled him out of the courtroom. Before the doors closed, his furious gaze bored into mine, and I gave him a grim smile as he disappeared from sight.

It's over. Without his magic, Hawker admittedly had an extra incentive to target the Death King, while Alban had lost an ally and also his main rival for the Death King's power. But if the Order didn't strip away his magic, they risked him escaping and launching another attack. The faster he was taken off the list of potential threats, the better.

Before we left the courtroom, I waylaid Mr Strong. "I have a question. How do you guarantee someone's magic loss is permanent? Do you use a cantrip?"

"That's classified information."

"Really." I looked him in the eyes. "If you'd used that magic on Hawker *before* he had the chance to launch a massacre, you might have saved lives."

"Some magic isn't licensed for public use."

"Is that so?" I said. "I don't know if you're aware, but there's currently a bunch of angry phantoms swarming around your basement, remnants of the victims of Hawker's experimental magic. I left the door open so they can leave the lab, but I'm not entirely certain they can find their way out. Soulless liches can be persistent."

That was a non-subtle dig in at him about the mages' history involvement in the liches' creation, but he didn't rise to the bait.

"It will be taken care of," he said, in calm tones.

Dickhead.

When we reached the lobby, Greyson turned to me. "I think our part in this is done. You can go home, and I'll make sure they have Hawker secured before his magic is stripped."

"Thanks for being here with me." I kissed him good-bye, while Dex made sick noises in the background. "Dex, behave."

To be fair, he'd mostly been quiet while waiting outside throughout Hawker's trial—apart from occasionally flicking sparks at the Order's guards—so I invited him home to hang out with Devon. The fire sprite spent the evening zooming around the house while Devon and sprawled on the sofa playing video games and eating take-out. All in all, not a bad way to celebrate the downfall of our enemy.

That night was the best sleep I'd had in weeks, and I might have slept half the day if I hadn't been woken in the early hours of the morning by Devon hammering on my bedroom door.

"The Death King's here," she said. "Thought you ought to know."

"Why?" If he'd come to my house in person, it must be important enough for him not to send warning. I shoved on clothes as fast as possible before grabbing my phone. No messages, so it must be Parallel-related. I ran down to where Greyson waited for me at the foot of the stairs. "What's going on?"

"Bria is back at the castle," said Greyson. "It's highly likely that I'll have to go and speak to the elves today."

"You woke me up to tell me you're going to see the elves?"

"The elves *leaders*," he clarified. "The Elders, they call

themselves. I can't say I know how long it'll take, but I thought I ought to let you know."

"Oh," I said. "That's a good thing, right?"

"I sincerely hope so," he said. "With Order on our side and Hawker incarcerated, we have a significant advantage, and convincing the Elders to join our side will only add to that."

"Guess so." My phone buzzed in my hand, and I glanced at the screen. A message from Mum. *I met your friend today.*

The phone slid from my grip. "Shit. *Shit.*"

"What is it?" Greyson picked up my phone. "Liv?"

"I think Alban paid a visit to my mother." I backed up the stairs. "Back in five."

I ran back into my room and grabbed my cantrip pouch and my bag, passing a bewildered-looking Devon on my way out. "They haven't gone after your mum, have they?"

"She told me she had a visit from a 'friend', which I'm guessing means Alban or one of his allies," I said. "Should have known the bastard wouldn't take one day off."

"Give them hell," said Devon.

"I will." I took the stairs two at a time and caught up with Greyson at the door. "Want to come?"

"Of course." In his Death King armour, he'd stand out dramatically in our mundane street, but there was no help for it. "Might the person who visited her be waiting to ambush you?"

"Potentially." I walked out of the house, striding alongside him. "Alban might have been trying to get my attention instead, but my mother also happens to have a pregnant wife at home, so he'll pay for messing with my family."

Luck was with us and nobody stopped to stare at the Death King's armour while we walked to Mum and Elise's house. I knocked on the door, and Mum answered almost at once. "Liv! You didn't have to come over."

"Are you okay?" I asked. "Is Elise?"

"Of course, sweetheart. Elise is resting upstairs." Her gaze went to Greyson—or to be more precise, his armoured clothing. "You're that young man who visited us a few months ago, aren't you? Are you going to one of those comic conventions?"

Greyson smiled, to my relief. "Something like that."

"This is Greyson," I said. "Who came here earlier? What friend?"

"Oh, he said he knew you when you were at school," she said. "Called himself your mentor."

Alban. "He's a liar."

"Is he?" Anxiousness flitted across her face. "He seemed charming. I know you had a tough time at school…"

"He…" The words stuck in my throat. "He's the reason for what happened to me when I was at school. For my memory loss. He broke the law and I got blamed for what he did."

Her eyes rounded in horror. "I shouldn't have let him in. I'm sorry."

"Don't worry," I said. "You couldn't have known. Anyway, he's the manipulative sort, and now I know he doesn't have my best interests at heart. He cares for nothing but his own gain."

"Well, I won't stand for that kind of nonsense in my

house," she said. "Especially with Elise's condition. She doesn't need any more stress."

I turned to Greyson. "Is it possible for us to set a watch on their house?"

"We can ask if anyone at the castle wants to volunteer to keep an eye out for trouble," he said. "I doubt Alban will be back yet, though."

"No." I shook my head. "This was a test. An intimidation check."

"We'll help you the best we can," Greyson said to Mum. "Elise, too."

Her admiring gaze followed him as he turned away, and she leaned in to whisper to me. "You said he wasn't your boyfriend, didn't you?"

"He is now." A smile tugged at my mouth despite the worry churning inside me. "It's a long story. Really surreal. Anyway, I won't let anything happen to you or Elise—or the baby. That I can promise."

14

Upon returning to the Parallel, Greyson and I asked the Spirit Agents if any of them wanted to offer to watch Mum and Elise's house in shifts when I wasn't around. I didn't expect anyone would say yes, given that spirit magic was technically illegal on Earth, but two of them volunteered, including Tate, Shelley's brother.

"Bound to be easier than guarding the castle, right?" Tate said.

"Be careful," warned Shelley. "Liv seems to have a lot of enemies."

"I have one fewer as of yesterday," I said. "Is it true that Bria is back?"

"She came back last night," Shelley said. "Then she ran off with Trix earlier. I think she was looking for you, Death King."

"I'll wait for her," said Greyson. "I believe she intends for me to speak to the elves' leaders in person."

"What were you planning on doing with all those

cantrips, anyway?" asked Tate. "There are boxes in every room, even the dormitories. We have to keep hiding the potentially dangerous ones from the kids."

I suppressed a groan. "I'll handle them."

While Greyson and Bria headed out to meet the elves, I spent an hour or so arranging boxes of cantrips, moving the more dangerous ones to the storage room so no hyperactive teenage mages accidentally set themselves on fire. At least it gave me something to occupy my thoughts, though it didn't quite quell the urge to go and watch Mum and Elise like a hawk. It wasn't like I had Alban's phone number so I could yell at him for visiting my family, and I'd be willing to bet he'd abandoned his recent hideout after my escape. Which made him as elusive as ever. He'd been careful to leave no trail behind him.

"Elements, stop crashing about in here," Dex admonished me from outside the storeroom when I put down a particularly heavy box of cantrips with a rattling crash. "You're giving me a headache."

"Someone has to sort out this crap." I lifted the box and stacked it on top of the others at the back of the room. "And besides, I have to do something to distract myself from being pissed off at Alban. He went after my *family*, Dex."

"You're not doing any good by storming around the castle," he said. "No wonder Aria's been hiding in a broom cupboard all day."

I blew out a breath. "I'll go and storm around outside, then."

The other sprites flitted across the ceiling as I walked through the lobby, casting shadows which looked almost human-sized from some angles. Did any of them remember their own former lives? Probably not, if they were anything like Dex, but for all I knew, everything Alban had told me in that vision had been as much a lie as his claims of acting in my best interests.

When I reached the foot of the stairs, a pair of liches approached me, shadowy and menacing. *Not this again.* I brought my hands up, prepared to call on my spirit magic. "What is it?"

"We saw you invited several members of the Order's upper room to the castle," said the lich on the right-hand side. "The very people who condemned us. You welcomed them into our home."

Ah, damn. "There wasn't another option. Hawker took refuge in the Order's headquarters and we had to call in backup to arrest him. We needed the upper room's support to bring him to justice."

"Lies," said the lich on his left. "Lies and false promises, like your claims that you intend to cure us of our curse."

"The Order doesn't have the cure," I said to the liches. "I searched their headquarters, but Holland was lying, as I told you. The Order would have brought you nothing but death."

"Alban has the cure," said the lich on the right. "We know. He sent us a message."

My blood chilled. "What? Why didn't you tell me or the Death King?"

"The Death King isn't here," said the lich. "And the message was for us, not him."

The liches' shadowy forms parted, revealing a pile of rotting bones and flesh lying near the gates. *Not again.*

"How did the cantrip get in here?"

"It didn't," said the lich. "He was out in the swamp

when someone threw the cantrip at him, and he managed to make it back in here in time to give us Alban's message before he died."

"Damn," I said. "I'm sorry, but I didn't know."

"They're picking us off one by one," he said. "What are you going to do about it? Are you and our so-called Death King too busy protecting your allies at the Order to care about his own people?"

"That's not true," I protested, my heart swooping downward at the murmur of agreement that passed among their group. "If we hadn't gone to deal with the Order and Hawker right away, he'd have come and attacked you next. As it is, Hawker is in jail, the Order won't bother us anymore, and our allies also took out the warehouse where those cantrips were being manufactured so the enemy's supplies are limited. Once we track down Alban's hiding place, we'll get the cure from him one way or another."

"And how many more of us have to die beforehand?" said the lich on the left. "How long before you admit you promise what you cannot deliver?"

"I'm offering you as close to a promise of a miracle as I can get," I said. "Look, the Death King hasn't steered you wrong so far. Considering what he's had to deal with, it's impressive that any of us have managed to survive at all."

"You call this survival?" said the lich on the right. "Only a spirit mage would dare."

"Only a spirit mage can save you," I retaliated. "I don't want to fight, but I'll defend myself if necessary."

"Hey!" Shelley ran across the grounds towards us. "Cut that out."

Another spirit mage moved in to join her, and I shot

them a look of gratitude when they stood alongside me against the liches.

"You're not gonna win this one," I told the liches. "Word of advice, summon up what little patience you have left, or you'll find yourself without a soul to return to your body."

The liches, thankfully, got the message and drifted away from us, returning to the pile of bones which had once been their ally.

"Thanks," I said to Shelley and her friend.

"Us spirit mages have to stick together," said Shelley. "What set them off?"

"One of the liches got hit by another deadly cantrip," I said. "Apparently, it's somehow my fault or the Death King's that their lich friend decided to leave the castle grounds and walked into a trap."

"I'm not surprised," said Shelley. "It'll get worse now they're cooped up. So are we, but we can at least walk around and leave the castle without risking being turned into a pile of bones... oh, there's the Death King."

I rotated on my heel, seeing Greyson walking through the gates, and went to meet him. "Alban left a message in the form of one of those deadly cantrips."

"Another one?" said Greyson. "Who was it this time?"

I pointed out the pile of dead flesh which had once been a lich. "They decided to blame me... and you. Fair warning."

"Did they, now?" Greyson switched smoothly into Death King mode as he approached the liches gathering near their fallen friend. "Are you cowardly enough to attack my Spirit Element in my absence?"

Nobody responded to him, and shame emanated from their faceless forms.

"I'm disappointed in you," he went on. "I'd advise you to think very carefully about where you wish to apportion blame for this atrocity. Meanwhile, my Spirit Element and I will search for the culprit. Now, go."

His very aura radiated menace, and the liches backed off quickly, leaving the pair of us alone beside the dead lich.

My mouth quirked. "My Spirit Element and I."

"You like that?"

"I think I do." I turned my back on the dead lich. "How'd it go with the elves?"

"Badly," he said. "The enemy got to them first, so they weren't in the mood for a meeting."

"Damn," I said. "Where's Bria?"

"On her way back, provided she doesn't run into trouble," he said. "I'll call someone over to deal with this."

I searched beside the dead lich and found the blank cantrip which had killed him lying in the mud. This one was marked with the Family's signature, too. "If there's nobody at the warehouse anymore, they can't still be manufacturing these."

"No," said the Death King. "I'd wager that there's only a few left. We need to sort this situation with the liches, however. Once I've disposed of their dead, I'll call them into a meeting and I'll plainly state my thoughts on them continuing to attack you."

"I'm not sure some of them will listen to reason at all until they have a cure," I said. "Alban keeps baiting them. As long as he remains the only person with access to the cure, the enemy has the Court's fate in his hands."

"Not entirely," he said. "Alban might have the cure, but he can't single-handedly use it on all the liches at once. Besides, it might be possible for us to find a way to replicate it on our own."

I glanced down at the mud-smudged cantrip in my hand. "Only with an active one of these cantrips, and we don't have a single one, let alone enough for everyone. I don't see how this is going to work."

"Regardless, I see no option but to tell the liches everything," said Greyson. "Including how I came to be cured, and why Alban has the power that he does. I have an inkling none of the liches truly know who Alban is... or what he did."

He killed the last Death King. Greyson had never told them that, out of fear of being kicked out of his position for not claiming the title legitimately. Yet we both faced that very possibility anyway, and maybe it was time to stop holding back.

"You aren't going to tell them that the easiest way to bring them back to life is to sacrifice a spirit mage's life for each of them, are you?" I asked. "Because they've tried to sacrifice me twice without even knowing that."

"No, but as long as they remain in the dark about Alban's true identity, they're going to keep pushing back against us," he said. "We need to stop these attacks, and the easiest way is to give them information. It's the only thing they want."

"No kidding." I nodded tightly. "Okay. I'll spread the word around. See how many have an iota of respect for the Spirit Element."

While the Death King had the remains of the dead lich removed, I walked around the grounds, conjured spirit magic to my hands, and sent a piercing blast into the sky which everyone in and around the castle would be able to see.

"All the liches present in the Court of the Dead are to come into the hall," I said loudly. "We want to talk to you."

I then repeated my message to every group of liches I passed in the grounds on my circuit of the castle. Once I was sure everyone had heard me, I made my way to the front entrance. By then, the liches had flooded the lobby, forming rows in front of the dais.

The Death King and I took to the stage, and my heart skittered with nerves. By giving the liches the details of how we'd removed the curse on ourselves, I'd give them double the incentive to sacrifice one or both of us to save their own lives. But it was that or let them work it out for themselves… or let Alban be the one to tell them.

I had to come clean about everything, including my own history with Alban.

When the last liches fell into line, the Death King spoke first. "It's come to my attention that a number of you are under the impression that myself and my Spirit Element are intentionally keeping the cure to the curse on the House of Spirit from you. Let me state plainly that that is abject nonsense. Hawker and his allies are intentionally manipulating you. For years, he hid among you, preparing to elevate himself above all others with no intention of ever helping anyone else. As for Alban? It was he who killed the last Death King."

A ripple of shock passed among the gathered liches.

"If not for Olivia's swift action ten years ago, Alban would have maintained control over all of you," he added. "After Alban's death at Olivia's hands, the former Death

King's power was left unclaimed, and would have dissipated without an owner had I not taken it myself. Unbeknownst to me, however, another of Alban's allies stepped in and bound his own severed soul to an amulet in the hopes of unearthing a way for him to rise again. Alban then waited a decade to return from death. Meanwhile, Hawker remained hidden among your very forces while plotting to take the former Death King's soul for his own. Have you forgotten how many liches the pair of them have destroyed between them? They are not your allies."

The others didn't say a word, merely watching us, and it was hard to gauge their reactions when they had no facial expressions to read. When the Death King didn't continue, I realised he wanted me to speak next.

"To people like Alban, souls are currency, living or dead," I said to the liches. "Even if he does have the intention of undoing the curse on all of you, he'll retract that promise the instant he has you where he wants you. You're more useful to him dead than alive. Even if you weren't, would you really want to act as his spirit mage shields, used for the purposes of taking damage so he walks away unscathed? That's hardly living in any sense, especially as he might sacrifice you again on a whim."

More whispering followed. It hadn't occurred to me before that the liches would have formed their own conclusions about the former Death King's demise, and that while the full story was between Greyson and me, that didn't mean it wasn't valuable for some of them to know the true reasons for Greyson's ascension to his position as their leader. If they chose to betray us anyway, at least we'd done all we could to convince them otherwise.

"Exactly," said the Death King. "We've witnessed how Hawker and Alban treat their fellow spirit mages: as shields and cavalry. If you have no loyalty to me left in you, would you not at least like to keep your dignity?"

He remained silent for long enough for his words to sink in, before continuing. "I will not tolerate any more deception. If you wish to take your chances and join Alban and Hawker, then you're more than welcome to retrieve your soul amulets and remove yourself from my service. I would remind you that you're simply trading one kind of bond for another, and that you'll find both of them considerably less merciful than I am. I will do my utmost to protect you as long as you remain here in the castle, but if you leave, then I will be more than happy to face you on the battlefield. There, I will show you no more mercy than anyone else."

Nobody made any response to that, so I cleared my throat and jabbed a finger towards the door at the far end of the lobby. "The hall of souls is that way. You're welcome to do us all a favour and take what's left of your souls if you really want to throw your lot in with a man who recruited me when I was fifteen years old, tried to force me to help him take the last Death King's place, and left me to face the punishment for his crimes."

Silence spread through the hall. Nobody made a move towards the hall of souls.

"Alban is not your friend." I told the gathering crowd. "He doesn't value you at all, but he has no more value for his fellow spirit mages either. Haven't you learned from the fates of his allies? The Crow, Cobb, and even Holland and Hawker have been abandoned as he's moved on to new targets. It's up to you whether you want to die with any sense of freedom over your own fate. Because I promise you all that we *are* going to find a way to undo the curse, before or after we bring Alban to justice."

"Precisely," said the Death King. "I think that is all. Do consider our words, and if you'd prefer to leave, then do so sooner rather than later."

As the liches dispersed, Greyson stepped off the stage and exited the hall via the corridor leading to his living quarters. When the door closed behind him, he groaned and rested his head against the wall. "Will nothing satisfy them?"

"It's no fault of yours." I walked behind him as he approached his living quarters and pushed the door open. "Maybe I should have told my story earlier. Do you think I should have?"

"It's your choice," he said. "Either way, they're growing desperate. I expect some might snap and go to Alban's side regardless of our attempts to convince them otherwise."

"Maybe, but I don't think any of them truly knew who Alban was," I said. "Unlike Hawker, he was never one of them."

"See?" He flashed me a smile. "I knew you'd find the right thing to say."

Warmth filled me despite the chill breeze sweeping in from the corridor. "I hope we don't go back down there to find a queue outside the hall of souls."

"I doubt they'll leave in high numbers," he said, "but give it a week and they'll find another reason to complain."

"You might have a point there," I said. "They ought to

know how good they have it by now. The last Death King wasn't nearly as merciful."

"It was obvious to them from the start that I lacked the experience of the former Death King, though," he said. "It's why I established the reputation I have. I don't blame them for doubting my intentions."

"Don't worry, you're still a scary bastard when you want to be."

"I'm choosing to take that as a compliment." A smile tugged at his mouth, but his gaze was distant, elsewhere. "It feels like we're living on borrowed time."

Didn't I know it. "I've felt that way since I returned from death."

I'd asked for a miracle and I'd got one—for both of us. Yet only when we'd undone the curse on the entire House of Spirit would the rest of the spirit mages truly be free.

Greyson turned to fully face me, his gaze deep and intense. "I understand that, Liv. I wish we had time to make all the memories I want to."

My heart fluttered in my chest. "We still have some time."

Our lips met, and heat sparked deep inside me as I deepened the kiss, wrapping my arms around him until the spikes on his coat dug into my skin.

I pulled back to breathe. "You don't have any pressing responsibilities at the moment, do you?"

"No." His lips met mine again and the heat rose, kindling to a flame. My mouth crashed against his, as did my body, his armoured coat poking me in the chest.

"*Ow.*" I jabbed the spikes with my fingertips. "How does that thing come off?"

"Judge for yourself." A wicked light shone in his eyes as

I struggled to pry the coat open, and I did a victory dance when it finally came off, revealing the shirt and trousers beneath. Much easier to get off. I said as much, and he chuckled before kissing me again. Seconds of feverish fumbling with clothes followed, interspersed with kisses, fast and urgent.

He pushed open the door to an ornate bedroom, not that I stopped to take in the details before sinking back onto the bed, where his fingers slid over my bare skin until he found the wet heat between my legs. I moaned against his mouth. He moved at my whispered commands, his devilish fingers stroking me until I lost all sense of reason and time. A gasp escaped as I orgasmed against his fingers, at which point he withdrew from me and reached for a condom from a drawer next to the bed. I was fairly sure *that* was a new acquisition, but he cut off my question with another kiss.

I was slick with need again as he slid deep into me with a groan to equal my own, and we moved against one another in a frenzy of lust. I was impressed he managed to hang on for as long as he did, before he came, whispering my name. *Liv. Liv.*

His orgasm brought me to a second climax. We lay together, breathing hard, legs tangled, and my thoughts quietened. For a moment, at least.

"Not bad for a dead man," I said.

He grinned and drew an arm around me, pulling me into an embrace which was welcome considering the chill of the castle was already beginning to pierce through to my flushed skin.

"For the record," I said, "you were worth coming back from the dead for."

"That's possibly the best compliment I've ever heard from you." His lips brushed the back of my neck, drawing a shiver to my skin. "I'm glad I waited for you, too."

"Liv!" called a voice from somewhere outside. *Dex.* Bloody sprite had the worst sense of timing.

"What?" I yelled back.

"If you two lovebirds can drag yourselves away from one another for a second," said Dex, "Bria's back and the Spirit Agents are throwing a party because she and Miles killed one of those low-life spirit mages who betrayed them. Also, Trix has some interesting stories about the elves and Harper wants to talk to you about her illusion skills, Liv."

I gave Greyson an exasperated look. "I can see why you're going mad with all the demands on your attention."

"I rather think it's you who's the popular one." A smile played on his mouth. "Let's go join the party."

15

The sound of my phone buzzing woke me, and I leapt out of bed at once. I'd wanted to spend the night with Greyson, but common sense had driven me to return home and sleep fully dressed. For one major reason, which also happened to be why I'd given the Spirit Agents permission to text me this early in the morning: my family was under attack.

After grabbing my cantrip pouch and putting in my contacts as fast as humanly possible, I left my room and nearly collided with Devon on the landing.

"They went after Mum again," I said over my shoulder as I ran past.

Devon swore. "I'll be right behind you."

I sprinted downstairs and into the hall. Shoving my feet into my shoes, I hopped through the node and landed down the road from Mum and Elise's house.

At once, I spotted several transparent shapes drifting towards their house. *Phantoms.* My hands sparked with spirit energy, and I blasted one of the oncoming phantoms, knocking it away from the door. Nearby, I saw the two spirit mages who'd been watching the house fighting off another one. Catching Tate's eye, I shot him a grateful look and carried on running until I reached the doorstep.

Elise screamed from inside the house. Cursing, I scrambled to grab the spare key under the doormat and unlocked the door. Up the stairs on my right-hand-side, a phantom drifted out of view. I launched myself after it, blasting spirit magic from my palms until the phantom turned on me instead. As it bore down on me, I grabbed at its life essence and tugged, pulling it into myself until the phantom evaporated into nothingness.

As I retreated into the hallway again, Mum ran downstairs, her dressing gown trailing behind her. "Liv, are you okay?"

"I'm fine," I said. "Stay back, okay? I'll make sure no more of those things are outside."

Judging by the quietness outside, the spirit mages had taken care of the others. I pushed it open and found both of the spirit mages standing near the door while several newcomers approached, all of them wearing the Order's uniform.

"What the—?" I broke off when a bulky redheaded Order guard roughly grabbed my arm and pulled me out into the street.

"Come with us," he said. "Your friends, too."

Oh, damn. I'd openly used magic in front of potential human witnesses, and while the Order and I might have come to a new truce, that most likely didn't include breaking one of their cardinal rules. "Hey, cut that out. We were attacked by phantoms."

"Spirit magic is illegal," insisted his friend. "Not only

that, those humans saw you use it, which brings you to at least two violations of magical law."

"Those humans happen to be my mum and step-mother, and they were the phantoms' targets," I informed them. "I figured it would be better for them to see me using magic than to get their souls sucked out by a phantom."

"Come with us," said the guy holding me. "We'll talk this over at our base."

"You're wasting your time," I said. "You have enough to deal with. Like Hawker."

"He has been stripped of his magic," he said. "He's no longer a threat."

"At least you did one thing right."

"How dare you speak to us in that manner?" said another Order guard. "You may be the Death King's Spirit Element, but here on Earth, you must obey the laws set out by the Order of the Elements."

"My family was attacked," I repeated. "I should remind you that it's supposed to be *your* job to ensure the safety of the non-magical inhabitants of the city. I know I'm tech-nically not an employee anymore, but nobody else would have got here in time to get rid of the phantoms if we hadn't been here."

Another of the guards seized Tate by the arm. "Come with us, or we'll have to use force."

They weren't just arresting me, but the spirit mages who'd had my back, too? I hadn't meant to get them into trouble, but the Order were seriously overcompensating for their failures at preventing Hawker's infiltration of their base. Regardless, I'd have to go along with them, if just to ensure the others didn't end up jailed for trying to protect my family at my request.

Without further ado, the Order members frog-marched the pair of spirit mages towards the node down the road. *I suppose it's fine if they use the nodes to hop around the city in front of potential ordinary human witnesses.*

Ignoring the guy holding my arm, I turned back to reassure Mum, who stood in the doorway looking considerably upset. Luckily, at that moment, Devon strode into view and figured out the situation immediately.

"I'll make sure your mum and Elise are okay, Liv," she said. "Promise."

"Cheers." I waved her off and obligingly let my captor steer me towards the node. He kept a tight grip on me all the way, as though he expected me to make a break for it. Which I might well have done if not for the two spirit mages they'd arrested along with me. Besides, I'd worked too hard to repair my relationship with the Order to throw out all that progress because they were throwing a fit over a minor misdemeanour.

We landed down the street from the Order's headquarters and wasted no time in catching up to the other Order members and their captives. While part of me expected to see Hawker on the other side of the automatic doors, the lobby had returned to normal, the damage from the battle wiped away entirely... and in the centre, Greyson stood waiting in the full armour of the Death King.

"They arrested us for using spirit magic to defend my family," I explained, before he could ask. He must have had an inkling I was in trouble, unless he'd already come here for another reason.

"Is that so?" He addressed the Order guards who'd brought the three of us here. "Have you such a strong desire to waste your time when there are more important matters to attend to?"

"It's hardly a good example if we let her get away with breaking the law," the guy holding me protested. "Spirit magic is illegal. Unequivocally."

"Olivia saved your lives," said the Death King.

"There are procedures," said another of the Order guards.

"A pair of ordinary non-magical humans were attacked by phantoms," I said, mostly for the benefit of everyone listening in. "The humans in question should have been on your safety watch list, which I'll be mentioning in my report if you insist on asking for one."

"Report the incident if you must, but if you punish Olivia or the others, you'll have to deal with the objection of the Court of the Dead," said the Death King. "And if Hawker's allies return to claim your base, you might well find yourself alone next time."

"Exactly." My gaze went to the two Spirit Agents. "These two offered to help protect my family because nobody here had any intention of doing so."

The man holding Tate by the arm shifted in an uncomfortable manner. "We'll report the incident right away. Come with us."

To my annoyance, they steered our group through the lobby and towards the elevator. *Not this bullshit again.*

"I'm not going down to the basement," I said flatly. "Neither are my allies."

The other two spirit mages wore alarmed expressions, but they knew perfectly well what the Order could do to us and they didn't have the years of experience dealing with them that I had. I didn't blame them for not saying a word of objection.

"It's a precautionary measure," said the guy holding me, gripping my arm harder than necessary. "We've spent the last day dealing with calls from the Order's branches in London demanding to know why we're letting spirit mages walk in and out of our headquarters without punishment when they're designated as responsible for that horrific attack a few weeks ago."

Ah, shit. It'd slipped my mind that they'd pinned the blame for the deaths on all the spirit mages for the lack of any other target. "Hawker was the one who killed those people and you know it. This has got to stop. We're in the middle of a war, for the Elements' sakes. You can't stick to the same rules as usual when Alban might walk in and attack at any moment. You might have taken care of Hawker, but—"

"He's gone." The voice came from the direction of the elevator, from which two ashen-faced Order members emerged. "Hawker's gone."

"What?" I looked between them in disbelief. "You're kidding me. You let Hawker escape?"

"I swear he was secured," one of them insisted. "He shouldn't have been able to get out."

"He didn't even have his magic," added the guy beside him.

Fucking hell. Hawker was out of jail and loose somewhere in the city. I'd bet *he'd* sent those phantoms. "Not having magic doesn't mean he can't slip away, you know. He's a clever bastard. Didn't you have people watching him?"

The Order guards ignored me, some of them running to request the permission of the upper room to track down Hawker, others grouping together to discuss their options. Who had let him out? Damn it to hell, there must still be people in this building who were in league with Alban. It was the only reasonable explanation.

"Olivia Cartwright?" Mrs Carlisle, head of the retrieval unit, shambled over to me. She looked much the same as always, if a lot more stressed, with lines under and around her eyes and her grey hair pulled back severely. "I'm told you want to report an incident involving an attack on several ordinary humans in which you used... *spirit magic*... in self-defence." She said the words *spirit magic* in a low voice, as though she found mentioning it as distasteful as swearing in a church.

"That was before your prisoner slipped his chains." I glanced at the other two spirit mages. "I asked these two to stand guard outside my mum's house because I had a suspicion the enemy might target her. Any magic they might have used was intended to protect innocent humans against magical assailants."

"I gathered," she said. "Come down to the retrieval unit. You can fill out the report there. Don't make me regret this."

Wait. Was she skipping over most of the procedures? That was a first. She'd never done anything to make my life easier during all the years I'd worked under her supervision.

Once we reached the retrieval unit, she took out a folder. "Your statement?"

I bit back my frustration and gave a quick summary of the phantoms' attacks, while the others gave near-identical reports. Then, after a mere half an hour of questioning, she let us go. I supposed that ought to be classed as miraculous by the Order's standards, but I remained irked at the wasted time and effort, especially as Mum and Elise remained vulnerable targets even with Devon watching them herself. *Hawker is out there, and the Order is more worried about paperwork than keeping people safe.*

Greyson met us in the lobby and our group left the building, at which point Devon texted me to let me know the Order had sent a few people to keep an eye on Mum and Elise's house after all. I replied telling her Hawker had escaped and warning her to set up as many defences on the shop as possible. Devon's horrified responses kept my phone vibrating right up until our group went through the node and landed in the swamp.

Several spirit mages ran over to us as soon as we reappeared, led by a panicked-looking Miles.

"What's going on?" asked Greyson.

"Bria's missing again," said Miles. "They captured her—the Family did."

"Shit." Given the timing, the enemy must have decided to strike on multiple fronts at once. "How'd they get to her?"

"We were in the elves' realm," said Miles. "The Family ambushed us and took her away."

"Dammit," I said. "Hawker escaped the Order's jail and is now sending phantoms to attack my family, too."

"Oh, that's just bloody perfect, isn't it?" Dex zipped into view. "Also, something's wrong with the hall of souls."

"The hall of souls?" Greyson shot me a concerned look, then followed the fire sprite through the gates.

While Tate and his spirit mage friend joined the other Spirit Agents, Greyson and I climbed the stairs and entered the castle. On our right, the door to the hall of souls had an odd glow around the edges as though a bright light shone on the other side. When Greyson led the way into the room, my heart sank. Every single one of the soul amulets emanated a vibrant white glow, which trailed off their surfaces like coils of smoke.

"What in the world is that?" I asked Greyson. "Has anyone else been in here?"

"No." His tone rang with quiet shock. "Not aside from myself, and the entire room is immune to all spells. Even spirit magic. I can't say I know what kind of spell that is, but it shouldn't have got in here."

"Might it be affecting the liches, too?" I hadn't seen any of them on our way in, but they tended to avoid the spirit mages after their earlier disagreements.

"I'll ask." He backed out of the room. "We'll get to the bottom of this."

Dex flew over to me through the partly open door. "Blazes and tides, that's one nasty spell."

"Do you know what it is?" I shielded my eyes against the glow, the magic radiating from the amulets leaving haloed imprints on the inside of my eyelids.

"It feels like something is sucking the life out of me," said the fire sprite.

"I can't feel anything." Dex was a spirit, though, which gave him sensitivity to things living people couldn't feel.

I crossed the room to the shelf which contained my own soul amulet, which emitted a similar glow, and picked it up. When I reached for the remnants of magic inside it, I felt nothing but an odd cold emptiness in its place.

The amulet fell from my hand. Something had sapped the soul amulet of any magic it contained, and at a guess, the same was true of every one of the amulets in the room. Dex whimpered and flew out of the hall, while I paced the row of amulets, wondering where in hell the strange spell had come from. And how to stop it.

The source wasn't inside the room, so I backed out of the hall of souls and closed the door against the bright glow. *Alban.* Somehow, he'd found a way to cast a spell on the liches from a distance. It had to be him.

The Death King strode back into the entrance hall via the front door. "The liches' magic is fading. All of them."

"Something is draining their amulets," I said. "Or *someone*. I think we know who it is."

"It's impossible," he said, "but he seems to have found a way to escalate the curse from a distance."

My heart leapt into my throat. If we didn't stop him, then I could only assume the remaining life energy would drain from all the amulets. What would happen to the liches when their soul amulets were rendered useless? Would they all fade from existence?

"Bastard," I said. "I should have known he'd find another way to target anyone who refused to join his army."

The Death King's expression was flinty. "I'm going after him."

"It's me he wants," I argued. "I'm the target. I can't stay behind."

"I know," he said. "We promised the liches that we'd

help them, and now… they might not have much time left after all. If they survive, they won't forgive this."

"Then… they can come with us." I hadn't counted on Alban finding a way to reach the liches even in here, but his lich-killing cantrips had already proved that his ability to harm the liches was in no way dependent on his access to their soul amulets. "I think it's our only option if we want to attempt to keep our word."

Until the end, whispered a voice in the back of my mind. I hadn't the faintest clue how Alban had caused the curse to accelerate, but it was the Death King's quiet shock that rattled me the most. If even he'd never seen a spell like this before, then how could I hope to undo it?

Would Alban even give us the chance to?

Outside, I began to spot a few liches drifting around, but it was no wonder I'd overlooked them on my way into the castle. They resembled faded shadows, drained of most of the magic which kept them anchored to the land of the living.

"Liches," the Death King called to everyone within range. "Alban is making an attack on all of you at once. He's attempting to put a spell on you to drain your magic from a distance."

"What do you want us to do?" said one of the liches, his voice thin and insubstantial. "You promised to save us. You lied."

"We promised to give you a chance to get the cure." I raised my voice so the shadows drifting around me could hear every word. "Alban has decided to attempt to destroy you before you have that chance, so we're taking the war directly to Alban. Tell every lich to come here if they want to come and stop his spell and wrest the cure from him by force. This is it."

Several minutes of rustling shadows ensued while the liches gathered in the castle grounds, a mass of faded darkness which resembled little more than smoke above the swampy ground. *Dammit. We did lie to them.* Not intentionally, of course, but how was either of us supposed to know something like this was even possible?"

"This is likely to be your only chance to be cured of the curse," the Death King told the liches. "I won't lie—you might perish in the attempt, as might any of us. It seems the enemy has accelerated the curse in an attempt to pressure us into surrender. If you stay here, the odds are high that you'll expire anyway. If you come with me, then I will do my utmost to pry the cure from his hands."

"This is a final gambit, then?" said one of the liches.

"It is." I glanced over at the Spirit Agents, who were listening in, too. "You can go and look for Bria if you like. It's the liches who need to come with us."

"It wouldn't surprise me if Alban's allies targeted the castle in my absence," added the Death King. "Miles, would you tell the other Elemental Soldiers where we're going?"

"Sure." Miles ran to the castle, while I watched the crowd of gathering liches, hearing snippets of their whispered conversations about the Death King's commands. It seemed a direct attack on Alban was exactly what the majority of them had been waiting for, despite the unlucky circumstances. Even with their power drained, they were still a formidable force collectively, but would it be enough to overcome Alban? I didn't know precisely how many allies he had… or how he'd managed to cast such a lethal spell on the entire Court at once.

If you hadn't come back to life, you'd have fallen under its effects, too. Not to mention the Death King.

Damn. If any of the liches survived and we walked away without the cure, they'd take us apart. Good intentions were one thing, but now everyone except for the two of us were on the brink of disappearing, I didn't blame them for being angry. Regardless of what they thought of the pair of us, though, this was their last shot.

While the liches arranged themselves into fighting formations, Death King gave them orders to prepare themselves to take on Alban. Some of them mounted zombie horses, while skeletal wights joined the growing army at his command. I hoped Alban would be easy to find, because if the liches all fell victim to the spell at once, the whole Parallel would know that the Death King had lost his entire army in one fell swoop.

Dammit, Alban. You had to force our hand, didn't you?

"I'll go ahead through the node," I told the Death King. "Your people can probably move faster on the ground, and it'll give me the chance to find more allies."

"You mean the vampires?" he asked. "They don't live in the middle of Arcadia any longer."

I'd forgotten, but it didn't matter. "Lord Blackbourne might offer to help. You never know. "

Unlikely, of course, but I had to try.

"Okay, but don't take too long." He gave me a brief kiss, and then I ran to the node. Hopping through the current of energy, I landed in the outskirts of Arcadia and broke into a run.

Breathless, I reached the door of the vampires' new

headquarters and knocked. The pale human from before answered on my third knock.

"Hey," I said. "I need to see Lord Blackbourne. I know it's daytime, but it's urgent."

"He isn't well," said the human. "None of the vampires are."

Worry spiked. "What's wrong with them?"

"I don't know."

"Let me see." I pushed past him into the hall, ignoring his feeble protests. In the room on my right, I spotted Lord Blackbourne slumping in a seat, his face looking paler than ever.

"I don't remember inviting you in, Olivia." His voice was awful, ragged and hoarse.

"What's going on with you?" I could hazard a guess. The curse, or whatever it was, was affecting the vampires as well as the liches. "Is something draining your power? Do you know where it's coming from?"

He pressed a weary hand to his forehead. "If I knew, I might be able to stop it. Every vampire was affected simultaneously. I don't suppose you'd like to offer an explanation?"

"Alban, but I don't know how he did it."

The spell must be aimed at the dead of all kinds, and if it had spread beyond the swampland, then I couldn't imagine the potential upheaval of the vampires being wiped out as well as the liches.

"Ah." Lord Blackbourne closed his eyes. "Do tell him I am displeased with his actions, won't you, Olivia?"

"I'll come back." I backed out of the door. "Whatever spell he used, it's affecting the liches as well. The Death King and I are going to put it right."

"Please do," the human said, his voice tremulous. "I don't have anywhere else to go."

I felt bad leaving the poor kid behind, but he wouldn't be much help against Alban, and I doubted the vampires had been the intended targets unless Alban had seriously been holding back beforehand.

After retracing my steps to the node, I transported myself to the centre of Arcadia, at which point I ran towards the citadel to find the others. By now, the army was beginning to congregate on a road near the central square, zombie horses and all, and a swarm of liches clustered in rows as though waiting for orders. I walked among them, shivering in the chill air brought by their presence. "Where's the Death King?"

"He's on his way."

I reached the square and the door to the citadel swung inward at my touch, revealing the empty room on the inside. I walked in, and a flash from above my head told me the transporter was active. *But who's using it?*

Whispers filled the air as I climbed the staircase, preparing a cantrip in my hand. At the top of the stairs, I opened the door.

Dirk Alban stood on the other side.

16

A gasp lodged in my throat. The door swung closed behind me, but I caught it in my palm without breaking Alban's gaze. "Are you out of your mind?"

Alban gave me the merest trace of a smile. "I take it you got my message?"

"Did you mean to kill the vampires, too?" I demanded.

"They aren't dead yet," he said. "They shouldn't be, anyway."

"What did you do?" I looked over his shoulder at the lights flashing on the surface of the machinery. The transporter? "How the hell did you hit all the liches at once?"

"How else?" The machinery glowed as if in response to his words. "Any spell can be amplified, with a big enough battery."

The light s brightened, revealing a cage had been hooked up to the side of the machine. Inside the cage lay a pile of gleaming discs that glinted with gold light.

Soul amulets.

"You *did* sacrifice your allies." *Holy crap.* "The spell you used only affects the dead. How do you plan on beating our living army with most of yours incapacitated as well?"

The Death King entered the room behind me with soft footfalls. "Dirk Alban. Care to explain why you've decided to abandon your attempts to convince my liches that you alone can undo their curse?"

"Oh, I *can* undo their curse," he said. "I can also do worse, but I think this spell is far more appropriate. It doesn't only affect the dead, you know. The effect will spread to any species who is dependent on magic to survive. Sprites, for instance, as well as vampires."

Sprites. Bile coated the back of my throat. Dex was in danger as well. Had he come with the Death King? I didn't see him, but the spell might have a worse effect if he and the liches got any closer to its source. Alban had used the citadels and their amplifying magic to spread the spell's effects all the way to the Court of the Dead. Maybe further. The platform linked up to the transporter was glowing, too, though Alban stood alone without any visible allies in the room.

My grip on the cantrip in my hand tightened. Alban had put himself in a vulnerable position, but if I made the wrong move, his spell might take down our entire army at once. "What do you want from me?"

"I want your allegiance," he said. "Nothing more, nothing less."

"Aside from your need to disable my entire army and send your forces into Elysium, too," added the Death King.

I tensed. "What's going on in Elysium?"

"The Family has claimed the Houses of the Elements," Alban said. "Except for the House of Spirit, of course."

My heart lurched. The Houses of the Elements had slipped my attention, but I'd been under the impression that the Death King had been hoping to recruit them as allies against Alban and his allies. So that was why Alban had been happy to sacrifice his liches. He already had an army. Worse, the Family had taken Bria captive, too.

"Do your allies know you're more interested in recruiting me than in helping them?" I asked. "Heard what happened to Hawker? Did he come back here, or did you spurn him now he doesn't have his magic any longer?"

"The others can play their war games all they like," he said. "It's of no interest to me."

"I thought the spirit mages' war was your idea to begin with."

"Not at all," he said. "My goals could easily have been achieved without bloodshed. I have no intention of getting my hands dirty."

"So much for loyalty." I swung back and threw my paralysing cantrip at him.

Alban deflected the spell with ease, spirit magic alighting in his palm which echoed the glow of the transporter behind him. Had he removed every one of the neutralising spells we'd put in the citadels? It looked as though he had, while the empty soul amulets behind him indicated he'd come here to use the machine for another reason aside from weakening the Death King's army.

"It would be quicker if you surrendered," said Alban.

"Then you'll undo the spell and remove the curse on

the liches?" I said. "Forgive me if I think you're full of shit."

I reached for another cantrip—this one a neutraliser spell--and flung it in a wide arc, over Alban's shoulder and towards the glowing machinery at his back. The spell turned on, striking the metallic surface, and at once, the transporter's glow began to dim. Alban deflected another spirit magic attack from the Death King and leapt onto the platform, vanishing in a flash of light, the instant before the neutralising spell kicked in and the transporter turned off.

"Where the hell did he go?" I ran over to the platform, cursing under my breath. The neutraliser had cut off our means of following him. Dammit.

"I'd hazard a guess that he went to wherever he activated the spell he used on the liches," said the Death King. "Look."

I spun around. A few liches had entered the room behind us, their bodies fading and insubstantial. Alban had tricked us. The spell draining the life from them wasn't in this room at all, and my neutraliser spell had only turned off the transporter, nothing more.

The Death King spoke to the other liches. "He's in one of the other citadels. The transporter in Elysium should still be working."

"Maybe that's where the spell is coming from." I didn't have any better ideas, so I headed downstairs with the Death King.

Our steps echoed in the empty tower, while the liches murmured to one another in the background. More of them waited outside, transparent and fading by the second.

Dammit, we need to fix this.

As I walked across the square, Dex came zooming from the node in the other direction. His bright orange form looked paler than usual, too, and my heart lurched when I saw how fragile he appeared. Aria, Mav and Terren flew behind him, and the other sprites were in a similar condition, as I'd feared.

"It's starting to affect us, too," said Dex.

"Shit." I turned to the Death King. "We need to find where it's coming from. It's got to be one of those machines. Elysium—"

"It's not Elysium," the fire sprite said. "The Family took over the Houses of the Elements and now they've swarmed into the citadel as well."

"They did *what?*" I fought the urge to shout in frustration. "Can they not give us a fucking break? Alban ran off to another citadel. I suppose he went to join them, too."

The Death King looked at Dex, then at me. "I'll bring the army with me to the outskirts of Elysium. It strikes me as a bad idea for us to land in the middle of the city when that spell might be inside Elysium's citadel itself."

Good point. The liches would draw attention wherever we landed, so we needed to get them somewhere out of the way—and then undo the spell before they all perished at once. Along with Dex and the other sprites. I'd brought Dex back from the brink of death once before, and I refused to lose him again.

At the Death King's instructions, we stepped through the node, landing in a street I didn't recognise somewhere in Elysium. A tide of liches followed, along with the rest of the Death King's forces—with the notable absence of the Elemental Soldiers.

"Should I go call Ryan and the others?" I asked. "And the Spirit Agents?"

"They're already here in the city," Dex said in my ear. "They reacted fast when Bria found out the Houses had been taken over and came here right away."

"Good. I expected no less." The Death King took a step towards the node again. "Stay here and wait for me, all of you. Liv and I will get closer to the citadel and see what's going on. The Houses might have capitulated, but I'm willing to bet some of their number refused to work with the enemy, so we might have more allies hidden in the city."

"Let's hope so." We'd taken the Order back, only for the enemy to go after the Houses instead, and most of the Death King's army was fading by the second. I didn't need to be able to see their faces to know that if they were pushed to the brink of death without a cure in sight, they'd do their utmost to take Greyson and I down with them.

"We'll come back," the Death King told the army. "I'll send the Elemental Soldiers here to join you, rather than challenging the Family and the Houses alone."

"I bet it was Bria's idea." It sounded like one of hers. We never should have left them behind, or the Spirit Agents, either, but I'd been certain Alban had set up that spell in Arcadia's citadel and would attack the castle as soon our backs were turned. Granted, he didn't need to access the hall of souls in order to take out the Death King's army. Not anymore.

What were those soul amulets in the citadel for, then?

Dex followed us through the node, and we landed closer to the centre of Elysium. The Death King looked up at the dark shape of the citadel and shook his head. "I'm not sure the spell is coming from here, either."

"How can you tell?" Admittedly, the building wasn't glowing as brightly as it had when the transporter inside had been linked to London, but it wasn't like we'd be able to sense the spell ourselves when it only affected the dead.

"The spell would get stronger the closer we get to the source," he said. "It's not here. Right, Dex?"

"It might as well be." The fire sprite whimpered. "Blazes and tides. I don't want to die again."

"Then where...?" I trailed off, recalling the other citadel I was familiar with. "I bet it's in the citadel where Hawker had those sprites captive in a cage and was test-driving the spell to bring the liches back to life. The spell's got to be there."

"Even if it isn't, that's the only citadel I know of which likely has a transporter we can use to move around without drawing attention." The Death King turned back to the node, and we both halted when a breeze drifted from nowhere and someone stepped out behind us.

"It's only me," said Ryan.

"Don't sneak up on us like that." I rotated to face the Air Element. "Where are the others?"

"We're taking back the Houses from the Family," they said. "Seems not all of the mages are keen to submit to a new boss, so we're going to help them amass an attacking force."

"Good," I said. "I hope they keep the Family busy so we can undo the spell affecting the liches before they disappear."

"What spell?" they asked. "What's wrong with them?"

"They're dying," I said quietly. "All of them. The

sprites, too. Alban used some kind of spell in one of the citadels to hit every single creature in the Parallel which depends on magic to survive."

Ryan swore. "Is there anything I can do?"

"Hold the fort here," said the Death King. "My army is assembled on the outskirts of Elysium. Feel free to give them orders if you like. Liv and I will be back as soon as we fix this."

"Be careful," Ryan said.

"Will do." Joining the Death King, I approached the node. "Ah… I don't know the location of any nodes near the citadel out in the wilderness. How are we supposed to get over there, walk?"

"I have an alternative." The Death King took my arm, and without further ado, he transported us directly to the front of the tower. We landed in the ruins of the collapsed town it'd once marked the centre of, scarred with the aftermath of the last war.

"You shouldn't be wasting your resources like that," I reprimanded him.

"It's that or waste valuable time." He strode up to the citadel's door and pushed it open.

I expected Alban to be waiting for us on the other side, but the room within was empty. Dex flew in, too, his glowing form lighting the way up the stairs. I followed, my legs protesting at all these damn staircases, until we reached the top and opened the door.

"False alarm," Dex called over his shoulder.

While the machinery in the upstairs room looked to be in full working order, a cage surrounded the platform, blocking it off entirely. We couldn't use the transporter, and it didn't look like the spell had been activated in here, either. Dex would know if it had.

"Is someone trolling us?" I remarked. "Why put a cage on the transporter?"

"There's a cantrip here." The Death King walked over to the machine and peered down at the engraved disc on its surface. "It's a memory spell."

Alban was playing some kind of game with me, all right. "I'm not taking his bait. We'll have to look elsewhere. He'd better not have blocked off every damn transporter in the whole Parallel."

Maybe we should have tried our luck in Elysium after all. As we descended the stairs, a lich appeared in the darkness ahead of us.

"It's me." Harper floated into view, her illusory human face appearing above her fading form. "I've been looking everywhere for you. We need you in Elysium. The Family has mages, assassins... we're overrun. The other Elemental Soldiers are trying, but they'll get themselves killed if we don't get help soon."

I swore. "We left the rest of the Death King's army in Elysium. I thought you were with the others."

"No, I went with Bria to try to stop the Family from overrunning Elysium," she said. "We think they're hiding in the citadel."

"That's where we need to be," I said. "We're positive the spell affecting all the liches is hidden inside one of them, but it's not in here and it's not in Arcadia. Dex said it wasn't in Elysium, but that's the only working transporter we know of."

"The citadel is in the middle of a battlefield," said

Harper. "You'd be hard-pressed to get near it without an army."

"I have an army," said the Death King. "And we need to go to Elysium's citadel to stand a chance of getting anywhere near the source of this spell."

"Unless it's a trap." But the army overrunning the city was no hoax. People would get hurt and die if we didn't help the Elemental Soldiers and the Houses fight off the Family's forces. "This all happened too damn fast. It must have been planned."

"The Houses were always a powder keg." He took my arm. "We'll meet you on the other side, Harper."

The two of us vanished and landed next to the army of liches and wights in Elysium's street. Some had already gone into battle, presumably led by the Elemental Soldiers, and the Death King wasted no time in giving orders to the others. The distant sounds of fighting echoed over the rooftops, while I watched the node, hoping Harper knew how to find her way back here. Admittedly, she was safer hiding out there in the wilderness instead, but there was no escaping the deadly spell creeping across the Parallel.

"Liv?" The Death King beckoned me over to the zombie horses assembling nearby. "It'll be quicker if we ride."

"Riding to war on a zombie horse, huh." I shot him a smile, then mounted one of the horses.

The Death King did likewise, and we rode straight through the node, emerging into the midst of the battle which now engulfed the centre of Elysium. Chaos filled the streets, mages on both sides clashing with one another and the Death King's forces riding through the melee. The

Elemental Soldiers were easy to spot among the crowd in their armoured coats, including Bria, but I scarcely had the chance to spare her a look before a mage blasted fire at my horse. I veered to the side to avoid it, returning his attack with a handful of spirit magic. Bria fended the mages off with fireballs as she darted over to join us.

"Got rid of that Family of yours, did you?" I asked.

"Not yet," she said. "I need to get into that tower. Then I'll have them."

"We need to get into the tower, too. We have to shut down the spell that's affecting all the liches." I wasn't sure she actually knew about the spell, unless she'd seen Harper, but it was Alban's doing, not the Family's.

"All right." The Death King's gaze was trained on the citadel as he climbed off his horse and walked straight through the crowd, deflecting any attack that got close to him.

I jumped down from my horse, too, joining Bria and Miles in approaching the citadel. As the Death King reached the tower, I spotted Harper making her way among the crowd. She must have come back from the ruins to join the battle after all.

When the Death King opened the door to the tower, a knife flew past my ear. Bria swore and charged ahead, blasting fire at the assassins lurking in the darkness. When our path was clear, we ran up the spiralling staircase, scarcely pausing for breath.

At the top, Bria kicked the door open and swore under her breath. Nobody was inside the room at all. I assumed the Family had fled elsewhere, given the glow around the transporter, but at least this one was still active. Miles, Bria and Harper approached the transporter while the

Death King and I examined the machinery for any signs of the spell, already knowing it must be in one of the other citadels. One we hadn't been to yet.

Along with Alban.

Bria jumped onto the platform. "Anyone who wants to chase down the Family, come with us."

"Is the spell here?" Miles asked Greyson.

"No," he responded. "We'll look elsewhere. Good luck, Bria."

Harper drifted onto the platform, and all three of them vanished in a flash of light. "Guess she wanted to join them after all."

"She didn't want to be alone, I don't think," Greyson said.

When she dies, I heard, and swallowed a lump in my throat. It was a horrible thing to contemplate, but we weren't out of time yet. "Where might Alban have hidden the spell? Can you even use the transporter to get to somewhere we haven't already been?"

I stepped onto the platform, sensing its magic humming below my feet. If I could astral project anywhere or use the nodes to follow other people to unknown locations, I ought to be able to find Alban, right?

"We might be able to sense him, if he's been here recently." Greyson climbed onto the platform at my side. "We'll try."

Already, I could pick up on Greyson's presence next to me using more than just my regular senses. My spirit magic was attuned to other spirit mages, and while I might not claim that level of familiarity with Alban, I'd laid my hands on his soul once before. I pictured his face as I reached for the magic at the heart of the transporter and thought, *take us to Alban.*

Light flashed, and the transporter carried us away.

As we landed on solid ground, sharp spears of white lightning shot at both of us. Greyson moved fast, knocking me down and shielding me with his body. Another bolt of lightning struck the ground nearby, and I rolled off the platform, my gaze landing on the caster.

Alban stood over us, a grim smile on his face. "I did warn you."

I rose to my feet, but Greyson remained lying on the floor, motionless. The attacks, though not physical, had pierced him all over, leaving jagged slashes behind that shimmered at the edges.

"Greyson!" I ran to his side, my heart sinking. The wounds went so deep that parts of his soul were torn right open.

"I can help you fix him," Alban said.

Raw hate shot through me, and I'd leapt at him before my thoughts quite caught up with me. A wall of magic slammed into me before I could make contact with Alban, knocking me onto my back beside Greyson.

Pain shot up my spine, but I rolled over and held my palms over his body in a desperate attempt to fix the wounds splintering his soul. The glow from my own hands seemed dim by comparison to the lightning-like spears which had ripped him open.

"Olivia, your magic isn't up to the task," Alban said. "You have considerable strength at your disposal, but you lack the skill and experience that I have. I alone can fix him."

Tears burned my eyes. "Damn you."

"Your choice, Olivia," he said. "I'd hate to watch you suffer as you lose someone you care for so dearly. If you join me, however… I will heal him, without any conditions."

Greyson wouldn't want me to ally with Alban to bring him back to life, but if I let him die, then it wouldn't just be me who'd suffer as a result. His Court would be without a Death King, leaving the survivors to fall under Alban's control, and none of us would stand a fighting chance of undoing the spell on the others, much less the curse.

"You once pledged to serve me," Alban said. "I'll gladly heal your ally if you keep that promise. I'd say that's an even trade. Your loyalty for Greyson's life."

Greyson's wounds gaped open, leaking trails of magical energy until his very soul dimmed at the edges. I could bind him to an amulet and turn him into a lich again, of course, but without undoing Alban's spell, he'd perish forever along with the rest of the liches.

The thought snapped the last shred of my resolve clean in two. "Okay. I surrender. Just save Greyson."

"That's all I wanted to hear."

Alban moved to my side and crouched down. A flood of energy filled the room, and before my eyes, Greyson's wounds sealed, the ragged holes in his spirit healing over until he might never have been damaged at all.

"Don't look so surprise." Alban stood. "I never had a quarrel with Greyson, Death King or not. I'll let him keep what's left of his Court as an expression of gratitude for having you at my side again, Olivia."

Nausea swirled within me, especially when Greyson stirred, his eyes flickering open. "Liv?"

My throat closed up. "I'm sorry, Grey. I have to go with him."

Greyson's expression turned horror-struck. "No…"

Alban put a hand on my shoulder. There came a flash of light, and Greyson's shout of dismay was the last thing I heard before the room disappeared.

17

Alban and I landed in a wide room which resembled a luxury hotel suite, with beige and crimson décor and framed paintings of landscapes on the walls. Not my style, but better than a hole in the ground. Pain seared my wrist, and I looked down to see a thin wire-like pair of cuffs anchoring the pair of us together. "The hell is that?"

"A simple guarantee that you'll keep your word," he said. "I'll take it off if you behave."

"What's this place?" I squirmed away when I felt his hands at my waist, removing the cantrips from my pouch.

"Your new quarters." He palmed the cantrips without breaking his gaze from mine. "I trust you'll find them comfortable."

After removing my weapons, he detached the chain linking our wrists together. One half remained looped around my arm like a thin metal bracelet.

"What's this, a security tag?"

"A precaution to prevent you from leaving the property."

And with that, he left via a door which closed behind him with the click of a lock. It shouldn't surprise me that he'd left me alone. He knew he'd won, and open gloating wasn't typically his style. The door itself was the only signal to my captivity, with a small window and a letter-box-like slot which I couldn't quite fit my hand through, presumably for someone to deliver my meals through.

I made two attempts to shove the door open before running to the window instead, finding it wasn't a window at all, but a large landscape painting of a verdant field bordered by lush forests. Was that what the Parallel had once looked like? Maybe. Despite the elaborate furnishings, I had an inkling we were somewhere in the Parallel ourselves, albeit a room even nicer than the Death King's suite at the castle. Through the other door in the room, I found an equally pristine bedroom complete with an en-suite bathroom so polished I could see my reflection in every surface. The bed was neatly made, while a wardrobe brimmed with new clothes. Had he looked up my size or had he just guessed? Whoever had bought the clothes didn't know my prescription, evidenced by the absence of any spare glasses to replace the ones I'd had to leave at home. I reached into my pouch and found that he'd at least left my spare contacts when he'd taken my weapons. Oh, and my lucky dice. How generous of him.

The bracelet on my wrist resisted all my attempts to tear it off. Runes were carved around the edges, indicating some kind of binding spell. Not a good start to our so-called partnership, but I wouldn't have trusted me either, considering I was already envisioning a dozen escape methods.

I reached for my spirit magic first, to no avail. *Dammit. It's like a neutralising cantrip.* That would explain why he'd attached the bracelet to my wrist so I couldn't remove it myself. Of course he wouldn't give me an easy way out.

I'd have to be sneakier, then.

Magical neutraliser aside, this place was clearly designed for a guest, not a prisoner, and he'd spent a while lovingly preparing the rooms for me. Did that mean he'd established a permanent base here? If so, the source of the spell on the liches might be elsewhere on the property, but I had my sincere doubts he'd have marred a nice house like this with a deadly cantrip.

I'd surrendered to Alban to give Greyson and the other liches a fighting chance at saving themselves, yet the ache in my chest only worsened with each passing moment. I'd abandoned my allies in the middle of a war, when the liches were already practically on their deathbeds. As long as Greyson was all right, I'd thought I could deal with the rest, but now…

I made my choice. Besides, undoing the curse on the liches had always been a long shot, and if it wasn't possible for them to return to their former lives, then perhaps quietly and painlessly fading away was the best possible outcome. Better than having their souls crushed the way Alban had done to the poor inhabitants of those soul amulets.

The thought brought a spasm of self-disgust. The spell had hit the vampires, too, not to mention the sprites, and they didn't deserve to be obliterated due to a petty grudge. There must be more I could do, even as a prisoner. Now Alban had what he wanted, maybe he'd be willing to listen to me.

Alban didn't return to speak to me until at least an hour later. By that point, I'd rubbed my wrist raw trying to remove the bracelet. I hadn't stooped to trying to kick the door down yet, though the temptation nagged at me all the same.

When the door clicked open, Alban entered with quick steps and closed the door behind him as though to ensure I didn't try to run out. I didn't move, as tempted as I was, because I'd be playing into his expectations if I did what he predicted.

"What's going on in Elysium?" I asked. "Who's winning the battle?"

"It doesn't matter," he said. "It's of no concern to either of us now."

"Screw that." I held up my wrist. "Our agreement didn't involve you cutting off my magic."

"I wanted to ensure you didn't do yourself any harm in an ill-advised escape attempt while you were alone," he said. "I'll take it off now."

He held out a hand. I hesitated, then figured it wasn't like I had anything to lose at this point and extended my own wrist. With a twist of his fingers, he unclipped the bracelet. My magic would probably take a while to return as it usually did when faced with a neutraliser cantrip, but at least I was no longer defenceless.

"You're welcome," he said. "Also, I thought you might want this."

He held up a cantrip with his other hand. I didn't recognise the markings until I looked closer, and then a trickle of familiarity slid through me.

A memory spell.

"This is what you always wanted, isn't it?" he said. "Perfect recollection of all the memories the Order took from you."

Not like this. "Nah, I gave up on the idea a long time ago. It'd be nice to remember some of the more pleasant parts, but you can't pick and choose. Besides, since it's you who's making the offer, you probably want me to remember all the nice things you did when you were pretending not to be a self-involved sociopath."

He didn't even blink at my insult. "Do you know how much I paid for a spell that specific?"

"I'd rather not, thanks."

He held out the cantrip to me. "There's no catch. I simply wanted to make your choice to join my side worth your while."

"You knew I'd end up here."

No surprises there. The calculating bastard had been planning this from the instant he'd returned to life.

"Yes, I did," he said. "When the effects of the bracelet fade, you'll be able to use that cantrip to get your missing years back. Within the hour, by my estimate. I'll send someone up here with refreshments in the meantime. I want you to be comfortable."

"All the best for your pet spirit mage, huh."

"I don't think of you as a pet," he said. "I have to admit it's been a difficult adjustment to make, having to consider you an adult rather than a child when no time passed for me during my years bound to a soul amulet, but I admire who you've become."

"Don't flatter me. It's weird." I took a firm step back, not taking the cantrip from him.

He gave a shrug and dropped the golden disc at my feet. "Your choice."

I stared at the cantrip's carved surface, while he retreated from view. The door clicked shut, leaving me alone with the memory spell tantalisingly close to my reach.

Lord Blackbourne had thought the answers to stopping the war lay in my memories. I'd seen enough glimpses into my history to know that I'd been involved with Alban's plans right up until he tried to take the Death King's soul, and who knew, maybe I *would* more answers within the lost memories I had yet to recover.

With nothing better to do, I waited for the effects of the neutralising spell to wear off while someone delivered a tray of food to my room via the slot in the door. I wasn't hungry, so I put the tray aside and continued to wait for my magic to return, snapping my fingers at intervals and keeping my senses attuned for any nodes in the area.

When a spark of light returned to my palms, I made no delay in trying to use it to blast the door open. Naturally, it didn't make a dent in the wooden surface. Alban had been careful to ensure I had no means of escape. Only one magical item remained in the room, and it lay on the floor, taunting me with the memories I'd sought for years.

I crouched and picked up the cantrip, turning it over in my hand. Alban wouldn't return for hours, for all I knew. He'd leave me here until he'd given me sufficient time to give into temptation.

He might be a liar, but memory spells showed only the truth.

I turned the cantrip on. A blinding white light flashed before my eyes, and then I tumbled headfirst into the past.

Dirk Alban faced my class at the academy, all of whom broke into awed laughter at something witty he'd said. I perched on the edge of my seat, intrigued and entranced by this man who seemed to spit in the face of the Order's traditional prissy attitudes without even trying.

"I'm a scholar," he said. "Ask me about my area of expertise after the end of this lesson and I might tell you what it is. Or I might not."

Charisma radiated off him, and my face heated when his gaze momentarily focused on me as though sensing my interest. I wasn't the only person who stayed behind after the lesson to speak to him. In fact, I almost didn't. I was shy and awkward and took my time packing my school bag in order to wait for the others to leave the classroom before approaching him.

Alban gave me an encouraging nod. "Come to guess my area of expertise?"

"Yes." I swallowed against my dry throat, my pulse thrumming with nerves. "Is your area of expertise magical talismans?"

"Good guess, but no." A smile curled his mouth. "Want to try again?"

"I—" My mind went blank. "Um. I don't know."

"Spirit magic," he said. "That's my speciality."

My mouth parted. "Isn't that illegal?"

"Not from a scholarly perspective."

His swift answer piqued my interest, and from the gleam in his eyes, he knew it did, too. "You're interested, are you?"

"Yeah," I said. "I always wondered why they didn't teach us about spirit magic at the academy."

"Curiosity is not a crime, though some might treat it as such," he said. "Here, take this. Email me if you want more details."

He pressed a business card into my hand and walked away. I looked at it for a moment, then pocketed the card before leaving the classroom.

I found Greyson Beaumont waiting on the other side of the door. Like the other boys in our class, he'd gone through a growth spurt over the last year or so and now towered over me in a way I might have found intimidating if not for the fact that unlike the other boys in my class, he didn't make a habit out of snapping girls' bra straps in the corridors, which set him above the rest in my fifteen-year-old mind. It didn't hurt that I found him undoubtedly attractive, along with ninety percent of my female peers, while he'd been nothing but polite on the occasions when we'd spoken to one another.

Not that it actually meant anything. I was a weirdo who played D&D and definitely wasn't in with the cool crowd. I hadn't a clue what *he* did outside of school hours, but I never saw him meeting with the sports teams or chess club. Not that it seemed to hurt his popularity. He didn't have any hangers-on at the moment, though, but maybe he'd stayed to speak to Dirk Alban, too.

"Hey, Liv," he said. "What were you talking to that Alban guy about?

Why not ask him yourself? If he'd been anyone else, I might have said exactly that, but since it was Greyson, I said, "I got curious about what he said earlier."

"What's his area of expertise, then?" asked Greyson. "Did he tell you?"

I found myself answering before I could question if it was a wise idea. "Spirit magic."

His brows rose. "Dangerous topic for a scholar, especially here. I'm surprised they let him come in."

Feeling tense for reasons I couldn't quite put my finger on, I said, "We're not forbidden to *talk* about spirit magic, are we? Why shouldn't he study it?"

I sounded more belligerent than I'd intended, but his interest had thoroughly flustered me. On top of Alban's offered business card, this was turning into an incredibly weird day.

Greyson blinked. "I didn't mean to offend you. He's free to study whatever he likes. I assume he's not a spirit mage himself."

"I doubt he'd come here if he was," I said. "He'd be locked up."

"If he was lucky," added Greyson. "You're not a mage yourself?"

"Nah, just a practitioner," I responded. "I hoped I might turn out to be a mage, but no luck. You?"

"No." He shook his head. "I carved my first cantrip over the summer. Might get lucky and end up having a knack for that."

"Really?" That was impressive, especially as we hadn't been taught more than the very basics of magical theory yet. "You want to work for the Order?"

"No," he said, with such certainty that I looked at him in surprise. "I want to work in the Parallel."

That, I understood. I'd never set foot in the place, but a longing for the Parallel had lodged itself in my heart and had persisted for the entirety of my time at the academy despite our teachers trying to play down the merits of living in a magical realm. I'd need top grades in magical theory to stand a chance of getting a job at the Order which would allow me to travel between realms, but maybe I hadn't considered all the options yet.

Like whatever Dirk Alban did. Since spirit magic had been banned before I was born, he couldn't be a practising mage himself, so he must have worked hard to convince the magical authorities it was safe to pursue his research without using it.

That night, I sat at the family computer, and I emailed Dirk Alban at the address he'd left on his business card. It took close to an hour to hammer out a draft which sounded formal and professional rather than overexcited and curious, especially with the lagging internet connection at home. Even then, a restless energy stirred beneath my skin, along with the sinking feeling that Alban was far too busy to deal with a fifteen-year-old student who wasn't even a practising mage yet.

Alban replied within the hour and sent me a few documents on spirit magic theory. I inhaled them in a single night, staying up late, and while I wanted to fire off a reply to him right away, I worried that might seem too eager. Instead, I gave it until the following evening.

His response invited me to come to one of his night classes at the academy.

I jumped so violently when I read the reply that I accidentally kicked the switch to the family computer and caused it to turn off. *Keep it cool, Liv. Keep it cool.*

I wasn't good at keeping it cool, but Alban didn't seem to mind. The memories continued, showing me the passing weeks where I studied with Alban in the evenings after my academy lessons finished for the day, building from theory to practical spirit magic over the course of two years. I didn't know at what point I'd accepted that his lessons were anything but theoretical, but once I'd used spirit magic for the first time, nothing short of the Order's intervention would have convinced me to stop. And I'd never set eyes on the Order aside from the occasional school visit from a smart-suited and dull careers advisor.

The world was far more exciting than that. I knew it was.

I had other things to distract me as well. Greyson and I had progressed from tentative flirting while revising Shakespeare to fooling around in the typical awkward manner of teenagers. We didn't flaunt our relationship at the academy, since it was nobody's business but ours, but my friends professed their envy at every opportunity. I found their comments vaguely irritating, but it was my lessons with Alban that I kept close at heart, a secret knowledge wrapping around me like a warm coat.

My present thoughts drifted back, momentarily. How could I have forgotten all of that? The old friends I hadn't spoken to in years, Mum's confused attempts to get me to tell her what my private classes were about, and how Greyson and I had gone from strangers to boyfriend-and-girlfriend without him ever stumbling upon my secret or vice versa…

And then—

And then.

One day, Alban asked me to meet him after classes were over. We weren't supposed to be having a lesson today, but I wasn't about to complain about an extra chance to talk to him, as he'd been busier than usual over the last few weeks.

Through the classroom window, though, I saw he wasn't alone in the room. Several students of varying ages gathered behind the desks, along with a few adults, too.

I'm not the only one he's been teaching spirit magic to. A bolt of jealousy shot straight to my core, followed by a rush of embarrassment. I felt like a complete fool for letting myself believe I was his only pupil. Of course I wasn't. He was clever and charismatic enough that everyone had wanted to get to know him, even if I was the only person in my class who'd ultimately taken him up on his offer.

The door opened and I watched the others leave the classroom, fighting a wave of conflicting emotions. Nevertheless, when he beckoned me into the room, I went inside and shut the door behind me. "What did you want to see me about?"

"The Order," he said, "is growing suspicious about my activities."

My heart lurched. "They know you're a spirit mage?"

"No," he said. "However, there is a certain individual who believes he ought to be the only spirit mage in existence, and I believe he intends to tip the Order off as to the nature of our lessons."

"Who?" What spirit mage could he possibly mean, and how did he know about our lessons? "Is it another of your students?"

"The King of the Dead," he said. "The king of liches is the most powerful of all spirit mages, living or dead."

Oh. Of course. Since the King of the Dead was, well,

dead, I hadn't thought of him as ever having been a spirit mage like the two of us. Everyone knew his title, but since he was feared throughout the Parallel, few had ever set eyes on him, and I'd never guessed Alban might have. "Why would he be interested in our lessons, though? Doesn't he live in the Parallel?"

"Because he's interested in anything that involves spirit magic," said Alban. "He's a dangerous, dangerous individual. You know how liches gain their magic, don't you?"

I nodded. We'd had several lessons on soul amulets, where he'd taught me about binding one's soul to an object to become a lich—a feat only achievable for a spirit mage.

"The liches and the Order have a binding contract," he went on. "A contract they signed after the war, when the Order banned spirit magic. As a result, the liches are the only people allowed to continue to have spirit magic at all."

"But they're dead."

"Exactly," he said. "I've been honest with you about the Order's views, but you know what will happen if they find out the truth."

We'd both be arrested. Fear clawed up my throat. "Were those students you were just speaking to learning spirit magic, too?"

"Yes, and they've agreed to help me out." He drew in a breath. "I see only one way forward, and it isn't a pleasant one. You see, it's the King of the Dead who has grown suspicious about me. Nobody else knows."

"Then... what?" I frowned. "He's still in the Parallel, isn't he?"

"Yes, he is," he said. "I don't like the idea in the slightest, but I think our only way forward is for me to take his soul amulet."

"You mean… kill him?"

"He's already dead, Olivia," he said. "He died a long time ago. Liches are tragic creatures. Many believe true death would be a blessing to them, and in their position, I would be glad for some peace. If we take the Death King's soul amulet and lay him to rest, then the truth will be buried along with him."

My blood pounded in my veins. *He's going to kill the Death King.* I didn't know how that was even possible, but to me, it seemed as though there was nothing Dirk Alban was incapable of.

"What do you want me to do?" I whispered.

"It's completely fine if you don't want to involve yourself in this," he said. "However, this will be the end of our lessons. Whatever you decide, if we don't remove him before he exposes us, then we'll all pay the price. Being underage won't mean the Order will spare you, Olivia. I am sorry."

I took a step back, my eyes stinging. "Then… okay. I'll help you."

I hardly heard another word he said. His revelation had dumped a bucket of ice-cold water over my head. Everything we'd discussed over the years had begun to unravel in the back of my mind. He wanted someone dead. Someone who was already dead, admittedly, but that didn't mean it was any less true. What if one of the others got cold feet and reported us to the Order? There were so many ways this could go wrong *before* I set foot in the Parallel.

The thought had never crossed my mind that he might want me to take the fall for him, but worry ate away at me from the inside for days following our conversation. I knew Greyson realised I was distracted, but he couldn't possibly guess what was on my mind. How could he? I'd kept my lessons with Alban a secret, the same way he remained cryptic about his home life.

I felt my conscious self in the background, struggling to pull herself free from the memories flowing towards me like an inevitable tide. After all, I didn't need to see anything more. I'd already recalled the day of the Death King's ascension in its entirety and most of what had happened since then had been relayed to me by people I trusted. Meeting Devon after failing my exams over the following summer and getting invited to join her new D&D group. Trying to apply for jobs at the Order, retaking exams only to fail again, and weeks of confusion and hurt, buried beneath a haze. The only major memory I'd been missing from the time had been my last meeting with Greyson before he'd left the academy for good.

Yet for all that I tried to fight my way back to consciousness, the flood dragged me under again.

The following morning after speaking to Alban, I met Greyson in the corridor of the academy. I confessed that there was something wrong, something which involved spirit magic, but I didn't want him to suffer for my mistake as well. Not when just talking about it would get him arrested as a co-conspirator.

I'd trusted the wrong person, but it was far too late to undo my mistake. Time ticked away until I found myself walking to meet Alban outside the academy. He greeted me with a nod. "I'm glad you decided to come, Olivia."

"Where are we going?" I asked, as he led the way down the street and away from the academy.

"Somewhere I think you've wanted to go for a while."

Worry fluttered in my chest. He'd taught me how to see nodes a year or so ago, and the current of light ahead of us was as beautiful as ever, but the fear persisted. I forced myself to focus on the glowing node, piercing and beautiful in an otherworldly way that made me want to keep staring at it forever.

Alban led me into the heart of the node, and the current leapt to life inside my veins and carried me to the Parallel.

Only when we reached the other side did I realise that Greyson wouldn't know where I was. I had no way to reach him from here.

I'd have to stop Alban on my own.

"Come on." Alban beckoned me to follow him through a winding street between the ruins of several abandoned buildings. The town we'd landed in was almost entirely formed of crumbling piles of stone and brick. Not a single building appeared to be intact—or inhabited. As we walked, a shadowy form floated past us.

"Phantoms," Alban murmured. "They won't bother us."

This is the Parallel. This is what it's really like.

This, I realised with a jolt of dread, was what the spirit war had done.

Alban led the way to a towering building which looked like it had been cut from night-coloured cloth, towering above the ruins and intact where everything else lay in rubble. He then opened the door and beckoned me into a circular room which appeared to be made out of the same obsidian substance, lit from within by curious runes carved into the walls which spiralled up the winding staircase. At the top, another door opened into a similar circular room filled with strange, glowing machinery. Runes glimmered on the walls, like downstairs, and a humming noise permeated the air. I remained quiet, taking it all in, my heart hammering in tandem with the sound of the whirring machinery.

"The original Council of the Elements used to meet in here," Alban told me. 'They used the citadels as their bases and were able to travel from one to another, rather like using a node."

"You..." I swallowed. "You mentioned that something went wrong back then. When the war started. Was this where it happened?"

"Yes, but don't look so worried," he said. "I never mentioned why the spirit mages turned on their fellow Elements, did I? It was for legitimate reasons. The truth is that the nodes between Earth and the Parallel were weakening, and the spirit mages were the first to notice. If the situation had worsened, the realms would have drifted further apart and maybe even become detached from one another altogether. As a result, the spirit mages made a request to the Council of the Elements to combine their strengths as they'd done during the Parallel's creation and to ask the other mages to help them, but the mages refused. The result was that the spell didn't work as it should have, and all of them died."

"That's awful." His revelation momentarily distracted me from my fear. "If they all died, does that mean the Parallel is still... drifting away from Earth?"

"No, because their spell did work as intended," he said.

"It also, however, resulted in a curse which affected the entire Court of the Dead. In fact, it created them."

"I don't understand." My voice was a whisper, yet the high walls of the citadel caught my words and echoed them back. "I thought you were here to take the soul amulet belonging to the King of the Dead."

"Oh, I already did that," he said. "It's right here."

He pulled the amulet from his pocket, and my heartbeat quickened as dread constricted my lungs. "Why did you bring me here?"

"Because you're going to be my successor," he said. "You need to witness this."

"Are—" I broke off. "Are you going to destroy it?"

"It's impossible to destroy a soul amulet," he said. "Not with any magic we possess, at any rate. No, the only way to remove the Death King's power is for me to take that magic for myself."

I'd been duped. If I hadn't already known it, I did now. He wanted the Death King's power, and to take his place. As for why he wanted *me* here…

"You're mine," he said. "My successor. My triumph."

No…

"Between us, we can do anything," he said. "We can kill death itself."

My heart pounded in my chest. "What do you want me to do?"

"Put this—" He held out the soul amulet towards me— "into there."

That was where it ended. The memory cut off, leaving me alone in the darkness.

18

The present day filtered back in as I came to myself, sitting on the floor of the guest room at Alban's house. My mouth was dry, my heart pounding in my chest. How long had passed? I'd seen two years of memories, but I couldn't have been trapped inside the spell for long, or else Alban would have come back. I was starving, thirsty and disorientated, but not as though I'd been gone for longer than a few hours. I didn't think so, anyway.

I downed the glass of water on the desk, my hands shaking, and placed the spell down on the smooth wooden surface. My heartbeat hammered in my ears, while a sense of unreality tilted the world beneath my feet.

That was it. Now I knew it all, from the very beginning. Sympathy for my teenage self warred with the certainty that she'd have *hated* to be pitied. She'd wanted to be respected. She'd wanted to be more than she was allowed to be, and that desperation had led her to seek out Alban.

As for his other apprentices? They'd died that day when I'd held his soul in my hands and the depths of his fury had struck them down in bolts of lightning, killing them all in the same instant. The ones who hadn't died had met tragic fates of their own, like Cobb and the Crow.

Leaving nobody behind but the two of us.

I lay down on the bed, my vision blurring. I thought about crying, but instead fell asleep, my emotions wrung out like an old sponge. Before my eyes closed, I saw an image of Greyson on that last day at the academy, when he'd come to see me for one final time before becoming the King of the Dead...

A sharp rap on the door woke me what felt like several seconds later. I jolted upright, then ran across the room, suppressing the urge to flinch when Alban greeted me with a smile. "Everything okay in here?"

Translation: *are you behaving?* I rubbed my forehead, still disorientated. "What day is it?"

"Oh." His gaze fell on the cantrip on the floor, and he positively beamed. "I should have warned you about the cantrip's side effects. Give it a few minutes and the dizziness will pass."

"I said, what day is it?" I repeated, louder.

"It's been two days since you came here. Does that help?"

No wonder I was so hungry. "Am I allowed to explore the rest of the house, or am I still grounded?"

A loud rapping noise came from somewhere behind me. Not my own door, but another one. Alban shot a frown over his shoulder. "Not yet. Be patient. I'll send someone up with refreshments."

He closed the door. I remained where I stood, listening out for more noises, but no other sound followed. Nor did he come back. The next knock signalled someone arriving with a tray of food, which they handed me through the slot in the door without speaking to me.

I took the tray and devoured the food, not about to turn down a free meal. With my strength returning and the dim confusion of the dream fading, the urge to escape returned. I paced the room and my foot caught on the slim shape of the bracelet which had once been affixed to my wrist. I took it in hand, examining the edges where Alban had unclipped it, which gave it the right shape to be an effective improvised lockpick.

Figuring it was worth a shot, I studied the letterbox-shaped slot through which my meals had been delivered. My hand wouldn't quite fit through, but if I got the right angle, I might be able to reach the lock. It took several minutes of painstaking manipulation before I slid the twisted end of the bracelet into the lock and jiggled it around until I heard a satisfying click.

Careful to make as little noise as possible, I eased the door open, halting at the sound of a crash from behind the door across from mine. Another prisoner? A second crashing noise sounded, like someone throwing a heavy object at the door from the other side.

Ah, screw it. I worked the lockpick on that door too until it clicked open. Then I pushed it inward and a blast of air shot from the room, nearly taking the door clean off its hinges and slamming my back into the wall. The breath hissed between my teeth. "Ow."

"Shit, Liv, sorry." Ryan stood behind the door, as intimidating as ever despite the cuffs securing their wrists. Not magic-proofed, evidently. "I thought you were him."

I stared at the Air Element. "What are you doing here?"

"Getting captured," they said, waving their cuffed hands. "I'm guessing this place wasn't designed to hold air mages."

"Damn." I slipped into their room and closed the door behind me so Alban wouldn't hear us. "How did he catch you?"

"I got careless," Ryan said. "The Death King has been driving us mad, so we've been avoiding the castle."

"In what way?" My heart gave a painful throb. "I mean, how's he dealing with all this?"

"The first thing he did after his army returned from Elysium was disband the Court and fire all his Elemental Soldiers, so I'd say he's coping wonderfully."

"He what?" Oh, damn. "Seriously?"

"Yeah, he's not thinking straight," said Ryan. "The castle is our home, so we all stayed anyway, but we've spent most of the last few days looking for you. The Death King wouldn't have had it any other way."

My eyes stung. Why had I assumed he'd return to running his Court in my absence? I had to get back to him, which started with getting Ryan out of their cuffs. I held up the bracelet I'd used to get the door open. "Lock-pick. Should work on the cuffs, right?"

"Sure, go ahead." Ryan extended their hands and I picked the lock on their handcuffs. "I've no idea where we are, by the way. The fucker knocked me out before he brought me in here."

"That figures." I let the cuffs fall to the ground and slid the bracelet into my pocket. "Look, I—I'm not sure I can leave yet. I haven't found a way to undo the spell *or* the curse yet, and if I get out of here before then, I wouldn't put it past Alban to turn Greyson into a lich again to ensure his fate is sealed."

"There'll be a way to undo both," said Ryan. "We just need to—"

Footsteps came from the landing, sharp and sudden, and a moment later, Alban opened the door to the room. "Enjoying getting reacquainted with my new guest, Olivia?"

"Eat shit," Ryan said.

I studied Alban. "I thought a condition of our bargain was that you'd leave Greyson alone."

"And I honour your wishes," said Alban. "However, it's in my knowledge that Greyson fired all his Elemental Soldiers. Since this one was causing trouble in the citadels, I saw nothing wrong with bringing them here."

Bastard. Of course he'd been keeping watch on the Court of the Dead despite his promise to leave them alone. "For what purpose? I thought this wasn't supposed to be a prison."

"It isn't," he said. "Olivia, you're allowed to have free run of the house for your good behaviour. This one, on the other hand, hasn't displayed any signs of cooperation."

"Go fuck yourself," came Ryan's response. "You were baiting us into looking for you. Don't deny it."

"I hoped to offer you employment," said Alban. "The Death King made a mistake firing you, considering his liches are no more."

My heart missed a beat. "What have you done?"

"Nothing whatsoever," he said. "The curse simply came to its natural end."

"You mean the spell *you* used to force the Death King's hand." I looked between him and Ryan in dawning horror. "The spell hit the sprites, too—and the vampires."

"Oh, I forgot you bonded with a sprite," he said. "I'm deeply sorry."

His words sank like knives into my chest. The other liches were dead. *Dex* was dead. "No. You *monster.*"

"I genuinely forgot, Olivia," he said. "My apologies—"

Ryan blasted air magic at him before he could finish his sentence. Alban raised a hand and Ryan's magic flew back at them, sending them flying head over heels into the opposite wall. Then Alban seized my shoulder, dragging me out of the room.

"Hey!" I squirmed out of his grip, but he'd already slammed the door on the Air Element, causing the lock to click into place again. "What the fuck was that? Did you just steal Ryan's magic?"

Taking someone else's magic without their permission struck me as a violation or at least impolite, but it was the least of Alban's crimes.

Dex. Alban had never intended to spare any of my allies, dead or alive.

"I'll give your friend the chance to calm down," said Alban. "And… I'm truly sorry about your sprite companion, Liv."

"You don't get to call me that." I backed into the doorway of my own room, fury building in my chest. "Were you hoping I'd sit back while you let my allies die through your own actions? While you captured the

Elemental Soldiers and forced them to join your team, too?"

"I hoped they might join me of their own free will." He exhaled in a sigh, sounding surprisingly weary. "The liches and the sprites alike were never long for this world. It's only the fact that the Parallel has a higher amount of magic than Earth that has allowed them to continue to exist."

"So you lied, blatantly, when you promised to free the liches from the curse." I blinked hard, determined not to break down in front of him. "You lied to Hawker, too. Where is he? Did you ever acknowledge that he lost his magic at the Order's hands without you lifting a finger to help him?"

I'd been desperate enough to make a bargain with Alban to save Greyson, but if he'd killed the sprites and liches without a second's thought and was busy trying to recruit the Elemental Soldiers, it was only a matter of time before his other promises evaporated like the illusions they truly were. Nothing he said was the truth, not even to his so-called successor.

Alban seemed to see my intentions in my face, because he raised a hand, which gleamed violet with vibrant power. Not just spirit magic, but something even more potent that brought a metallic taste to my tongue and raised the hairs on my arms.

"You don't want to challenge me, Olivia. You'll lose."

"What the hell kind of magic is that?" I reached for his life essence, only for him to grab *mine*, his hand closing over the very heart of my spirit magic. Pain speared my chest, and all the fight went out of me in a chilling rush of weakness.

"I'll give you the chance to calm down before I speak to you again, Olivia. Remember our bargain."

He released me and gave me a shove into my room, gentle but firm. Once he shut the door on me, I heard him walking out of sight.

As for me, I sank onto the floor of the room, despair rising like a tidal wave. His regret had to be faked, but the liches *had* been dying when I'd left, and he'd given me no reason to believe he'd brought the spell to a halt now he had what he wanted.

Because… if not…

Dex. Elements, Dex. It wasn't even his first death. He'd been a living fire mage before he'd lost his mortal life, and he'd never known. Regret swamped me for not telling him what I'd learned. Unbidden, a memory of astral projecting out of an underground cell to find Dex rose in the back of my mind, and I bit back a scream of grief and fury.

Dammit, I couldn't give in. Alban might have given me my memories back, but he was the reason I'd lost them to begin with. I would never bow to anyone. Even Alban. *Especially* Alban.

I pulled out the improvised lockpick again, then hesitated. Getting out of the room might be easy, but there must be other defences on the house itself as well as security guards. Not to mention Alban's new magical skills. I hadn't seen energy the violet colour he'd held in his hands before. What kind of new magic was he carrying? Was it to do with those soul amulets which had lain abandoned in the citadel, stripped of their power?

I jumped to my feet when I heard the sound of a scuffle from somewhere downstairs. Adrenaline surged at the unmistakeable crash of something heavy being thrown across a room.

Ryan? Or had Alban caught one of the other Elemental Soldiers and brought them here?

I scrubbed my eyes with my sleeve. Then I walked to the door and pushed it open as another crash sounded from somewhere below my feet. "Ryan? You in there?"

Ryan's muffled voice came from behind the door to their room. "Sure. What's that noise?"

"Let's find out."

My fingers fumbled the lockpick when another series of crashes came from below, but nobody interrupted. Once I'd let them out of their room, Ryan led the way downstairs on quiet feet.

We arrived in a pleasant hallway with white wallpaper decorated with a flowery motif, where a locked front door stood ahead of us. Its windows were tinted, but not enough to hide the bright flash which came from outside.

The door flew open. Ryan shouted a warning, and I threw myself out of the way as air magic rippled through the hall and slammed into the person who'd opened the door. A yelp drew my eyes open to see none other than Trix facing off against Ryan in the hallway.

My mouth fell open. "Holy shit, Trix. How in the world did you get here?"

"I followed Ryan's trail," he said. "Um… sorry I startled you."

"Sorry I hit you." Ryan grabbed Trix in a hug that made the elf gasp in surprise. Or possibly pain. The Air Element's spiky armour was still intact, after all. Nevertheless, Trix hugged them back just as tightly.

I cleared my throat. "Not to interrupt, but where's Alban?"

"Was he the man I knocked out at the gate?" said Trix.

"You knocked someone out?" I said. "I doubt it was Alban. He wouldn't have been easily surprised."

Though I doubted he'd seen the elf coming. I certainly hadn't.

"Come on." Ryan released Trix and took a step towards the door. "Let's go."

The door swung open again. Alban entered the hall, an expression of utter fury etched on his face. A shimmering light surrounded him, a shield formed of spirit magic.

So much for an easy escape.

Trix spun on him, but Alban raised a casual hand and blasted the elf off his feet into the wall. Ryan stepped in, only for Alban to turn their own air magic back at them. I tried my spirit magic, but as I expected, Alban's shield was faultless.

So I reached into my pouch for my last weapon… my lucky dice. What the hell. At least I was going down fighting.

The dice flew from my hand and smacked Alban in the forehead, as though his magical shield wasn't there at all. His eyes widened in surprise—then he fell backwards, out cold.

"What the hell?" I scooped up the dice and ran over to the others. "How'd I break his shield?"

Trix sprang to his feet. "The dice are magical, didn't you know?"

"I'm sorry, what?" Since when were my dice anything other than, well, dice? Admittedly, this wasn't the first time I'd used them to knock someone out, but the odds of rolling a natural twenty were the same as any other die.

He blinked. "I thought I told you when I gave them to you. They're elf-made. Why else would they give you such an accurate shot?"

Elves. Honestly. I'd deal with that one later, because now we needed to figure out how to get the hell out before Alban woke up. "I hope you remembered the way back to the swamp, because I have no idea where we are."

"I know the way," Trix said. "Also, I should mention I didn't manage to knock out all the guards."

"At least we're forewarned." Ryan's hands glowed with air magic as they took the lead and we ran outside.

Sure enough, several armed guards in dark clothing closed in to block our path. I didn't know whether they were mages or otherwise, but I was done holding back. I reached out with both hands and drained the life force of two of them at once, causing them to collapse. Ryan's air magic lifted another guard into the air, creating a tornado which blasted the entire security force backwards. Glad they were on my side, I launched into a run towards a fence which encircled the property.

Trix beckoned to a tall gate, already partly open. "The node's that way."

Ryan and I let the elf take the lead, skirting the fence until the bright current of a node came into view. Despite the burn in my limbs, I picked up speed and didn't stop until I reached its bright embrace.

The instant we landed in the swamp, the sharp pain of Alban's revelation hit me again like a blow to the chest. *Dex.*

Eyes swimming, I looked up at Trix. "Is it true? I mean —that the liches have gone?"

"Gone?" he echoed. "You mean left the Court?"

"Alban was lying," Ryan interjected. "Unless something changed in the last day, the liches are—"

Alive.

A trail of sparks flew through the air as Dex soared towards me. "There you are. I knew you'd get away."

"Dex!" I tried to hug him, only for him to slip through my arms and cause me to narrowly avoid falling on my face in the swamp. I wouldn't have cared if I had. *He's alive. The sprites are alive, and the liches haven't fallen victim to the curse yet.*

"What are you doing?" Dex zipped overhead. "Did you forget I'm not solid?"

"I thought you were dead!" I said. "I thought…"

The words died in my throat as an armoured figure appeared in my peripheral vision. Greyson's shocked eyes took me in. "Alban let you go?"

"I knocked him out first." I gestured to my companions. "Trix found me. How did you manage to track him down, anyway?"

"With difficulty," said the elf.

Greyson continued to stare at me as though I was a ghost. "I thought you were bound to him. I thought you couldn't leave."

"He tried to bind me at first, but he said he wanted me to choose to stay with him. Maybe he honestly expected me to keep my word. Which might be understandable if he hadn't led me to believe Dex was *dead.*"

Greyson stepped forward and wrapped me in a hug. "Thank the Elements. He didn't hurt you at all?"

"He locked me up at first in case I tried to run, but he didn't push boundaries or even make me use my magic. He also... gave me my memories back."

Greyson froze in my arms. "All of them?"

"Everything about us." I squeezed my eyes shut and rested my head against his chest, and for a brief moment, I forgot all the pain and darkness of the last few days.

Then reality intervened with the memory of the utter shit show I'd left behind here at the castle.

"Ah, shit." I released him. "How's Devon? And the others?"

"Devon was fine the last time I saw," Ryan said. "I've been checking up on her. The rest of us are staying in the castle, except for Bria. She went back to Elysium with the Spirit Agents when it was safe for them to return to their base."

"Wait, what happened with the Houses?" I asked. "Did the Family get kicked out?"

"Ask Bria," said Ryan. "The elves helped her out a lot… and I might add that it would be a lot easier for us to deal with Alban's potential retaliation if *someone* bothered to take them up on their offers of meeting in person."

"They asked for the Death King," said Greyson. "I wasn't capable of acting in that capacity."

My throat closed up. "What do you mean?"

His expression was stark with pain. "I thought I'd never see you again."

"You seriously thought I'd chosen him over you?" I said.

"I didn't know what to think," he said. "The man has no morals. He might have manipulated you into doing anything for him."

"He told me all the liches died, and the sprites, too," I said. "He might have given me freedom to pick his side of my own free will, but he was still a lying piece of shit. He captured Ryan, too."

"In fairness, I might have provoked him," Ryan said. "Not that he didn't deserve it. The bastard said all this crap about how he was going to find one mage of each type to serve as his soldiers. I'm guessing he sees himself as the new Death King in all but name."

"That was always his goal," said Greyson. "And since stealing my soul amulet is no longer an effective option for him, he intends to take me down using another method."

"Then why hasn't he actually killed the liches yet?" I asked. "I never did find out how he put that spell on them."

"Neither have I, unfortunately." Anger rang through his tone. "I know it's a spell, but either he hid it somewhere it can't be detected, or it's not him who's causing the liches' magic to fade."

Then who could it possibly be? And why would he brag about using a spell when he wasn't the one responsible? It couldn't actually be a new side effect of the curse on the House of Spirit, could it?

"Wait, is Lord Blackbourne okay?" I asked. "And the other vampires? I forgot they were affected by the spell, too."

"The vampire lord hasn't made an effort to contact me, but he was alive the last I heard," said Greyson. "Lying low, I think."

"Has anyone found Hawker yet?" I asked.

"No," he said. "He might have perished in Elysium during the battle three days ago, for all I know."

Three days. I'd been gone less than a week, but it felt like much longer.

"The spell wasn't in his house," I said. "I don't think it was, anyway. He was careful to remove my access to anything magical, but I'd assume it needed a citadel's machinery to have that magnifying effect across the Parallel."

"I didn't look around the whole house," Ryan said, "but I don't think he would have put it in there in case any of his prisoners used it to their advantage."

"Alban's plan isn't complete, then," I said. "Speaking of which... I remembered more about the day he first brought me to the Parallel."

Greyson's expression clouded. "You mean the day he tried to take the previous Death King's soul amulet?"

"Yeah... I saw the rest of the memory," I said. "I didn't know, at the time, that he was coming here to the Parallel. I should have guessed. I was so pitifully naive."

"Don't blame yourself," insisted Greyson. "He manipulated you, told you half-truths, and kept you in the dark."

I hadn't helped the situation by not telling Greyson any of it, but he'd already forgiven me for that. "He implied the real cause of the war was the spirit mages trying to stop the realms from drifting apart, but it backfired on them because they didn't have the support of the other mages on the council."

"You're sure it wasn't a lie?" asked Greyson.

"Might have some truth in it," I said. "It's not the first time he's talked to me about the spirit mages creating the Parallel by combining their magic with one of each of the other four types of mage."

And, a voice in the back of my mind whispered, *he's looking for one of each mage himself.*

"I think that's true," said Trix. "The elves might know more."

"The *elves?*" I glanced at him. "I heard the elves originally built the citadels, but not that they were involved in the Parallel's creation."

"They did build the citadels," he said. "They also had their own realm which has existed since long before the Parallel was ever created. That's where the spirit mages got the idea of creating their own realm to begin with."

"Seriously?" The day wasn't out of surprises yet, it seemed. "Alban said the spirit mages created the Parallel by combining their powers with other elemental mages until it created a loop of power and turned into a node. Not sure if the elves can do anything similar."

Yet Hawker had hinted that the nodes had been created by sacrificing innocent lives. Which was the truth, then?

"The elves can't do exactly the same, but our magic was the inspiration for the machinery in the citadels," he said. "Our artefacts have been here since the Parallel was first created."

"Speaking of which." I pulled out my lucky dice. "You never told me these were elven artefacts which can break through a spirit mage's shield."

"Your dice?" Greyson gave Trix a bewildered look. "They're an elven artefact?"

"Not a very powerful one," said the elf.

"Bullshit," said Ryan. "If not for them, we'd never have got out of that house."

"I knocked out Alban and escaped," I explained. "He took my weapons but left the dice behind. Pity for him, because they broke straight through his magically enhanced shield."

A smile broke out on Greyson's face like sunshine from behind a cloud. "You never cease to amaze me."

Ryan cleared their throat. "We have company."

Sure enough, Felicity and Cal strode towards us from the gates. Cal almost looked happy to see me for the first time ever, while Felicity grinned. "Glad you're back, Liv."

"Me too," I said. "I'm glad Alban didn't capture you as well as Ryan."

"The others had more sense than to poke around the citadels," Ryan said. "The scumbag even hijacked my magic and used it against me."

"He did." I thought back to our brief struggle, which he'd won. "He has some new tricks he didn't have last time. Some kind of new magic I've never seen before. Did anyone ever find out what he used those soul amulets in Arcadia's citadel for?"

"No," said Greyson. "Speaking of which… you might want to see the soul amulets."

"Sure." I'd already seen them, but with the other Elemental Soldiers bombarding Ryan with questions, I wouldn't mind a moment alone with Greyson.

We entered the castle, where he led the way into the hall of souls. He then paced along the shelf and picked up his own soul amulet. He regarded the skull carved into its surface with a frown before putting it back down.

"Is that one fading, too?" I asked.

"Yes, but I don't feel it." He drew in a breath. "Liv, there's something I have to tell you."

"What is it?"

"I wasn't myself during your absence. I turned my back on the others, shut down my Court, and…"

"And what?" I said.

"I thought he bound you with a spell and that I would need to use unnatural force to get you out."

My heart leapt into my throat. "What did you do?"

"I went looking for some old research belonging to my predecessor," he said. "Illegal magic. Very illegal… and dangerous."

"Research into what?" I asked. "Greyson? What kind of illegal magic?"

"The kind even the last Death King decided against using."

Uh-oh. "That bad?"

"The previous Death King had a backup plan ready in case he found himself deprived of his lich army," he said.

"I should add that at the time, there was no known cure for the curse, not even an imperfect one like those cantrips. He would have needed to hire an independent spirit mage."

"To do what?" I said.

"To enact a ritual designed to open the doors between life and death," he said. "One that requires each of the five elements to be represented. The spirit mage acts as the conduit and the catalyst for the spell."

My mouth dropped open. "What? That sounds like the spell that created the Parallel."

Greyson nodded. "That's because it's almost the same. To create a node, each spirit mage had to channel enough energy to create a permanent link between the two realms. The same is true of spells requiring similar levels of energy, and there is nothing that surpasses the bond between five elements. When all five combine together, the boundaries of life and death itself can be breached."

"You're not making any sense," I said. "You were dead. So was I. Pretty sure we've both tap-danced over the boundaries between life and death at least once already."

"Yes, we have, but here… it's not the same." He waved a hand at the nearest shelf of amulets. "Liches exist in limbo between life and death, not quite belonging to either. True death is another realm entirely, inaccessible even from the Parallel."

A chill broke out on my skin. "What, like the afterlife?"

"Like oblivion." His voice was soft. "Many spirit mages in times before have tried to create a path between life and death, on which one may wander freely."

"Why would they do that?"

"Curiosity, mostly," said Greyson. "I can't pretend to

understand their reasons, but the former Death King had another motive. He believed that if he used a similar spell, he might be able to undo the curse on the House of Spirit."

"I thought he was the one who agreed to the curse in the first place," I said.

"I doubt the Order gave him a choice," said Greyson. "Remember, they had his soul amulet. They had total control over the House of Spirit until he agreed to become their King. I'd wager that he spent his entire leadership trying to find a way around it."

"But did he?" I said. "I mean, he had no guarantee that opening a path between life and death would actually undo the curse on his people, did he?"

"No," he said. "No, most of his experiments involved the manufacture of energy. It's not unconnected, though. We know that to use a cantrip to return the dead to life, another life needs to be sacrificed."

My heart lurched. "So he'd create a loop between five mages until enough energy was generated that if he'd be able to return to life? That's what he wanted to do?"

"Perhaps," he said, "but he never tried it on himself. It sounds like one of his liches volunteered as a lab rat, but his notes don't reveal what ended up happening to that lich."

"That... doesn't sound like a good idea."

"Maybe it wasn't," he said, "but Alban killed the former Death King before he had the chance to attempt to undo the curse on the other liches."

"But... why would *Alban* want to build a bridge between life and death?" I asked. "He's already very much alive. He was alive back when he took the Death King's amulet, too. Unless he wants the mages for some other spell entirely, but what might that be?"

"Similar ideas appear in the former Death King's records," he said. "He wasn't opposed to the idea of being an immortal, but he'd have preferred to stay as a living human instead of a lich. Becoming an immortal human, if such a thing is possible, would involve freely moving between the realms of life and death."

"Why did he want to live forever so badly?"

"Before the curse, many liches weren't in that state permanently," he said. "They could switch back and forth between lich and human. Perhaps that's what he meant."

Switch back and forth between lich and human.

I rubbed my forehead. "If that was possible until the war, why did it take the former Death King so long to figure out how to do it?"

"The records were lost, and by all accounts, those who practised that kind of magic were incredibly rare," said Greyson. "I only knew a little of the theory myself, and it wasn't until I found the former Death King's notes that I began to put the pieces together. Nothing like the curse had ever been seen before, either."

"Damn," I said. "You know, I'm starting to doubt any of the stories about the events which kicked off the war are strictly true. They say the spirit mages slaughtered their fellow council members, but Alban claimed they were trying to use a spell which backfired on everyone. Granted, he's already proven himself a blatant liar."

"Yes, he has," said Greyson. "Did he give any more information about the spell the Council was supposedly trying to do when the war started?"

"He said the nodes were weakening and driving Earth

and the Parallel further apart," I said. "The spirit mages tried to fix the damage, but they couldn't get the other mages to agree to help them conduct a similar ritual to the one that created the Parallel. Allegedly, they tried anyway and died in the process, but he said *that's* the reason the Court of the Dead ended up cursed."

"Really," he said flatly. "So, he doesn't lay the blame at the feet of the Order?"

"I have no idea who he blames." My gaze skimmed over the soul amulets in front of us. "He did say the sprites are remnants of the original elemental mages who were sacrificed and that the spirit mages became liches. Is there anyone here we can ask to verify the story?"

"No," he said. "None of the liches in my Court were part of the group who are believed to have instigated the war."

Then who? "Phantoms?"

He blinked. "You'd be hard-pressed to get a straight answer from a phantom. Most of them can't even speak."

"I'm aware of that." Frustration bubbled up within me. "Are you sure there isn't more information in the last Death King's research?"

"Not of the war," he said. "None of the instigators was left alive or was capable of confessing to anything. I doubt Alban was telling the truth, given what he said about the nature of the curse. I assume he hoped that when he took the former Death King's place, the truth would never be known."

Hmm. Alban thought the spirit mages had been wronged by the rest of the Council of the Elements, which stood in contrast to the accepted story about the spirit mages being responsible for the war. Which, then, was true?

"What were you even planning to do with that ritual?" I asked the Death King. "How would combining your magic with four Elements have helped you to find me?"

His mouth parted. "I wasn't certain, but I got the impression from my reading that a similar ritual can be used to undo a magical bond without harming the victim."

"Like… the bond between a lich and a soul amulet?"

We stared at one another for a moment.

"Was he onto something?" I asked, when Greyson didn't answer. "The last Death King, I mean?"

"Maybe he was," said Greyson, "but I can't see why Alban would care. He has more than enough ways to free liches from bindings himself, if he cared to."

"Yeah, but it sounds like *he* wants one of each Element to combine his magic with, and that's why he captured Ryan," I said. "Question is, which spell does he want to cast that requires that level of power?"

"I'd rather we didn't give him the chance to show us," he said. "A spirit mage with four other mages as conduits… such a thing has likely not been seen since the war."

Damn. Good job Ryan and I had broken out when we had, considering he'd already hijacked Ryan's magic at least once. The image of those dead soul amulets came to mind and my mouth went dry. That energy must have gone somewhere…

"Can a spirit mage take an unlimited amount of the life force of others into themselves?" I asked.

"Depends on how strong they are," Greyson said. "Alban is… uncommonly strong. As am I. If I wanted, I could drain the life out of every soul amulet in this room and store it within myself."

I gripped the shelf with one hand, nausea rising in the back of my throat. "I think he did that to those soul amulets. The ones donated by the liches he recruited. He—linked them up to the machine first, though."

"Did he, now?" Greyson wore an expression of distaste. "Yes... I remember. If he *did* absorb their magic, then he'll have made himself dangerously unstable in the process."

"It's that or he used their lives to fuel a cantrip." The idea of Alban gaining the combined power of all five types of magic was not a pleasant one, but it wasn't like there was any *point* to it that I could see. Unless he intended to declare war on the Death King after all.

Greyson drew in a breath. "I'm going to look at the research notes again. Can you go to Elysium and find Bria?"

"Bria?" I echoed. "Oh—you need all your Elemental Soldiers to be here."

"Yes," he said. "Exactly. I hope she and the others will forgive me for dismissing them."

"They will, I'm sure." My thoughts spun in circles. While Alban had undoubtedly moved further towards his goals than Greyson had, the research was similar enough for me to suspect both had had access to similar knowledge. If it was possible to undo the bond between the soul amulets and the liches and return them to life again, then the curse would be permanently undone.

Alban knew that, too, but he'd had no intention of helping. It was all on us.

The Death King left the hall, while I made a pit stop at

the bathroom for a shower and a change of clothes. I then went to the break room to grab sustenance. As I was downing my second glass of water, Dex appeared at my shoulder. "Boo."

I damn near emptied the glass on his head. "Dammit, Dex."

"Didn't take long for you to get over my untimely death, did it?"

I gave him an eye-roll, trying to suppress a smile. "You'll never let me live that one down, will you?"

"Definitely not," he said. "What were you and the Death King doing in the soul room? Please say you weren't boning. That's disrespecting the dead, that is."

"No, we weren't." As I watched him zipping around the ceiling, it hit me that he and the other sprites were likely a product of a spell gone wrong. Or rather, a ritual. Like the one we might have to use ourselves. Could we really risk the lives of the other Elemental Soldiers in the same manner?

Dex waved a hand in my face. "You're zoning out. What's your plan now you're back in the land of the not-quite-living?"

"I'm heading to Elysium." I grabbed a snack bar from the cupboard. "I need to find Bria and tell her the Death King wants her back."

"This, I gotta see," he said. "Do you remember the way to the Spirit Agents' house?"

"Well… not precisely," I said. "Okay, you can come with me, then."

Dex flew alongside me out of the castle and all the way to the node, which we used to transport ourselves to Elysium. No signs remained of the battle, at least in this part of the city, and I let Dex lead the way to the Spirit Agents' house.

I could see why they'd chosen to leave the castle and go home, since the house was swanky by Parallel standards, with well-tended gardens complete with a group of resident vampire chickens. From what I'd gathered, Bria had somehow been responsible for the latter.

When I knocked, Bria answered the door. "Hey, Liv."

"Oh, hey," I said. "The Death King said you'd moved in here, after…"

"After he fired me," she finished. "Did he do the same to you?"

"Not exactly."

A young woman with long dark hair walked into view behind her, then ducked out of sight. She looked oddly familiar… wait a moment.

My mouth fell open. "Is that Harper?"

Bria glanced over her shoulder. "Yeah."

"She's not a lich anymore." I stared, befuddled, as Harper sheepishly came back into view. "What did that? Not a cantrip?"

"Ah, it wasn't a cantrip." Harper looked embarrassed. "It was an accident."

"How can you come back to life by accident?"

"She got hit by of one of the elves' weapons, thanks to the Family," said Bria. "I thought it killed her, but it turned out to have the opposite effect on the dead as it would have on someone living."

"You're kidding." There had to be a catch, surely. "The elves can't bring back the dead, can they?"

"Not usually," Bria said, "but we were standing on top

of the citadel when the machinery was going haywire and it caused the weapon to misfire."

An elf-made weapon? Trix *had* mentioned the elves had originally come up with the ideas which had inspired the citadels' machinery, so maybe the two were more closely linked than any of us had known.

"Believe me, I think it was a one-off," said Harper. "I wasn't under the same curse as the other liches, either. I was only a part of the Court of the Dead for a short while and Miles was the one who bound my soul to an amulet."

"Ah." That would make her situation differ from the others, all of whom were bound to the Death King. "What kind of weapon would have that effect? Would you be able to get hold of it again so we can have a look?"

"No," Bria said bluntly. "The elves have it for safekeeping. It nearly levelled the whole of Elysium."

Damn. I'd missed a lot during my capture. "The spell draining the liches' magic is still in effect and we haven't figured out how to undo it yet."

"Look, I have *no* idea if the weapon would work in the same way twice," said Bria. "It wasn't supposed to happen the way it did. I don't want to be responsible for killing all the liches instead of saving them."

Behind her, Miles walked into view. "Hey, Liv."

"Hey." To Bria, I said, "Can you ask, then? Didn't the elves and the Death King have some kind of new agreement?"

"Oh, fine," Bria said. "I'll pay the elves a visit. Hope this one doesn't take too long."

Gratitude flooded me. "Thanks."

"Why do you need to speak to the elves?" Miles wanted to know.

"Might need to borrow something of theirs," I said. "To help with undoing the liches' curse. Since we haven't found the source of that spell, our time might be limited."

"Oh, that," said Miles. "I swear Grey and I have visited every citadel in the damn Parallel and haven't found any signs of that spell."

Strange. I'd been certain it must be one of the citadel's machines amplifying the effects of the spell so that it reached all the liches across the Parallel. Not to mention the vampires and sprites. I scanned the garden for Dex and saw him hovering above the fence, looking in the direction of the dark shape of the citadel visible over the rooftops. The enemy must have given it up, but I hadn't checked if anyone had put in a new neutraliser spell to block it from linking to London…

Oh. Elements.

"Fuck," I said. "I know where the spell is."

Bria frowned at me. "Where?"

"It's on Earth."

20

I broke into a sprint down the road, and Dex flew in behind me. "Hey, don't run off. What spell?"

"The spell which is draining the liches' power." I jabbed a finger at the citadel. "The transporter got turned back on during the battle, right? I bet you anything Alban activated the spell on the other side of the node and relied on the chaos to hide his trail. I'm not sure how much is left of that hotel in London, but I bet nobody realised that anyone could hide a spell on top of the node buried inside it."

We needed to shut that thing down, without any delay.

"You're heading there now?"

"I'll explain to the Death King later." If we broke the spell, we wouldn't need to resort to drastic measures in an attempt to undo the curse if we managed to bring the liches back to their full strength in time to take on Alban's inevitable attack.

"Good luck with that." Dex flew over my shoulder as we neared the centre of Elysium. Marks of the battle littered the streets in the form of shattered windows, scorched walls, and gaping holes where roofs should be. Yet the citadel was unguarded, and the door opened without any resistance. After all, Alban already thought he'd won.

Dex and I climbed the spiralling stairs until we reached the top floor. Part of me expected to find Alban waiting for me on the other side of the door, but the room was empty aside from the gleaming bank of machinery and the raised platform. A faint glow around the edges of the transporter indicated it was still linked up to the other citadels, but it was difficult to tell if it was open to the newly created node in London.

One way to find out. I stepped onto the platform and called on my spirit magic, picturing the hotel which had once stood on this very spot in London. Before Hawker had destroyed it, that is.

Brightness flashed, to be replaced with a mass of shadows so dark I couldn't see anything except for the faint glowing shape of Dex on my shoulder.

"Help me!" gasped the fire sprite. "I'm being sucked away! I'm dying!"

Shit. Why had I let him come with me? I stumbled through the darkness, crumbling stone and shattered glass crunching beneath my feet. *The hotel. We're in the hotel.*

I'd guessed right, but what the hell was this dark pit I'd landed in? Dex moaned and clung to my shoulder tightly enough for his flames to burn my skin, but I didn't dare ask him to loosen his hold in case I lost him for good this time.

. . .

"Hang onto me, Dex." I'd once returned him to life by bolstering him with my own magic, so I ought to be able to do the same again. "Wait a second. I've got you."

Focusing on my spirit magic, I did my best to push the energy into his small transparent body, and Dex's faintly glowing form merged with the halo of spirit magic surrounding me. "That's better."

"Good, because I have no idea where the exit is." More to the point, how could I turn off Alban's spell if I couldn't see where it was coming from? I didn't see any cantrips or other indications of hostile magic, but the hotel resembled a black hole in the middle of the city. How the hell had nobody noticed? Unless it was visible only to the magically inclined, like nodes were. It did kind of resemble a node, except shadowy instead of bright.

Dex's grip on my shoulder tightened when Hawker loomed out of the darkness ahead of me. The former spirit mage's face was pale against the shadows, and his eyes glittered with malice. "You just don't know when to quit, do you, Olivia?"

"How did you escape the Order?" More to the point, how had he got all the way here without any spirit magic?

"With difficulty," he said. "I struck a deal with someone who was sympathetic to my plight and they helped me escape. Thanks to you, I've been unable to return to the Parallel."

"You're hiding in the ruins of a place you blew up in a mass murder," I said. "Forgive me if I don't extend any sympathy to you for not being able to get through a node."

"I've been reduced to waiting here for days in the hopes that a spirit mage would wander through and reactivate the portal again." said Hawker. "And you did just that."

I folded my arms across my chest. "If you want me to give you a lift back into the Parallel, you're out of luck."

I'd left the others behind, except for Dex, but Hawker had no magic of his own to speak of. To get to London, he must have used public transport instead of magic, which was amusing enough to think about, but without nodes, he'd had no choice but to go back to the scene where he'd committed mass murder in the hopes of finding a way back through to Elysium.

"I know what you're thinking," Hawker said. "You think I have no power. You're wrong."

He took a step forwards, and a light shone from an amulet around his neck. A soul amulet. Hawker had got his hands on someone's soul and claimed their magic along with it. "Where the hell did you get that?"

"From one of Alban's allies."

My brows shot up. "With or without permission? What did Alban think?"

"I don't give a shit about Alban," he said. "All I want now is for Greyson Beaumont to die, along with his army."

"*You* were the one who drained the liches' power. Not Alban." The conniving shit had been lying all along, to hide the fact that it'd been Hawker who'd kicked off the spell and not him. That Hawker and Alban cared little for one another didn't mean they wouldn't gladly take credit for one another's ideas if it suited them.

"I opened a gate, that's all," he said. "The spell is acting on its own now."

"The hell does that mean?"

"It means this is a giant magical sinkhole," Dex said in my ear. "The spell he used has seriously fucked with the node. That's why it's gone all shadowy and weird."

My stomach sank. He was right. The pillar of darkness *did* resemble a node, yet despite the inherent wrongness of its warped appearance, it must remain connected to the Parallel. If it didn't, I wouldn't have been able to travel through it from Elysium.

"Where'd the magic from the Parallel disappeared to, then?" I asked Hawker.

"Nowhere," he said. "Like mine, it's going into oblivion."

Damn him. Was this some kind of revenge for losing access to his own magic? Had he decided to unleash his revenge on the Parallel at large instead of just on me? The shadowy node must be sucking in magic from the Parallel like a vacuum, with a knock-on effect on all the magical beings within range. That meant the liches would be the first to expire, because they were more magic than anything else, and so were sprites. The rest of us would lose our magic gradually, and I didn't even want to think about what might follow if the spell didn't stop. The Parallel itself was built on magic, and if the effect spread to the other nodes, it might mean disaster for everyone living there.

I raised my hands, conjuring spirit magic to my palms. "Then I'm guessing you won't mind volunteering to be the first to dive into oblivion along with it?"

The torrent of shadows swallowed up the magic that poured from my hands. Dex threw a handful of fire at Hawker, only for that to be swallowed up into the abyss, too. How could we possibly get rid of the damn thing when it sucked any nearby magic into its depths? For the moment, it was confined to one region, but how long would that last before it started spreading, not just on Earth but throughout the Parallel, too?

Hawker raised his hand, and a jet of spirit magic shot at me from the amulet on his chest. I deflected using a shield and returned with another attack, but as long as he kept standing on top of the shadowy node, I didn't stand a chance of landing a hit on him.

"Dex," I whispered. "Want to lend a hand?"

"With pleasure."

The fire sprite's magic mingled with mine, and flames sprang from my own hands. Unlike Alban, I wasn't taking his magic against his will. Dex was giving me his power willingly, because he trusted me, and the result was a torrent of fire that even the shadows couldn't suck away.

Hawker realised the danger and tried to dodge, but Dex's fiery magic rippled from my hands and engulfed him from head to toe. He screamed, high and reedy, as the magical fire burned through his defences. As the flames dimmed in my hands, he flung himself to the ground in an attempt to put out the fire, and the soul amulet fell from his neck and clattered to a halt amid the swirling shadows.

On instinct, I crouched down and picked it up, an idea occurring to me. Hawker lay in a heap, flailing and moaning, his clothes smoking at the edges, and I leaned over him. "Care to tell me how to undo the spell?"

"You can't," he whimpered, arms over his face. "I won't let you."

"Maybe I'll give you an incentive." Holding up the

amulet, I reached for the power swirling within it. He must have killed its owner or stolen it from their corpse, because only a thin trickle of magic rose when I tugged it instead of the usual human-like shape which could be formed into a lich. Nevertheless, the brightness transferred to my own hand, bolstering my own strength until the soul amulet was empty. As Hawker twitched at my feet, I reached forward and grabbed his life force. Dex exclaimed as I gave a firm tug on Hawker's soul, oblivious to his frantic screams.

Hawker's spirit came free of his body, hovering above my glowing palm. In vain, he tried to pull away, but he had nowhere to run. Not without disappearing entirely.

"I will not submit to you!" he bellowed.

"Fine, then." I held up the amulet and pushed down upon his spirit, and Hawker's transparent figure sank beneath the surface of the disc. At the same time, a shadowy cloak shaped like a person rose into view before me, and his corporeal body turned to dust on the spot, instantly swallowed up by the darkness.

"You bitch." Hawker's voice came from the newly created lich. "What the hell did you do that for?"

"That spell of yours is sucking in all the magic in both realms," I said. "Now it'll affect you, too. Are you any keener to tell me how to undo it?"

"I told you, it's impossible." His cold lich-voice sounded higher than before, frightened. "You've doomed me."

"Stop lying." No spell didn't have a solution. Did it? My conversation with the upper room's members slammed into my mind and I took a horrified step backwards. He hadn't stolen it from the Order, had he? *Please tell me he didn't.*

"I'm not lying," he said. "Also, you forget... as a lich, I can sense the node now."

He glided into the abyss, becoming one with the shadows. I lowered his soul amulet, then pocketed it, but he didn't return. Apparently, he'd rather risk death than be bound to me.

He can't have been telling the truth. There must be a way to undo this spell.

I stared at the growing torrent of darkness, wondering how in hell I could possibly turn the node back to normal. While it'd been created by sacrificing lives to fuel the transporter on the other side and create a link to Earth, this version which sucked magic into a black hole was beyond my understanding.

I stepped into the middle of the shadowy mass, searching for any signs of a cantrip or another indication of the spell's starting point. There must be a focal point somewhere, but the whole hotel was like an empty dark pit. Nodes didn't have an obvious start or end point either, but this was different.

"Don't step in there again," said Dex. "It looks like a portal to hell."

"It does a bit, but we can't just leave it sitting around in the middle of London." I conjured spirit magic to my hands to make a torch, only for the pit to suck the magic straight into its depths. "It's like a magical black hole."

The Order presumably hadn't been checking up on the site of the attack, but the dark node might not even be visible to non-spirit mages. They wouldn't know the portal was here unless they stood directly on top of it.

We have to shut it down.

"Yes, it's a black hole," said Dex. "Or a reverse node. It feels similar to a regular node, except twisted and weird."

"I can sense it, too, but I guess you can probably feel it more intensely because sprites are made out of magic," I said. "Same as liches... I guess they were affected first because they have more magic inside them, even though their magic comes from the same source."

"Come again?" Dex peered at me. "What do you mean by 'the same source'?"

Ah, shit. I still hadn't told him. "Dex... sprites and phantoms used to be mages."

"What the hell do you mean?" said Dex. "I'm not a mage."

"I think you used to be." I looked into the swirling shadows below my feet. "I'm sorry, Dex. I didn't know how to tell you, but during the spirit war, some of the mages who died became sprites, keeping their magic but losing their bodies. I don't know how you lost your memories of your past life, but it makes sense, given that liches and phantoms were once spirit mages."

Dex went silent for possibly the first time in his life. After a pause, he said, "You're kidding. Who told you that?"

"Alban told me, but... it fits." Not that I knew what to do with that information. It wasn't like I could bring him or the other sprites back to life, and I doubted the cure would work on them like it did on the liches. "I think it's because the mages died while taking part in a ritual which ripped them from their corporeal forms."

"Well, that makes me feel *so* much better." Dex sniffed. "I'm a ghost."

"Nothing wrong with that," I said. "Don't forget I used to be a lich. I *am* sorry I didn't tell you right away, but I needed to process it and figure out what it all meant."

"How do you know Alban was telling the truth?" he said. "Maybe he was trying to screw with your head."

"He didn't tell me in the present day," I clarified. "I saw the memories of our lessons while I was a prisoner, and he told me right before he tried to take the former Death King's power. He also claimed the spirit mages weren't trying to start a war when their spell backfired and killed everyone involved. They were trying to save the Parallel instead, but something went wrong and all the mages ended up being ripped out of their bodies."

"Uh-huh," he said. "The guy's a compulsive liar. Don't trust a word he says."

"The former Death King's research notes back him up, though," I said. "It makes sense that a ritual killed the entire mage council at once. If they were all linked up via a magical connection, it's no wonder there were no survivors."

"Nice theory, but does it even matter?" asked Dex. "If I died as a noble sacrifice to save the Parallel, it'll mean bugger all if I meet a permanent end when this black hole sucks the life out of me."

"I know. I'm trying to figure out how to stop this." What would Alban have to gain by draining all the magic out of both realms? After how hard he'd fought to gain power, you'd think he'd want to keep it, but perhaps Hawker had acted alone. Either Alban had let him go ahead because he didn't care about losing his magic... or he knew how to stop this.

I can't ask for his help. He'll laugh in my face. He certainly wouldn't accept a bargain with me again, anyway, not after I'd wriggled out of his last one. Yet the answers weren't here, so they must be elsewhere.

"Hang on tight," I told Dex. "We're going back to the Parallel."

21

Dex didn't like the trip back any more than I did. I braced my feet on the carpet of shadows and pictured Elysium's citadel clearly in my mind's eye. Black hole or not, it functioned the same as a regular node, so I opened my eyes to find myself on the platform in the citadel with Dex clinging to my shoulder.

"Never again," the fire sprite said. "Next time we're going in through a normal node, that clear?"

I scanned the room. "Hawker isn't here." Not really a surprise, but I couldn't help wondering how long it would take before people in Elysium began to feel the effects of the spell on the other side of the portal. It'd begin to affect the mages at some point, given their proximity to the citadel. "C'mon."

I ran downstairs with Dex at my shoulder. Outside, I firmly closed the door, as though that would stop the magic-sucking effect of the portal from seeping out into the city.

We have to stop that spell.

Once we found our way to a node, we travelled back to the swampland, where Dex let go of me with a shudder of relief when we drew closer to the castle. He looked better already, his colouring deepening from pale orange to vivid flames.

As I entered the grounds, Devon barred my path. "It's nice to see you, too."

"Devon!" I strode over and hugged her. "Sorry I didn't come to see you sooner. There's a situation in London—"

"You went to London before coming to tell me you got away from Alban?" she said.

"I had to fetch Bria from Elysium," I said apologetically. "It was supposed to take a minute, but then I saw the citadel, and—the spell draining the magic from the liches and sprites is on the other side of the node Hawker created on top of Elysium's citadel. That's why nobody has found it yet."

I gave her an abbreviated explanation of what I'd found on the other side of the portal, including my encounter with Hawker.

"You turned Hawker back into a lich?" she said. "Why?"

"I was hoping he'd tell me how to turn the spell off, but he said he didn't know," I admitted. "I may have screwed that one up."

"He's back here in the Parallel, then?"

"For now, but he's just as likely to perish from that spell he unleashed as anyone else." Which meant that if Alban did have a way to undo it, then Hawker would have gone straight to him.

Behind Devon, the door to the castle opened and

Greyson strode out. "I thought you were going to fetch Bria. What's going on?"

"There's been a change of plans," I said. "I went to see Bria and found Harper—you know, the one who used to be a lich—and she said she got in the way of an elf's weapon and it turned her from a lich back into a human again. So I thought…"

"You thought that might undo the curse," said Greyson. "I can't say the elves would be happy for us to borrow their tools to experiment with. Is that where Bria went?"

"She volunteered to ask them," I said. "Dex and I were on our way back here when I realised the spell affecting the liches wasn't in the Parallel at all. It was in London."

Understanding flared in his eyes. "The node?"

"You've got it," Devon interjected. "Unfortunately, she found Hawker on the other side, and turned him into a lich."

"You did what?" said Greyson.

"Not the important part!" I said. "I'm ninety percent sure that Hawker stole a spell from the Order which turned the node into some kind of shadowy black hole. Instead of magic flowing back and forth between realms like a regular node, it gets sucked into this weird abyss instead. It's like a leaking hole in the middle of the Parallel, slowly draining it of magic."

Greyson stared at me. "That's why it's affecting the liches so badly."

"And the sprites," Dex said. "And on that note, when were you people going to tell me I used to be a mage when I was alive?"

"You what?" said Devon. "You used to be a mage?"

"All the sprites did." I looked up when a chorus of gasps came from somewhere nearby, and spotted Aria and Terren listening in. Ah, hell. "I'll explain later, but we have to deal with that giant magic-sucking portal on top of London if we want any magical being in the Parallel to survive the week. I couldn't figure out how to undo the spell, and Hawker said there was no reversing it. Like the spell the Order uses to strip someone of their magic. In fact, I think that's exactly what it was."

"The Order has a spell that takes away people's magic, and they let Hawker steal it?" Devon said incredulously. "Damn. That's what I get for assuming they finally had their shit together."

"I know, right?" I said. "According to the upper room, stripping someone's magic is irreversible and so is the spell. There's no solution. Not one the Order has made public, anyway."

"Then we'll have to ask them," said Greyson.

If they'd tell us, which was debatable. But if we were to stand a chance in hell of undoing the spell before it drained the Parallel of all its magic, we'd need to ask the Order ourselves, and hope they'd be willing to share their most closely guarded secrets.

———

With little time to delay, Greyson and I gave the Elemental Soldiers a brief explanation of our plan to meet with the Order's upper room. Needless to say, none of them were thrilled that Hawker was once again at large—as a lich, no less—but they agreed to stay and guard the castle in case he showed up. The sprites kept firing questions at me about what I knew of their history as mages, but Dex took over the explanation so I'd have the chance to find Devon. I suggested she stay behind with Trix and the Elemental Soldiers, but she refused.

"I'm done avoiding the Order," she said. "I want to give them a piece of my mind."

"I don't blame you." They'd better have a good answer about how Hawker had wound up in London when he was supposed to be locked in a secure cell, and how he'd stolen a spell which had enabled him to turn the node into a death trap. He and Alban were likely reunited by now, and while the slim chance that Alban had a solution remained, I couldn't discount the possibility that this had been his plan all along. A second chance to force my hand, in case his first attempt to gain my trust backfired.

I'd ask the Order before I considered going to him for help again, and pry answers out of them by any means possible.

Upon crossing through the node into Birmingham city centre, the Death King took the lead, striding towards the Order's headquarters with Devon and I behind him. I didn't hear what he said to the guards at the doors, but they parted to let us in without a word. To no surprise, everyone in the lobby gawked at us when we walked in.

"We're here to see the upper room," the Death King told a bewildered secretary.

"You can't see them without an appointment," she insisted.

"It's urgent," I said.

"In what way?"

"I found Hawker," I said, losing patience. "You know, your escaped prisoner? I found him in London, hiding in the hotel which he destroyed in a lethal spell to create a node linking to the Parallel. He claimed to have stolen a spell from you which turned the node into a black hole which is slowly sucking in all the magic from both realms. Is that a good enough reason?"

Shocked silence reverberated through the lobby. I hadn't bothered to keep my voice down, since at this rate, everyone would know about the spell soon enough, and if it got us to the upper room without being mired in red tape, I was willing to let the entire magical world know what Hawker had done.

"Well?" said the Death King.

"I... yes. This way." Hands trembling, the secretary led us towards the staircase which would take us to the upper floor. She then cast a nervous glance at Devon. "You can't come upstairs. Only the Death King can. Olivia..."

"Olivia will come with me," said the Death King. "She and I have met with the upper room before. They know her."

Devon scowled. "Okay, I'd like to talk to Mrs Carlisle of the retrieval unit. I'll meet you when you're done, okay, Liv?"

"Sure." I turned to follow the Death King up the stairs.

A white-painted corridor waited at the top, where the secretary led the way to a mahogany door bearing a gold-plated emblem and gave a hesitant knock. A hush came from behind the door, which then opened.

Mr Choudhary peered out at us. "Death King... and Olivia. What are you doing here?"

"We found an emergency situation in London which the local Order branches seem to have overlooked," said the Death King. "Involving your escaped prisoner, Hawker."

"Hawker?" he echoed. "You'd better come in."

We did so, while the secretary slunk away downstairs. Nobody else acknowledged my presence, but the Death King's summary of the situation didn't take long. The moment he finished speaking, the upper room broke into conversation among themselves.

I cleared my throat a couple of times to get their attention. "What I'd like to know is who got Hawker out of jail. He said he convinced someone in this very branch to help him escape, but it doesn't look like anyone has even been searching for him."

"We certainly haven't been ignoring him," Mr Strong said indignantly. "We've been chasing up every possible lead. We'll send a team to London right away."

"Bit late for that now," I said. "Hawker isn't there any longer. Unless you know how to turn off the spell he used on the node?"

"If it *is* one of our spells, then it won't stop until it runs its natural course and removes all magic from its target," Mr Strong said. "If the spell could be reversed, it would defeat the purpose of stripping someone of their magic."

"What if the target is a node, though, and not a person?" Dread clenched around my chest. "What will happen if it carries on?"

"It..." Mrs Bell glanced across the table at Mr Oliver, whose face had paled. "The effects will take a while to spread. It's only one node, but its central location will cause it to spread faster until it reaches the other nodes in the area."

My throat went dry. "And they'll turn dark as well?"

"Exactly," said Mr Strong. "It's a self-perpetuating cycle. The nodes feed off one another, and with one node draining the magic from the region, the others will either start to do the same or they'll simply disappear. It'll affect Elysium first, and then…"

"And then it'll spread," I concluded. "So the Parallel might end up being cut off from this realm entirely?"

"Eventually," said Mr Oliver. "It would be disastrous for the parts of the realm which are dependent on supplies from the other side of the nodes."

"Not to mention everyone will lose their magic." Mages and practitioners depended on the nodes to make a living. Their ability to survive in the Parallel was precarious enough already, yet most of them had nowhere else to go.

"Precisely," said Mr Strong. "It might take several months to spread, which would be enough time to evacuate the Parallel—"

"Get real," I said. "You seriously want to evacuate millions of people in a short time and expect them to adjust to living on Earth without creating absolute havoc? That's not feasible at all."

"It's that or leave them to die," he said. "The Parallel is dependent on supplies from this realm, in addition to the magic that holds the realm together, and the latter is disappearing."

"I can't believe this." I shook my head at them. "Whose idea was it to create a spell with the potential to suck all the magic out of the world without any way of undoing it?"

"The spell isn't supposed to be used on a node," insisted Mrs Bell. "Hawker created a node which was already far more unstable than any other, since it exists on top of a magically amplified portal which also links up with the other citadels. As a result, an incredibly large amount of magic is flowing in and out of it."

"If we use neutraliser cantrips to cut off the transporters between the citadels, will it slow the effects down, then?" I asked.

"Yes, but there's no permanent solution," said Mr Strong. "Not without employing the kind of magic which hasn't been used in years."

"You mean spirit magic," I said. "Spirit mages are the ones who originally opened the nodes, aren't they? Surely they can use a similar method to fix this."

"We can't take the risk," Mr Choudhary said. "There were no real regulations on the spirit mages who created the Parallel, and despite all their knowledge, if their spell had gone wrong, innocent people might have been killed. Now, with so few spirit mages left, let alone in possession of the right knowledge… it can't be done."

Damn. The people who'd created the Parallel might have been able to undo the spell, but they were long dead along with the former Council of the Elements. I was willing to bet Alban *did* have access to that knowledge, but he hadn't handed it to me even when he'd thought I was his willing ally.

Which left one option: gather the remaining spirit mages and improvise with the little knowledge we did have, preferably without destroying both realms in the process.

"You should know, Hawker is hiding in the Parallel in the form of a lich," I told the upper room. "He went to join

Alban, which means it's highly likely that he'll come back to Earth. Got a plan for that?"

"We'll be in contact with our branch near the site of the node in London," said Mr Strong. "As for Alban, we have people searching the Parallel for him as we speak."

"With no luck, I'm guessing," I said. "He's more slippery than Hawker is, and that's saying a lot… but I happen to know where he's hiding."

"Why is that?" He gave me a considering look. "Have you been negotiating with him?"

"Wouldn't put it like that, but he did keep me imprisoned in his house until a few hours ago." The people in this room might be able to take away my freedom on a whim, but that seemed insignificant in light of the threat facing both realms at once. "If you want to send a team to attempt to bring him in, I'd be more than happy to tell them his location."

Assuming he was there… and assuming the Order could handle him. Which was debatable, given that I wouldn't have escaped without the use of my incredibly lucky dice.

"Alban will not be as easy to restrain as Hawker was," the Death King warned.

"He's been sacrificing his own liches in order to absorb their power," I added. "I got away by a fluke, but even a spirit mage would be hard-pressed to take him down."

Mr Bell flinched. "He's been doing *what?*"

"Using the machinery in the citadels to absorb the magic from every soul amulet in his possession… including ones he took from the Court of the Dead when he promised their owners to free them from the curse." I looked around the table at the members of the upper room. "This is what your decision to punish the entire Court of the Dead has led to. Their people were forced to trust in Alban or die, and they'll be the first to expire when the spell Hawker took from you drains away their magic. By your own laws, that would make you murderers."

"We are *not* responsible for what that madman Hawker did," said Mr Oliver.

"He was under the curse, too, did you know?" I felt the Death King's disapproving stare on me, but I pushed on. "He survived the war only to end up cursed himself. He's been wanting revenge on your people for a very long time, and it looks like he might just have got his wish."

"We'll mobilise a force to find him," said Mr Strong. "Alban, too. Without delay. Death King... we will let you know when we're ready."

That was a dismissal if I ever heard one, and I had to admit I didn't have much faith in their ability to capture anyone, let alone someone who'd taught spirit magic under their noses without being caught until he stole the soul amulet of the former Death King himself. Let's face it, we were on our own, and the best we could hope for was that they didn't stand in our way.

As we reached the lobby again, I spotted Judith talking to Devon. Judith gave me an awkward wave as I walked past, while Devon extricated herself from the conversation and came to join us. "That was a waste of time. Mrs Carlisle knows nothing about Hawker's spell. Please tell me you had more luck upstairs."

"They can't fix the spell," I told her. "Instead they're going after Alban in the hopes that *he* might tell them how to fix it."

Which wasn't likely to backfire at all. Alban did nothing for free, and I wouldn't be able to bargain away my loyalty this time. He knew I was no longer his, and I never would be.

"Come on." The Death King beckoned to me, and the three of us walked out of the Order's building and headed back to the node.

Once we landed in the swamp again, I released a sigh. "I'm starting to regret sparing Hawker's life. I hoped turning him into a lich would be enough of an incentive for him to tell me the solution to that spell."

Instead, he'd run back to Alban. He'd be affected, too, eventually, but I'd bet he'd be happy to wait for us all to die before deigning to undo the damage. After all, he'd be the most powerful person left in the Parallel, with nobody left to challenge him.

"What's he doing here?" Greyson walked towards the gates, his gaze fixed at a point on the other side.

I peered over his shoulder, where Lord Blackbourne of all people stood next to the suspicious-looking Elemental Soldiers. The vampire lord looked even paler than usual and somewhat unsteady on his feet, and I was surprised he'd walked all the way here on his own. "Lord Blackbourne."

"I heard you managed to get away from Alban," the vampire said. "Well done."

"Don't get too excited," I said. "You know that spell that's draining your magic, as well as the liches'? It's worse than it sounds."

"The Elemental Soldiers told me." He nodded to Ryan and the others. "You're going to stop it, of course."

"The Order just told me it was impossible." I'd bet the

vampire had zero intention of lifting a finger to help us anyway. "They created the spell, so they should know."

"No spell lasts forever," he said.

"A spell that's trapped in a node which keeps feeding power into it in an endless loop, though?" I said. "It's been going for days."

"I haven't seen the situation worsen, though," said Lord Blackbourne. "It seems to be stable."

Was he not taking this seriously even as it ate away at his own life essence? "If we ignore the fact that it's a giant black hole in the middle of Elysium sucking in any nearby magic."

"He has a point," Devon said. "No spell lasts forever. It's one of the first things we learn at the academy."

"Yes, but it's not just a spell," I said. "It's plugged into a battery, with the machinery in the citadel on the other side. We can delay the effects by using neutraliser cantrips to sever the link to the other citadels, but it can't be turned off."

"I have little doubt a spirit mage of your skill level can find the solution."

"A spirit mage..." Wait a moment. "You were alive before the war, Lord Blackbourne. You knew the Council of the Elements, didn't you? Didn't *they* have a solution for this kind of spell?"

"Ah..." His gaze flickered to Greyson, and then to the Elemental Soldiers. "I'm afraid that by the time of the war, they'd grown somewhat complacent after years of peace and prosperity. They saw no need to keep their skills fresh, and they were out of practise."

Greyson stepped in. "Lord Blackbourne, did you witness the Council of the Elements conduct a ritual similar to those the previous Death King was researching?"

"I cannot say I know what you mean, Greyson."

"You know perfectly well what I mean," he said. "I *told* you about the notes when I found them hidden in the hall of souls a decade ago when I moved into the castle."

I cleared my throat before the pair of them devolved into bickering. "We had an agreement, Lord Blackbourne, that I would tell you everything I remembered of Alban's plans once I remembered. And now I do."

His gaze slid to me. "Do you, now?"

"Every lesson," I said. "Every word we spoke to one another. I can tell you the specifics later, but shortly before he killed the former Death King, he told me a story about how the war started. He said that the nodes between realms were weakening and only the spirit mages noticed, but they were unable to fix it without the other mages' help."

Lord Blackbourne's expression sharpened. "Is that so?"

"Yes," I said. "He told me they tried to fix it anyway, but the ritual backfired and killed everyone involved. Granted, he might have been lying or wrong, because it's not like *he* lived through it, but it's certainly true that they all died, right?"

"Yes," said the vampire lord. "Yes, that is precisely what I wished to know. I heard a ritual caused their deaths, but I always wondered what the Council's mages were hoping to accomplish."

"Alban claimed the ritual did fix the nodes and that's why we haven't heard anything of it since," I added. "Which would be believable if it didn't contradict the story of the spirit mages turning on their fellow Elements. Which is true?"

"Like I said… I didn't witness the ritual myself," he said. "As for Alban, I rather hoped you'd tell me what *he* was hoping to achieve."

Disbelief flooded me. Was the information I'd given him not enough? "Aside from becoming the next Death King? Actually, I think he's looking for mages to enact a similar ritual, but I can't say why. He never told me."

"Oh, is he now?" Lord Blackbourne's eyes gleamed. "Interesting. Very interesting."

"Does that mean you're going to help?" I asked. "The Order's sending a team to bring in Alban, but I'm not convinced they can restrain him. He's been bolstering his strength by draining his lich allies' soul amulets."

"How distasteful," said the vampire lord. "You know his location?"

"Yes, we do," said Greyson. "I expect him to either go on the run when the Order shows up or stand his ground, no doubt causing considerable damage in the process. Can you truly spare no volunteers to help us?"

"I can ask, but I can't promise the others will say yes," he said. "We are quite risk-averse creatures… the polar opposite of you spirit mages. Thank you for the information, Olivia."

He glided past us, out of the gates, while I watched his back with a mixture of incredulity and annoyance. Bloody vampires.

Greyson shook his head after the vampire lord. "In the notes I found from the previous Death King, there *is* a mention of how to use the ritual to stabilise nodes, but not to counter a spell of that nature."

"And Lord Blackbourne thinks I can do it anyway?" I said. "Yeah, he has too much faith in me."

"I never said that."

"No… you're one hell of a spirit mage," said Devon. "Just because it hasn't been done before doesn't mean it's impossible."

"It's too risky," I said. "If we try to do some unknown ritual on top of the node without first trying to wrangle more information out of Alban, it might go as badly wrong as the ritual which killed the Council."

What choice did I have, though? He'd backed me into a corner. If I didn't find a way to stop the spell, I didn't want to think how everyone in the Parallel would react when all the mages and practitioners started losing their magic at once. The Order certainly wouldn't be able to do anything. With the resources Alban had, it was a safe bet he'd outlast most of us and then build his own empire from the ashes of the world he'd destroyed.

"You want to join the Order in their pursuit of Alban," said Greyson. "Not again, Liv. You know he's waiting for you to come back to ask him for answers."

"That's not why I want to go," I said. "I'm probably the only one who can catch him off guard at this point. Not saying I can talk some sense into him, mind you, but I might at least be able to convince him that Hawker's lost his damn mind."

"I'll go with her," Dex said. "I want to throw some sparks at that bastard for making Liv think I was dead."

"Fine," said Greyson. "We'll go with the Order and we'll ensure Alban gives us the solution to the spell."

22

The Order's first team showed up within the hour, consisting mostly of mages... with one highly visible exception.

"Judith?" I said. "You're volunteering to come to snag Alban?"

"I guess I am." She didn't meet my eyes, and her hands were trembling so hard she'd have trouble keeping hold of a weapon. Still, if she wanted to come, that was her prerogative.

I counted two dozen volunteers, including Ryan, Felicity, Cal and Trix. Craig and Carla weren't among them, which didn't come as a surprise. They were happier working behind the scenes, like Devon, who would also be staying behind. Along with...

Greyson walked to my side. "I need to stay here with the liches. I don't like sending all my best soldiers after him as it is."

"I know." I looked into his eyes. "He won't take me again. I'll come back, Greyson."

After a swift kiss goodbye, I joined Trix and Ryan in leading the rest of the team to the node. Since the three of us alone knew the location of Alban's hideout, we'd been put in charge. Bria still wasn't back from meeting the elves, but we had no time to delay.

I stepped into the node, picturing the grounds outside Alban's house in my mind's eye. In a flash of light, we landed in front of the large manor. More flashes signalled the rest of the team's arrival, but the gates stood open, with no sign of any guards outside.

Had Alban left? Perhaps he'd guessed that I wouldn't hesitate to share his hiding place's location with everyone I could, but I'd assumed he'd be ready and waiting to counter our attack. Along with Hawker.

"Hold on," I warned, as several Order members headed through the gates towards the manor house. "I reckon he gave us the slip. Or he's planning an ambush."

"Liv," Dex hissed in my ear. "I can sense something magical. Whatever it is, I don't like it."

I trod in behind the Order members, and my skin tingled with static. The smell of burning rose, sharp and sudden.

"Get out!" I spun around and ran towards the node as a fiery blast went off behind me, loud enough to make my teeth rattle in my skull. Flashes signalled some of the mages fleeing through the node, and at the second blast, I flung myself flat, hands pressed to my ears, until the sound faded enough for me to lift my head. Dex's flames singed my sleeve as he clung on for dear life. I could see Trix and the Elemental Soldiers crouching behind an earthen shield Cal had created using his magic, but the Order's team hadn't been so lucky.

I rose to my feet, and my stomach lurched at the sight of the burned bodies lying behind the gates, scorched beyond recognition. Nausea choked me, and I swallowed down bile. "Guess Alban decided to nuke the place once his address got out."

Question was, where had he gone? Had he expected me to be within range of the blast myself, or had it simply been a warning? Likely the latter—but he hadn't cared if anyone else had got caught in the aftermath. At least two or three inferno cantrips had obliterated the area in front of the manor, and the members of the Order's team who hadn't been able to escape via the node had all met the same end.

Cal's earthen shield collapsed into a pile of soil. "Where's the bastard gone?"

"I don't know." I felt numb, my ears ringing with the blast and the sight of the burned bodies imprinting itself on my vision. Judith lay among the dead. She hadn't got away in time.

Legs shaking with the aftershocks, I retreated towards the node. The Elemental Soldiers crowded in behind me, along with Trix.

"Are we heading back?" Dex asked from my shoulder. "I'd say yes, before another one of those cantrips goes off."

"Not yet," I said. "I'm going to see if I can find Alban's trail. You don't have to come."

"As if we'd let you go alone," said Ryan.

"It might not work." I stood in the centre of the node and pictured Dirk Alban's' face in my mind's eye, recalling the twisting wrongness of his magic...

The node's light swallowed us up. A heartbeat later, we landed in the centre of Elysium, close to the citadel.

"Alban was here?" said Felicity.

"Apparently." I stepped out of the node, frowning up at the citadel. "Is it just me, or does that thing look… weird?"

The citadel's obsidian shape looked oddly smudged around the edges. When I trod closer, the smudges resolved into shadows… shadows as dark as the black hole engulfing the remains of the hotel.

"The fucker turned on the transporter and boosted the spell," Dex said in my ear. "I can feel it from here. The effects are spreading."

Crap. The Houses of the Elements were right here. Had they begun to feel the effects, too? Ryan, Trix, Felicity and Cal looked at the darkness surrounding the tower, each wearing expressions of shock and disbelief.

"*That's* the node?" said Ryan. "The one inside the citadel itself? I thought we shut it down."

"Not permanently." I glanced down at Dex, who'd already began to pale again. "Alban must have turned on the transporter. I bet you anything he's hopping around between the other citadels and doing the same, so the effects of the spell will spread faster."

"What?" Trix's expression was aghast. "Elves have more magic than humans. We might be the next to be affected."

"No," Ryan said. "We'll catch him before that happens."

"What about the people in the city?" asked Felicity. "The Houses of the Elements are right next to the citadel."

"They are, but mages won't die if they lose their magic," I said. "Vampires will, and so will liches, sprites, and other magical beings. Not sure about elves, but if they're anything like mages, using magic near that node will cause it to get sucked into a black hole."

"I have to warn the Elders," Trix said.

"Wait." Ryan caught his arm. "You can't run off now. The elves in their own realm will probably be fine, besides. It's the Parallel which is in trouble."

"Someone needs to warn the Houses, too," said Felicity. "And the Spirit Agents."

"Forget the Houses," said Cal. "The spell won't kill them, right? Losing their magic is better than dying. Might teach them a lesson, too."

"We might need their help," I said. "I need to go and warn the Death King. Get word back to the Order and find what's left of their team, too."

Alban had already killed half the Order's team, but he'd be able to do much more if everyone else in the Parallel lost their magic. Since he'd taken on the magic of his own liches to boost his own, his reserves would be far deeper than usual, and he might well be the last mage standing by the time the dust had settled.

"All right," said Felicity. "I might not like the Houses, but someone has to tell them to move out of range of the tower."

"We'll split the Houses between us," Cal said. "It'll be faster. Ryan…"

"I'll come." They glanced at Trix. "Go with Liv."

"I can't," said the elf. "There's a path to the elves' realm open in the citadel out in the wilderness. Bria left it open so we could easily contact the elves again, but if the spell is spreading through the transporters, it might end up reaching them, too."

"Wait, there is?" Oh, damn. "Is that where Bria went?"

"Yes, and someone needs to tell them what's going on." Trix briefly hugged Ryan. "I'll come back as soon as I can."

Dex cleared his throat. "Since nobody else is volunteering, I'll tell the Spirit Agents, if they haven't already figured it out."

"Okay, but make sure you stay away from the citadel," I said. "I'll meet you all back in front of the castle. If you see Alban, don't fight—run."

The others dispersed, while I hopped through the node again, landing in the swampland. My mind whirled with thoughts. Warning everyone was a necessity, but without a solution, Elysium might well devolve into outright panic. Particularly the Houses, who'd suffered enough of a shock during the battle only a few short days ago.

My feet caught on a piece of fabric. A cloak… attached to a body which lay sprawled in the mud. I came to a halt, my heart leaping into my throat. The rest of the Order's team lay dead in the dirt, their bodies unmarked with any wounds, as though someone had sucked the life out of them with a touch. My shoulder blades prickled at the sight of a lone figure standing in front of the gates to the castle, behind the scattered bodies.

Alban. He'd heard me coming, of course, and he turned to face me with his usual placid expression. "There you are, Olivia."

"Where's Hawker?" More to the point, where was the Death King? *I shouldn't have left him behind.*

"I have no interest in Hawker," said Alban. "I expected you wanted to speak to me, so I decided to come to you instead."

"You killed people." My hands clenched. "You booby-trapped your house and then killed anyone who ran away."

"I assumed you'd have more sense than to go near the place, Olivia," he said. "As for the Order, my expectations weren't as high."

Bastard. "Why did you let Hawker use that spell in London? More to the point, why'd you lead me to believe you were the one who did it?"

"I hoped it would be easier for you to let your lich allies go if you felt their fall was inevitable," he said. "Which it was, due to the curse… as your Order friends knew full well when they enacted it. This is in everyone's best interests."

"You're not acting in the interests of anyone except for yourself."

"Untrue," he said. "I have a select number of people whose fates I care for, and you are one of them."

I gave a derisive laugh. "Yeah, and that's why you led me to believe my friend was dead. That's why you manipulated Hawker, hoping to push him into murdering the Death King in my absence despite the fact that you promised to leave him alone."

"The Death King should have expired a long time ago," he said. "I never concealed that fact."

"By that logic, I should have, too." I stared into his pitiless eyes. "Did you know Hawker murdered me, and I turned into a lich myself? If Hawker hadn't accidentally reversed my fate, I'd be under the effects of this spell of yours, too. Would you be so keen to bleed the magic out of both realms if I'd ended up being one of the first victims?"

"If you won't come with me of your own free will," said Alban, ignoring my words, "how do you feel about making a deal? If you agree, I'll undo the spell my ally foolishly unleashed, nobody has to lose their magic at all, and the liches can continue with their dissatisfying existence."

Dammit. He does know how to undo it.

"You chose me once before," said Alban, when I didn't respond. "You walked into an apprenticeship with me willingly."

"You're still on about that?" I said. "I can't change the past. I can't undo my choices. But you? You don't even *want* to make amends. You want to keep being a manipulative scumbag and murdering innocent people. You're the one who intentionally accelerated your ally's spell, without a hurt for the innocent lives you endangered."

"No lives are in danger," he said. "Only sprites, phantoms, liches and the like, and they don't count as people, do they?"

"More than you do," I fired back at him.

"I assumed you'd be keener to agree to a deal with me if you really did care for them as people, Olivia," he said. "Your decision to continue to resist me says it all."

Anger gnawed at me. He had me by the throat and he knew it, but making an agreement with him would only end in disaster. He'd either put a sting in the tail of our agreement or go back on his word, and then my sacrifice would be for nothing. No... I'd have to find a way to do it myself. "You can make all the conclusions you like. I'm not agreeing to anything you put before me, Alban. We're through."

"Hey, dickhead." Dex zipped over from the node, a torrent of fire flying from his fingertips. "This is for what you did to Liv."

Alban deflected the fire sprite's flaming attack, but he

looked almost uncertain, as though he'd honestly expected me to say yes. "You see how little she values you, sprite."

"You don't know what that even means, Alban," I said. "You've never valued anyone in your life."

Lights flashed, and the Elemental Soldiers ran out of the node to join Dex, exclaiming in shock at the sight of the dead mages. I tensed, yet Alban didn't move to attack them. He merely gave me a searching look and then vanished in a flash of whiteness.

"What the hell was he doing?" Ryan caught up with me, fury in their eyes. "Aside from murdering the rest of the Order's team?"

"Trying to convince me to join him," I said. "He does know how to stop the spell."

"You're not going to say yes?" said Felicity. "We warned the Houses, but they're hopping mad and they want answers. From the Death King."

"Why do they think it's *his* fault?" I marched towards the gates, where several liches flitted about, their faded forms transparent instead of shadowy. Where was the Death King? I walked up the steps and into the entrance hall, where the door to the hall of souls lay partly ajar.

Inside, I found him standing with his back to me, his gaze fixed on the shelves of soul amulets.

"They're vanishing," said Greyson, without turning around.

I stepped closer, seeing the lights around the amulets were paler than ever, and some had gone completely dull. "The spell accelerated. Alban turned on the transporter again."

He lifted his head. "I take it he also gave the Order the slip?"

"Not without booby trapping the house and killing their entire team." I blinked hard. "Greyson… he was outside the castle. He wanted to talk to me."

"He was?" He rotated on his heel, wearing a stunned expression. "I didn't sense him."

His magic is fading, too. Mine must be as well, but I hadn't been paying attention since my body was abuzz with adrenaline. "I turned him down, but he does know how to undo the spell. He told me."

"Right." His voice was quiet. "I won't have you sacrifice yourself. I will go with him instead."

"That won't work." I shook my head. "He wants a successor, not an equal, and I think it's finally dawned on him that I'm the latter and not the former. Anyway, Lord Blackbourne thought *I* could undo the spell. Or you."

If the Order insisted the spell couldn't be reversed, and they'd created the damned thing, then it was beyond me to figure out how to bring it to a permanent end. On the other hand, the Order had purposefully stamped out all research into spirit magic after the war. Their wilful ignorance didn't mean there wasn't an answer.

"Lord Blackbourne prefers to stay out of any conflicts if he can avoid it," said Greyson. "I wouldn't take his lack of responsibility for permission."

"No spell is infinite, though." Even a neutraliser spell had its limits. If the spell burned itself out, for instance… but that wasn't possible with a spell which kept going in an infinite loop. Besides, some magical objects could exist indefinitely if left untouched. Like soul amulets…

My gaze travelled along the shelf of dimming amulets,

drained of their power. Any cantrip might be drained in a similar way, right? If we could unplug it from its power source… or rather, remove it from the node.

"Perhaps not." Greyson dragged his gaze away from the cantrips. "The Elemental Soldiers are back?"

"They are now," I said. "They sent a warning to the Houses and the Spirit Agents, but what we need to do for a starting point is close off all the transporters. All of them. Use neutraliser cantrips, or even infernos. Whatever it takes. Once the link is reduced to existing between Elysium and London alone, I'll try to remove the spell."

The idea sounded simpler than it actually was, considering I hadn't even been able to *see* the source of the spell in the giant black hole of a node.

"We can do that," said Greyson. "The Order's second team will be here soon. I'll send them to the citadels to turn off the transporters."

"I hope they don't meet the same fate as the first one." Poor Judith. "The Houses of the Elements… um, I think they want answers from you."

"Of course they do," said Greyson. "They can wait while we prepare. Did you see Hawker?"

"Nope. Seems he and Alban still aren't friends."

"You can control Hawker using his soul amulet, anyway," he said. "He's not long for this world."

Too bad the other liches might join him. "That just leaves Alban, but we'd be hard-pressed to back him into a corner unless we hit him with a neutralising cantrip. Honestly, though, I'm not sure he wouldn't figure a way to slither out of that one too."

I held Hawker's soul amulet, so I had little doubt I'd be able to deal with him myself if I needed to. Alban was trickier, but our first priority was bringing the spell to a halt… which meant a little experimental spirit magic of our own.

"What do you want to do, then?" asked Greyson.

"Give it a practise run," I said. "The ritual formation, I mean."

His brows shot up. "Are you sure?"

"Don't you think that if the ritual can be used to create a node, then the same spell can be used to return a damaged node to its former state?" I said. "I know that particular node was created by sacrificing a bunch of lives, but I'm not sure it's a requirement. Not if we do it right."

Greyson gave a thoughtful nod. "I think I know what you mean, but if you want to perform this ritual, you'll need one of each mage. Do you want to borrow my Elemental Soldiers?"

"I'll give them back in one piece." My heartbeat kicked up. Considering I was pretty sure a similar ritual gone wrong had kicked off the war, even if Alban had smudged the details, I wouldn't blame the Elemental Soldiers if they said no. Since I was all out of any better ideas, though, this was all we had.

"I'll bring the former Death King's notes," he said. "You ask Ryan and the others."

Here we go. I left the hall of souls and returned to the castle grounds, where the three Elemental Soldiers milled around and Dex flew up to meet me. "The Spirit Agents are on their way to the castle, by the way. Thought you should know."

"Good." I beckoned to Ryan and the others. "Hey. I

have a massive favour I need to ask, and I need four mages to volunteer to help me."

Cal's brows shot up. "Massive favour, huh? You mean the life-threatening sort?"

"Depends whether or not you trust me." I wouldn't lie to them. They'd need to walk into this with the full knowledge of what was at stake.

"I do," Ryan said immediately, to my surprise.

"As do I," added Felicity. "What's the favour?"

Greyson interrupted by descending the stairs, holding a thick leather-bound book in his hands. "There are certain rituals which require one of each type of elemental mage to combine their own magic with a spirit mage. Liv wants to try it out before attempting to use the same ritual to shut down Hawker's spell in London."

"Ritual?" echoed Cal. "Like… human sacrifice?"

"Only if it goes wrong," said Greyson. "Which it won't, because I trust Liv."

"You need all four of us?" said Felicity. "Including Bria?"

"Shit, she's not here." She and Trix both hadn't returned from seeing the elves, in fact. "I shouldn't have sent her away."

Dex gave me a pointed wave. "Did you say you need all four elements?"

"Not you," I said firmly.

"I *am* a fire mage," he said. "Stop being pedantic. I want to help you shut off that damn spell. And I trust you with my life, so there."

I opened and closed my mouth. As far as I knew, there was no reason I couldn't use a sprite in the ritual, since he'd once been a mage. "Okay, get in line. You need to stand in a circle with me in the centre."

The three Elemental Soldiers formed a circle, following Greyson's instructions, while Dex settled into line with them. I stood in the centre and reached for my spirit magic, my hands outstretched. A glow spread around my body, centred on my palms.

"Now you need to draw on the others' magic, too," said Greyson. "All four of them at the same time. Are you sure you don't want me to try instead?"

"I want to give it a shot." Theoretically, he'd be able to do the ritual just as well as I could, but he had countless liches depending on him for their survival. I didn't. "All four of you... use your magic. You don't have to do anything fancy with it. It just makes for easier access."

Fire, water, earth and air stirred in the air, raising the hairs on my arms. Now for the tricky bit. I had to draw on all four of them at once, without taking too much from one person.

I reached out, the same way I did when I pulled Dex's power into my hands. He was the easiest, and fire mingled with the spirit magic in my palms. Then I reached for Felicity and felt the cool rush of water magic as a ribbon of blue connected us—but in the same instant, the fire went out.

"Hang on." Holding the cool essence of water in my hands, I reached for Cal's earth magic, and a bolt of brown-yellow light appeared connecting us, churning the magic in my hands. Ryan's air magic was even more volatile, and the connecting current of green light nearly knocked me on my back when I called it into my hands.

With difficulty, I managed to stay upright, and when I'd caught my balance, I called for Dex's fire magic again.

Fire flooded my veins, mingling with the light in my hands. The colour shifted from orange to green to blue to brown and then back to the pure white of spirit magic again—but brighter than before. As bright as a node, a swirling pool of light between my palms.

Now what was I supposed to do with it? The ritual book hadn't mentioned that part. My body trembled with the effort of holding onto five conflicting forms of volatile magic and trying not to let them all go at once. "How do I break the circle?"

"Don't ask me," Ryan said through clenched teeth. "I can't move."

I braced my feet against the muddy ground, holding the swirling light in my hands. Within, the threads of the individual types of magic were visible, but when they became one, they balanced out. The five elements.

Devon walked out of the castle gates and gave an approving whistle. "Nice going."

"Aren't you supposed to be at home?" My momentary distraction made my attention slip, and a bolt of magic shot from my palms at the sky. "Oops."

"Like I'm gonna miss this one," said Devon. "I'm all set with my neutralising cantrips. I'll help the Order's teams in case they need some pushing around."

"Fair enough, but be careful." I focused on my trembling hands and the current of magic in my grip. Gingerly, I pushed the magic away from me, thread by thread, and the four streams of light separated from one another. Since each was naturally drawn back to its owner, it took less effort than I'd anticipated to give them a push in the right direction. The tremors in my limbs halted, while the glow in my hand died down enough for me to risk lowering my palms.

Cal stumbled out of the circle. "That's better."

"Yeah." Felicity shook her hands. "That wasn't bad at all, though. Didn't hurt a bit."

"I'm glad." I'd successfully channelled all five elements. Now all I needed to do was repeat the same ritual and undo the spell on the node in London before Alban got there first.

The game was drawing to an end. Almost time to face the final boss.

23

Within minutes, the Order's reserve teams showed up, with the expected furore as they stumbled upon the corpses of their fallen members. Most were less than thrilled at the Death King's instructions to turn off the transporters in the citadels rather than hunting down Alban, though since nobody knew where Alban had run to, the citadels were as good a place to start as any.

The Spirit Agents went with them, too, along with Devon. After the events at Alban's house, the last thing I wanted was for her to go running into danger, but she insisted. The quicker the links between the citadels went out, the better, since I didn't know if it would do any good if I attempted the ritual beforehand. Once they'd dispersed through the nodes, I gathered my team of Elements and headed that way myself.

I stood inside the node and pictured London's street clearly, but while the node continued to glow, my feet remained planted firmly on the ground.

"It's not responding," said the Death King. "Try Elysium instead."

Crap. Is the spell affecting the other nodes already?

I fixed an image of Elysium in my head, and in a flash, our team landed on a street I didn't recognise. Judging by the distant smudge of the citadel visible over the rooftops, we were miles out on the outskirts of the city.

"We're nowhere near the right place," I said. "We can't run to the middle of London on foot. It'd take way too long."

I might have been able to try using my spirit magic to travel between realms without a node, like the Death King did, but that would wipe out my reserves at a time I really needed them. Especially if I needed to take three people and a sprite with me.

The Death King stepped up to my side. "I'll help you."

Magic flooded me, bolstering mine with a rush of dizzying energy. "Whoa. How'd you do that?"

"I asked my liches to volunteer their strength," he said. "They know this is our last shot."

As the spiralling current of energy rushed through me, I called the others to come closer. Dex and the three Elemental Soldiers stood close behind the Death King and me as we drew on the depths of the node, magic swirling between us. Then, with his guiding hand on my back, I stepped through...

...and landed in a web of shadow. The darkness had spread even further since last time, leaving the area around the hotel awash in blackness too dense to see through. Any node in the area might well have been snuffed out altogether.

The Death King spoke from behind me. "The ritual

won't work until Elysium's citadel is turned off or weakened as much as possible."

"What do you mean?"

"I mean we can't afford any setbacks," he said. "I need to go and destroy the transporter in Elysium's citadel in person. That will wipe out all the extraneous magic flowing through to the node. I won't put my faith in the Order."

"Good call." I didn't want to conduct the ritual without his steady presence at my side, but we had to stop this madness before it was too late and I doubted we could pull it off with the endless loop of power from the citadels flowing through the transporter and feeding straight into the shadows on the other side. Who even knew what the humans in the middle of London thought was going on, if they could see the shadows creeping across the city? Even if it wasn't visible to ordinary people, anyone who walked through the general area would have the sense that something was wrong.

Greyson's hand brushed mine. "Trust me."

"I do." As he vanished in a flash of white, I beckoned to the others. "Back into formation."

My nerves jittered as the others circled me. Poor Dex was practically transparent, and I kept an eye on him as I prepared to draw on the others' magic. Taking in a steadying breath, I called my spirit magic to my hands, but the shadows swallowed up the glow a second later.

"Crap." I shuffled back. "Not so close."

"We have to stay close to the node," said Dex. "Otherwise our spell won't reach the damn thing."

"I know." Standing on top of it was out of the question, though. "Okay. Let's try again."

I conjured a ball of light and held it tightly, ignoring the tugging of the shadows under my feet trying to draw it from my grip. I had to make this quick, but getting hold of the others' magic was even more difficult than the last time. Every thread I grasped escaped my fingertips, drawn into the abyss, while Dex faded more and more by the second. I called his fire first and held fast, feeding my own magic into him in a desperate attempt to keep him in one piece. Threads of water, earth and air slipped through my fingers, but I reached for them, again and again until the glowing ball in my hands brightened. One thread at a time. Four elements mingling with mine.

Yes. That's it.

Magic flowed in my hands, all five Elements, growing brighter until I could hardly see for the glowing light. The shadows veered towards me, greedily sucking at the magic in my hands, but it kept going. I'd created a looping current like a node.

"Don't move," I warned the others. "I've got this."

The brightness in my hands shifted as I directed the stream of energy to point into the heart of the shadows. The others exclaimed, knocked off balance by the sudden shift in energy, and I found myself struggling to keep my footing as the shadows threatened to snatch the magic from my grasp. I focused my attention on the swirling current of light in my hands instead, its stability keeping me grounded.

The original spirit mages had formed bonds with the other four Elements in order to open each node, and their mutual relationship of trust had forged an unending balance. Likewise, as long as our formation held, the balance of the five Elements couldn't be broken.

A sudden flash of energy rippled through the shadows, which briefly shrank away from our circle, granting me a breath. The darkness momentarily turned transparent, revealing the street of London which appeared mercifully free from shadows from this angle. They'd weakened... but how?

Greyson. He must have shut off the transporter in Elysium, confining the spell to a single node. Without as much magic fuelling the spell, it became a single column of darkness, leaning towards the glowing beam of light in my hands like a plant towards the sunlight.

Ryan sucked in a breath. "Is it weakening?"

"It is, but we need to find the source." I held onto the current of energy, tensing when the darkness touched its edge, but the light didn't bend. Instead, a stream of brightness shone from the pulsing light in my hands and illuminated the area around the shadows.

Including the outline of a disc shape which lay among the ruins. *There it is.* I gingerly moved the current of light until it pointed straight at the cantrip, pushing against it.

The disc rolled over on its side, carrying the darkness with it. Another push sent it tumbling out of sight, and abruptly, the crumbled ruins of the hotel appeared beneath our feet.

"Holy shit," Dex breathed. "Was that it? The spell?"

"Yeah." The node was almost invisible, without the shadows sucking the life out of it... but I'd lost sight of the cantrip when I'd knocked it out of the way. "It's not in the node, but I didn't turn it off. Hang on..."

I took a step forwards, but the current of magic holding all five of us pushed me back like an invisible barrier. I needed to break it first, but despite the absence of the darkness, something held me back. This couldn't be it, surely.

"Well done, Olivia." Alban rose from the ruins of the building, holding the shadowy cantrip in his hand. "Catch."

The cantrip flew into the centre of our formation. Darkness crashed into light, and at once, the shadowy disc began sucking in everything it could reach. The others staggered, knocked off-balance, while Dex yelped in panic, straining to break free of the circle.

"Dex!" I tried to push the fire sprite's magic back towards him, but the torrent of darkness ricocheting around me made it impossible to separate the strands of magic merging in my hands. Worse, the node ignited again, its current of light piercing the sky and adding its strength to our lopsided circle of power.

The cantrip's smoky shadows cut through the heart of our formation, poisoning the light and turning it into darkness again. If I let go of the circle, the shadows would spread through the heart of the node and all we'd done would be for nothing.

Alban watched us, not smiling. Only then did I see people gathering around the ruins of the hotel, including the Elemental Soldiers and various Order members, all of whom stared up at Alban. Yet the true focus on their attention was the current of magic visible in my hands and the shadows threatening to take it apart.

Alban raised his voice to address the crowd. "If the current of magic in Olivia's hands is broken, the cantrip will once again fall into the node and all magic will drain out of both realms if none of you can replicate the spell my admirable apprentice has enacted. I should point out that nobody has managed to complete this ritual in thirty years."

"Is this the time for theatrics?" Ryan glared at Alban from their position within the circle. Dex, meanwhile, pulled a face at Alban, defiant despite his fading form. I couldn't keep draining his power, but if I let go of any of them and the circle broke, the shadows would escape and take over the node. As Alban had intended.

I crouched down and picked up the cantrip, gasping when the shadows burned through the light on my hands. I held on regardless and pushed the light into the cantrip, but the darkness cancelled it out. We were at a stalemate. I could think of only one solution: to take the spell somewhere it couldn't cause any more damage to any of the nodes, and then break the circle. But every ounce of magic in me fuelled my resistance against the shadows and I had none to spare.

The cantrip's shadows sucked at my magic, urging me to let go. This was the manifestation of the threat the Order held over spirit mages like me. Losing their magic had driven both Cobb and Hawker to madness, while I'd been willing to do almost anything to escape the same fate. Yet far worse was the notion of the spell killing Dex, sapping the life out of the other liches, and giving Dirk Alban the power he craved.

"Greyson," I whispered.

"Yes?" He was closer to me than I'd thought, facing Alban with unmasked hate. "I can kill him."

"Don't," I breathed. "He's ready."

No doubt he had enough defences to resist almost anything. He'd even picked up the shadowy cantrip with no visible effects on himself, while it was all I could do to keep from surrendering to the shadows. Cold sweat slid down my spine, while my knees threatened to buckle beneath me.

The Order members apparently hadn't got the memo, because several guards climbed up the hotel's ruins behind Alban. One took aim and threw a handful of flames at him, only for his attack to vanish before making contact. A heartbeat later, the mage screamed, falling to the ground, devoured by his own flames.

Greyson gave Alban a hard stare. "I wouldn't try the same on me. You'll lose."

Don't! I wanted to shout, but I could hardly speak through my chattering teeth. I gripped the shadows tightly, determined not to let them spread any further, but my hands ached and my whole body trembled. If not for the shadows, I had little doubt I'd be able to keep generating magic via our shared connection until I created enough to form a new node, but that wasn't the plan.

Greyson strode past me towards Alban. *No. Don't do it.*

Alban sighed. "I did warn you."

A strangled cry caught in my throat as Alban raised a hand. A shimmering gold barrier formed around him, similar in colour to the torrent of magic in my hands. The lives he'd sacrificed had belonged to mages of all kinds, and he'd taken their collective life force into himself.

Yet Greyson kept approaching him, and a shield of pure white light appeared in front of him, too.

"You killed them, Greyson?" Surprise coloured Alban's tone. "I thought you were loyal to your people."

"I didn't kill them," he said. "They were already dead."

Beneath my feet, the node flared up, and I stumbled as

the light crashed against the shadows in my hand. *I have to go. Now.*

"I'll come back, Alban," I shouted.

Then I called on all the spirit energy burning inside me, all the magic shared between the five of us, and pictured the most distant place in the swampland I could possibly imagine.

Magic burned through my blood and built to a crescendo, then our entire group vanished into the node, carrying the shadow-wreathed cantrip along with us. Alban's shout faded to silence as we landed in the swampland, near the fence circling the castle.

Dammit, that's too close. Yet I didn't have enough power to move us again. All three Elemental Soldiers had fallen to their knees, while the cantrip's shadowy magic remained trapped within our circle.

I had to break the spell, but did I dare take the risk with the other liches in the castle so close? Wait…

My heart climbed into my throat. The faded forms of several liches trickled out of the gates, drawn to the brightness of the light in my hand.

"Go!" I warned them. "Back away. This cantrip I'm trying to contain… it's killing you. It's the source of the spell Alban wants to use to destroy every one of you."

Yet they weren't backing off. Instead, the lichees swarmed around us, drawn to the darkness and light battling in my hands. Drawn to oblivion.

Do they want to die?

Maybe they did, and that was what the last Death King had been looking for the whole time. A way to end his infinite life. A way to move on.

Understanding crashed over me. The unnatural bond

wasn't between the liches and their amulets, but between the liches and the very Parallel itself, which kept them imprisoned, unable to die, unable to truly live as they once had. Phantoms had begun to appear, too, joining the liches' swarm, while the shadows remained in my hand, a solid lump of darkness clashing with the combined power of the five types of elemental magic.

"Liv!" Devon waved at me from near the fence. "Need help?"

"Yes." Inspiration hit me. "Can you throw me a neutraliser spell?"

The shadows might be lethal to any magic they touched, but the cantrip *was* a spell, technically. Would a neutralising cantrip be enough to cancel it out?

Devon reached into her pocket and pulled out a cantrip. "I don't want to break your circle."

"Do it. I'd rather temporarily lose my magic than the alternative."

"Olivia Cartwright!" Alban appeared in a flash in front of our circle, causing Devon to stumble back in shock. The Death King appeared a moment later. His eyes flew wide at the sight of the liches crowding around our group, but his expression hardened when Alban turned on him with a manic glint in his eye.

"Very impressive," he said. "Truly... you're a master at work, Olivia. Now break the circle, and nobody else will have to die."

Like hell was I breaking the circle before I'd extinguished the shadows, not with the liches surrounding me like moths drawn into flames. Beneath the shadows, five kinds of magic ran through my veins, invigorating, bringing me to Alban's equal level. I'd never felt so alive.

Alban's mouth pressed together, then he said, "I really didn't want to do this, Olivia."

He raised his fist, but the Death King got there first, tackling him off his feet. Not with magic but with pure unexpected brute force—and in that armour, it had to hurt. Alban crashed onto his back, cursing explosively. Before the Death King could reach him, he flung a wild handful of magic at the circle.

The shadowy cantrip flew from my grip, *out* of the circle and into a pool of shadows. The liches recoiled from its dark presence, while the three Elemental Soldiers around me dropped to their knees, Dex flopped over in the air with a groan, and the magic in my hands became infinitely heavier. My arms shook. My entire body trembled, yet the combined force of the five elements remained in my hands—sharper, without the shadows to dampen them.

I tilted my head at Alban. "Where *did* you learn the secrets of spirit magic? Who was *your* mentor?"

Alban, back on his feet, gave me a baffled stare. "What does that matter?"

"Oh, it matters." He'd wanted the former Death King's soul amulet for a reason, and he'd known exactly where to find it. "Like the story you told me about the spirit mages trying to save the realms from destruction and accidentally causing the war instead."

Alban continued to look at me with incredulity in his expression. "What of it?"

I held up the shimmering current of golden light, which suddenly felt lighter in my grip, the threads still connecting me to the four mages in my circle. "The last Death King realised your true identity, but you didn't want the secret getting out, did you? Not when you'd taken care to leave no witnesses alive to reveal the cause of the Council of the Elements' demise."

"What are you talking about?" he said.

"The truth is that the nodes between realms were weakening, and the spirit mages were the first to notice." I quoted his own words back at him. "As a result, the spirit mages made a request to the council... but how would you know that if you weren't there?"

Dex flipped upright. "Uh. Liv. He wasn't alive back then."

"I beg to differ," I said. "He was. He just went by a different identity. I assume he changed his name after the former Death King's experiment brought him back to life."

Alban's expression froze. "How on earth did you come up with that absurd theory?"

"The former Death King's records," Greyson cut in. "You and Hawker knew one another before the Court of the Dead ever existed, didn't you?"

Damn, he'd caught on fast. I hadn't considered Hawker's role, but like him, Alban had survived as a lich—at least until the former Death King had turned him back into a human again during an experiment intended to find a way to end the curse. I doubted he'd known *who* he'd brought back to life, considering his own fate.

"Have you any idea how long I've been waiting to bring down the Order?" Alban said, not denying Greyson's statement. "I thought we'd finally done away with them, but they insisted on surviving in their mockery of a current state."

"*You* killed the Council of the Elements?" said Dex. "It

was your farce of a spell which backfired and left everyone dead? You're the reason I died, you fucker."

"What?" said Alban blankly. "You don't remember your past life at all, do you?"

"Not being able to remember doesn't mean it didn't happen, dickhead," snapped Dex. "Let me guess—you staged a coup, along with another bunch of jumped-up spirit mages, and managed to get yourselves killed as well as the rest of us."

"He's right." I gave him a pointed stare. "What did you really do to the original Order of the Elements? Tell me the truth."

Alban's gaze drifted among our group, then he gave the faintest shrug. "Yes, it was something like you guessed. The ritual of the Elements is quite versatile, you know. It can be used to restore life, as well as remove it. Not quite the bridge to the afterlife my predecessors envisioned, but it certainly enabled the spirit mages who agreed with my plan to access the closest to immortality as is possible for humans to attain. Not only that, we might have brought magic to Earth as well as the Parallel and ruled over both."

"But you didn't, because the others refused to help you," I said. "And they didn't take kindly to being sacrificed."

"No," whispered a voice. "We didn't."

A phantom drifted nearer, joining the others clustering around the liches who'd come to listen in. Alban frowned, seeming to notice them for the first time.

"Didn't know you had an audience, did you?" I said to him. "Want to tell them to their faces that you don't think they count as people?"

"That's ancient history," he said. "They died. I was

reborn, and now I carry the souls of a thousand inside me. Nobody can defeat me."

"You killed them," said the phantom, and a dozen voices echoed the same words back at Alban. If I were him, I'd have been a little concerned, but Alban simply gave them his usual calm stare.

"Your master did the same," he said. "He's drawing on your power right this second, in fact."

"I didn't kill them," said Greyson. "They gave me their power willingly. And I can give it back."

Give it back. The glowing light in my hands continued to burn. The combined magic of all five elements, forming one, the element of life. *The ritual of the Elements...* according to the former Death King's research, it could undo any bond.

Spirals of brightness unfurled from my hands, washing over the liches surrounding me, and bathing their incorporeal forms in its golden glow.

Alban saw the light and turned back to me. "See? You didn't need my help after all, Olivia, but you know I can't allow you to stand in my way any longer."

He raised his hands and sent a bolt of magic straight at my hands. The power knocked me flat, and the circle snapped like a piece of elastic, throwing all four of us to our knees. I shouted a warning to everyone within range, but the magic I'd been holding shot straight past the liches and straight into the node near the castle instead, becoming one with its glowing torrent of light.

Alban gave another manic laugh, tinged with anger and fear in equal measures. "Get away from there, Greyson Beaumont."

I spun around, my heart sinking when I realised

Greyson had somehow crossed the grounds to the node. Stepping into the centre of the current, he began to glow all over. He was absorbing its magic—or rather, the magic I'd channelled, a combination of all five elements at once. *What is he doing?*

Golden light ignited in Greyson's hands, washing over the liches assembling in the swamp. He wasn't seriously attempting the ritual single-handedly, was he?

No. He wasn't, because he wasn't alone. A number of sprites soared over the fence from the castle in a cloud of bright colour, and tendrils of magic spiralled from each of them into Greyson.

He was prepared for this. He hadn't simply read the Death King's notes... he'd been ready to put the ritual into action himself. Light spiralled around Greyson, swirling in currents, turning from white to pure gold. More threads appeared in the air, linking him to each of the other liches. An echoing roar came from the direction of the castle, and my mouth dropped open when a flood of soul amulets came soaring through the open doors, drawn by the power radiating around Greyson. Even Alban staggered under the sheer force of the magic Greyson channelled, while the soul amulets joined the swirling hurricane within the node.

"I give you life," Greyson said to the liches. "I return it to you."

Of course it had to be him. Greyson was the one who held their lives in his grip, and it was his hands which held the current of magic connecting them all.

One of the liches took a step forward. A *step*, on a solid foot...

"That's enough." Alban reached for the shadowy

cantrip on the ground, but I threw my lucky dice at him. They snapped through his shield, knocking his hand aside, and I leapt over and clamped my hand over the cantrip.

The shadows bit into me like teeth, while the effects of the golden magic from the combined force of the five elements continued to spread among the liches, turning them into more solid-looking forms. Alban's body glowed with light, coalescing into bolts of lightning in his hands… until I threw the shadowy cantrip into the path of Alban's attack.

The shadows swallowed up the light at once, but as I made another lunge for the cantrip, the last bolt of white-hot magic speared me through the chest.

Alban's face twisted with regret, but beneath it lay resolute determination. "So be it. I will be the last spirit mage standing in this realm."

"Liv!"

I could see the Elemental Soldiers running towards me, but my knees hit the ground and my legs refused to stand up. Dex reached me first, and as the fire sprite's insubstantial form landed on my shoulder, I pushed the little energy I had left into his trembling body. I didn't want to go to the other side alone, and if I had to die, at least Dex would be with me for my last seconds. At least I wouldn't be alone.

My vision blurred and my body tipped to the side. Something sharp dug into my hip. Assuming I'd landed on the shadowy cantrip, I reached for its cold shape, determined to hold the shadows back from reaching the liches until my last breath.

A chill breeze whispered over my skin, and Dex

yelped. My eyes flickered open as a human-shaped shadow fell over me from behind.

"You have something of mine," a voice rasped.

Hawker. His soul amulet must have fallen out of my pocket, and the cool rush of energy in my hand prompted a reminder that some life still remained inside the amulet. *Thanks for that, Hawker.*

I clung onto the soul amulet and drew its energy into myself, ripping out what was left of Hawker's spirit. His scream cut off abruptly as the magic flooded me, bolstered my flagging strength, but it wasn't enough to repair the damage to my soul.

It *was* enough for me to launch to my feet, straight at Alban. My fist slammed into his jaw, hard. Since I'd been holding Hawker's soul amulet at the same time, the hit drew a shrill scream from him. Damn if it wasn't the most satisfying sound I'd ever heard in my life.

Alban staggered backwards, straight into the path of several rapidly solidifying liches. Or rather, mages.

I bared my teeth. "Thanks for the magic lessons, Alban."

"Liv, hang on!" Greyson caught me before I dropped to my knees again, sudden weakness crashing over me. Spirit energy leaked from the wound in my chest, while golden light bathed everyone within sight.

I fought to keep my eyes open, to be rewarded when Devon appeared behind Alban, a neutraliser cantrip in her hand and her face screwed up in concentration as she took aim…

Greyson shouted my name. "Liv!"

I tried to hang on. I really did. But darkness drew me into its embrace, and I knew nothing more.

24

When I next came to awareness, I found myself floating near the ceiling of the hall of souls. Dex hovered across from me, his form brighter than I might have expected. Maybe I'd given him some of my flagging life force after all… but I'd been so sure he was going to disappear.

"Hey," I said to Dex. "I'm a lich again, aren't I?"

"Sorry, Liv."

I swore. Just my luck. At least I'd endured in some form, but it was a poor substitute for life. I'd thought Greyson had managed to bring the others back, but maybe it didn't work on those of us who hadn't originally been part of the curse.

"Did it not work?" I said. "Breaking the curse, I mean? Greyson… shit, where's Greyson?"

"Relax, he's fine," said Dex. "He can't watch you all the time, not with the castle suddenly full of living people who need attention."

"Living people?" I echoed. "What in the world—?"

The door opened and Greyson walked into the room, his gaze rising to meet mine. "Liv."

"Here we go again." I sighed. "Don't suppose you've got any more of that element of life saved up?"

"I don't need it," he said. "Your body is unconscious, but I managed to repair the damage. I'm afraid I had to temporarily bind you to a soul amulet in order to do it, however."

"What... what do you mean?" I looked down at my shadowy form. "My body is dead. I'm a lich. Aren't I?"

"The curse is broken." Greyson smiled at me. "If you like, you can switch back and forth between lich and human."

"You... really..." I floated down to ground level. "How is that possible?"

"You saw it yourself, didn't you?" He turned around to leave the room, while I stared after him in confusion.

"Go on, you should be celebrating." Dex flew down to the same level as me. "Binding a soul to an amulet no longer turns you into a permanent vassal for His Deathly Highness."

"You're still here, though," I said to the fire sprite. "I thought you were fading away."

"You managed to give him enough of your own energy to stabilise him." Greyson halted in the doorway. "At a risk to your life, I might add."

"Nah, I think it was Hawker's life force I gave to him," I said. "I drained his soul amulet."

"So that's how you did it." Dex snorted. "Aria and the others are fine, by the way. They hid in the hall of souls to avoid getting caught up in the madness."

"But..." I paused. "Didn't you want to... I mean, I saw

some of the other sprites disappear. There was no way to recreate their physical forms like the liches, so I guess they chose to move on."

"Yes, I *could* have moved on, too," Dex said, bumping into me in a shower of sparks, "but who else would keep you from dying every five minutes?"

"Hey, watch it. Did you forget how flammable I am like this?" I couldn't hold back a grin as I followed Greyson out of the hall of souls, across the lobby, and upstairs to his suite.

Dex flew ahead of me and pointed to my body lying on the sofa. "Now do you believe us?"

"Damn." I looked down at my body, which hardly had a mark on it. "How do I get back?"

"I'll undo the binding." Greyson held up a soul amulet, which glowed around the edges.

The amulet's light brightened, and I floated downwards into my body, the shadows around my lich form dissipating as I sank into my living form like slipping into a cool bath.

Opening my eyes, I sat up, then grimaced at the rush of vertigo, gripping the side of the sofa with my hand. My other hand reached for the soul amulet Greyson held, from which I felt the merest trace of lingering magic. "What should I do with this?"

"Whatever you like," said Greyson. "You can leave it behind or carry it around with you. The amulet has some of your life essence inside it, same as the others, but the binding isn't permanent."

"The others kept their soul amulets?"

"Everyone who wanted to return," he said. "When the curse unravelled, they were given the choice. Not all of them wanted to stay, but those who did mostly opted to remain in the castle for the time being."

I drew in a breath. "And... Alban?"

"The Order took him into custody," said Greyson. "Devon threw a neutraliser spell at him before he could do any more damage, but you were already... I feared it might be too late to save you."

I rose to my feet and wrapped him in a hug. "You did. And you saved your people from the curse, just the way you promised."

"I couldn't have done it without you."

"Or me," said Dex. "I was the most important."

"Sure you were." Grinning, I released Greyson and spotted my cantrip pouch lying on the sofa. Along with... "Hey, my lucky dice."

"Devon brought them in," said Greyson.

"Speaking of whom." Dex jabbed a finger towards the door, which opened to reveal none other than Devon herself.

"Liv!" She gave me one look and grabbed me in a hug, half-strangling me in the process. "Fair warning... the liches know she's not in the hall of souls any longer."

"And that matters because..." I asked warily.

"They want to thank you," Devon said. "Keeping them away from you has been a full-time job over the last day. We traded shifts outside the hall of souls to give you some peace."

A day? I'd been knocked out for a full day? "Thanks for bringing back my lucky dice. Wait... where's the Order's magic-sucking cantrip? Is it still active?"

"It's sealed in the hall of souls for now," Greyson replied.

That couldn't be a permanent solution, not with the insidious magic remaining inside it, but it wasn't as much of a threat to the inhabitants of the castle, who were no longer dependent on magic to survive. "Good enough for me. Devon, can you tell the other Elemental Soldiers I'll be down in five minutes? I'd like the chance to clean up a little before I show my face."

"Sure." As she retreated, I grabbed Greyson again and drew his mouth down on mine.

"I see you," Dex said in my ear. "If you want to show up in front of the elves looking like you got dragged through a swamp backwards, feel free."

"The *elves?*"

"They're at the castle?" said Greyson.

"Yes, and they're waiting outside your door," said Dex. "Bria needs to work on her punctuality."

I released Greyson, with reluctance. "Never a dull moment, huh. Trix is with them, too?"

"You bet." Dex zoomed out of the room, while I ran to the bathroom to change my contacts and at least wash the mud off my face and hands. Not much I could do about the state of my clothes, but that could wait.

I ran downstairs to join Greyson, finding him and the Elemental Soldiers greeting a group of people wearing odd-looking armoured clothing with a texture which appeared more like wood than metal. They all had long hair and the same pointed, graceful features as Trix did. *Elves.*

Bria gave me a sheepish look when she spotted me. "Sorry we're late."

"Liv!" Ryan hurried to my side. "You're awake."

"Just about." Not only was I awake, I was still wearing

my muddy clothes from the battle. Faced with the impeccably polished elves, I felt distinctly underdressed, but the elves were more interested in talking to Greyson than to me. Dropping my voice, I faced Bria. "Did the elves bring their magical weapons?"

"I thought you didn't need them now the curse on the liches is undone," she said. "Not sure it'd have worked anyway, to tell you the truth."

"Not for that," I said. "There's a cantrip which I'm pretty sure no human means of destruction can make a dent in."

"Really?" said Bria. "Let me check with the elves."

She moved over to the elves and they exchanged a few words in a language I didn't know. Spotting me, Trix scooted over to my side and hugged me. "Sorry we missed all the action, Liv. Ryan was telling me about it all."

"Do *you* know if the elves have the means of destroying a cantrip?" I asked. "Ryan mentioned that shadowy magic-eating cantrip Hawker stole from the Order, right?"

"Yes, of course." Trix's expression turned thoughtful. "I don't see why that wouldn't work."

Part of me remained sceptical, but the other elves backed up his word. When I passed on the message to Greyson, he went into the hall of souls himself and brought out the cantrip, a slight grimace on his face as he fought to keep its shadowy power from eating away at his magic.

The elves, meanwhile, held up a glowing tree branch which I assumed was one of the artefacts which had accidentally brought Harper back from death. It didn't *look* too impressive, but when its vibrant glow came into contact with the cantrip, light swamped the shadows at once. Within seconds, the cantrip crumbled into to nothing more than dust.

"That was dramatic," said Dex.

"What did you expect?" I watched the remains of the cantrip drift away as a breeze swept through the castle's lobby.

"I expected more sparks," he said. "Maybe I'll set the ashes on fire."

"Feel free." The elves had got rid of what was left of the spell, and nobody would be able to use it again. Including the Order.

Not if I had anything to do with it, anyway.

———

The upper room of the Order of the Elements faced Greyson and me across the long conference table. It'd taken us forever to get a face-to-face meeting and I still wasn't entirely sure why they wanted us here.

"We have successfully caught and jailed the member of the Order who set Hawker free," Mr Strong said.

Did they expect a standing ovation for doing the bare minimum? "Good. And Alban?"

"Secured."

Alban was jailed. Stripped of his magic, in fact, though I'd made it quite clear what I thought of *that* spell. In fact, I'd threatened to set the elves on them if any more slip-ups happened.

"In that case, I'd like to know why you invited me here," I said. "What did you want to speak to us about?"

"We want your input on the new laws concerning spirit magic," he said. "Both of you."

"Seriously?" I glanced at Greyson. "In what way?"

"We'd like your perspective on the current status of spirit magic, for a start," said Mr Choudhary. "We witnessed the events in London and saw the terrible danger you put yourself in to fix the node. I understand that the magic you used was a modified version of the spell used to create the Parallel itself."

They'd got the story from the Death King directly, since Alban wasn't exactly a reliable witness. To the end, he'd denied everything he'd already confessed to in front of the entire audience of liches. The Order didn't know his previous identity yet, but I had little doubt someone would figure it out eventually. Besides, he'd committed enough crimes in his present life to spend the rest of his days behind bars.

"If there had been no spirit mages present, then Alban would have succeeded in his plan," I said to them. "He survived the war by hiding among the liches and always planned to return to his former life as a spirit mage. If he hadn't taught me everything he knew, I would never have been able to stop him."

"If spirit magic had been legal, more spirit mages would have been there to help him," said Mr Strong. "More lives would have been lost."

"Alban never let the law get in his way," I said. "Spirit magic was banned, yet even being dead didn't stop him from taking advantage of his position among the liches to return to life. Besides, there *are* more spirit mages out there than you want to admit. Not just the Spirit Agents in the Parallel, but with the curse broken on the House of Spirit, the numbers will increase even more."

"Far more than you'll be able to control," said Greyson. "Besides, it would be a waste of talent for them all to be confined to the Parallel."

"What are you implying?" Mr Oliver said. "You expect us to let people like Alban train the next generation of mages?"

"All I want is for spirit magic to be legalised," I said. "Of course they'd have to follow the regular laws, but it's not always practical for the mages to live in the Parallel. If they're born into a regular family like I was, for instance, or into a family of other magic users. Most of the Spirit Agents were forcibly separated from their families."

"Precisely," said Greyson. "I spent most of my teenage years living in a house of underage mages who'd been estranged or torn from their families, directly because of the Order and the Houses of the Elements' laws. It's no way for a child to grow up, and if anything, it fuels the likelihood of them turning to lawbreaking out of desperation."

"Understandable," said Mrs Bell. "But we can't let dangerous magic run rampant either."

"I agree," said Greyson. "The laws against crossing into the Parallel without a permit make it almost impossible to train an Earth-born mage, whether in spirit magic or otherwise. As it is, they're forced to pick one world by default. Most choose the Parallel, which both deprives the Order of their talent and leaves them vulnerable to those in the Parallel who are out to take advantage of desperate mages."

"Treating people like criminals only pushes them in

that direction," I said. "You've seen the evidence for yourselves."

We went through a few more points before they closed the meeting. While I doubted that we'd get our way on all fronts, the upper room had at least made notes of our suggestions. There was no denying the population of spirit mages had soared after the liches had returned to life. Most had opted to stay in the castle for now, but others had moved elsewhere, and sooner or later they'd run up against the Order's rules. While spirit magic remained illegal here in the UK, I hoped that we might be able to convince Order to relax their rules. In time, we'd forge a future where nobody would end up facing the choices I had.

As for Alban? He'd spend the rest of his days in a secure cell, without magic, without influence, and without power. Everyone knew what he'd done, including his role in the war, and even the Order's rules preventing the former liches from leaving the Parallel hadn't stopped word spreading about the fate of the House of Spirit. According to Bria, the Houses of the Elements were gradually reforming, too, aided by the Spirit Agents, and there was also a campaign to bring back the House of Spirit with Greyson as the head. He had yet to reveal his thoughts on that particular request, but frankly, he had more than enough demands on his attention already. I should know.

As we walked out of the Order's headquarters, Lord Blackbourne glided past and gave both of us a nod on his way into the building.

"What are you doing here?" I asked the vampire lord.

"I've been invited to discuss the future relationship

between the Order and the vampires of Arcadia," he said. "I believe we're going to start with cantrips. I've often thought about getting into the trade."

I wonder what brought that on? The Death King was still the official owner of the Collective of Spells, though they'd gone back to selling cantrips to the Order again now they were no longer under Alban and Hawker's command. Of course the vampire had taken the Death King's acquisition as a personal challenge. It seemed their rivalry would never cease, at least on the vampire's end.

"Good luck with that," Greyson told him.

As the automatic doors closed behind the vampire, I grinned. "He doesn't know what he's getting into, does he?"

"Not in the slightest." Greyson slid his hand into mine as we walked away from the Order's headquarters. "Do you think they'll relax the laws? The Order?"

"I think they will," I said. "Then again, I was naïve enough to spend years hoping they'd stop being dicks to me."

"And I gave up hope altogether," he said quietly. "I think the upper room is starting to see things our way, though. I'd like to give some of the other spirit mages the chance to speak to them."

"Does that mean you don't want to be the head of the new House of Spirit?"

Greyson was silent for a moment. "I'm not sure the former liches will *let* anyone else be the leader, to be perfectly honest."

"No, we won't," I agreed. "Even Dex wants you to lead the House and he isn't even part of it."

"I've wondered about letting sprites join," said

Greyson. "If they want to. Since the other Houses don't recognise them as mages."

"Dex and Aria will be happy to join, I'm sure." Mav had gone back with Harper, as far as I was aware, but while the other sprites who'd been freed from the citadel had free run of the Parallel, they tended to prefer hanging out near the castle, because there was less chance of being caught by unscrupulous mages.

Some things didn't change. Including the Death King's fearsome reputation, for instance. Though the Court of the Dead was much less creepy than it used to be, evidenced when we crossed over into the swampland and were greeted by an enthusiastic *neigh*.

Neddie, now a bay with a glossy coat, butted his head against my hand when I walked up to him. "Hey, there."

"He's much less temperamental than he was before," said Greyson.

"That's because he's alive again." The life energy which had flooded the swamp when the liches had returned from death had had some other unexpected consequences as well. "I know I'm not complaining. Anyway, will I see you at our D&D game this afternoon?"

"I might be a little late," he said. "I have another meeting with the Houses of the Elements."

"They're not that important."

"I'm trying to make a good impression."

"I'd prefer it if you scared the shit out of them." I didn't mind him being a bit late to the game, though. It'd give Devon and I the chance to figure out how to incorporate an extra character into our team. "Let me know when you're on your way."

"Sure." He kissed me goodbye. "See you later."

———

"Natural fucking twenty!" I punched the air. "Thank you, lucky dice."

The others cheered as Devon flicked over the miniature dragon I'd defeated with one decisive stab. Our living room was a tad more crowded than usual, since all four Elemental Soldiers were crowded around the table along with Trix, Craig and Carla. The latter two had kept their jobs working for the Order, though they'd made their views on the new spirit magic laws clear when asked. So had Devon, though she joked that she'd rather the former liches stayed in the Parallel so they wouldn't keep asking to join our D&D group. I didn't know who'd decided to tell everyone, but we were inundated with requests lately.

Maybe if I talked Greyson into setting up his own game as the DM, they'd start their own. I had yet to hear from him, but he was probably stuck in the Parallel dealing with the Houses of the Elements.

With the last dragon defeated, Devon moved the campaign along. Naturally, our first interruption came when Dex was in the middle of mimicking a volcanic eruption which accidentally caused an actual fire. As we were trying to fan the flames away from the cardboard, the doorbell interjected with a strident cry of "INCOMING!"

"Invite anyone else?" I asked Devon.

"No." She shooed Dex away from the table and doused the flames with a swiftly applied cantrip. "Nobody who rings the doorbell, anyway."

I went to answer, prepared to tear the Order a new one if they dared to interrupt our game, and found Mum and Elise on the other side. The latter was heavily pregnant by now, and positively glowing with it.

"Are you busy?" Mum said. "Oh, we'll wait until you finish your game."

"Sorry, it's my fault for calling a daytime gaming session," I said. "It's the first chance we've had in a while. You can come and watch if you like. We have about an hour left, but we can curtail it."

"Oh, don't stop on our account," Elise said. "We'll watch."

And I'll make sure Dex behaves himself. It was their first unexpected visit in a while, but I'd brought it on myself by telling them we'd handled all the trouble and that they were welcome to drop by any time.

When I led them into the living room, I gave Dex a stern look telling him not to freak everyone out. Typically, Mum spotted him right away. "Is that part of your game?"

"Am I what?" said Dex, making her jump. "Yes, I'm part of the game. The best part, in fact."

"Dex." Ah, hell. They'd seen him already. I might as well attempt an introduction. "Mum, Elise, this is Dex. He's a friend of mine."

"Isn't he adorable?" Mum said. "What is he, a fairy?"

"A *what?*" If steam had come out of Dex's ears, I wouldn't have been surprised. "No, I am *not* a fairy."

I bit back a grin, but Elise looked less certain. "Is he like those creatures who came to our house?"

"Not at all," I said. "His name's Dexter, Dex for short. He's a fire sprite."

"I used to be an important mage," he added. "It's an honour to meet you."

To my relief, that seemed to suffice. My family didn't need to be burdened with all the details, but I'd been keeping them at arm's length for too long. Since I'd lost my memories, I'd effectively cut them out of my life rather than attempting to find a way to reconcile my past and my present. I didn't want that to happen with my new sibling, too. As Mum smiled up at Dex while he cartwheeled around the ceiling, hope sparked inside me that I'd be able to find a compromise that would work for everyone.

As I went to introduce the other players to Mum and Elise, the node lit up and the Death King stepped out of the air into our living room. Dex released several sparks in fright. Mum jumped, steadying Elise by her elbow. Everyone else leapt to their feet, while Greyson rotated to face me. "Is this not a good time?"

The players jostled to make space for one more at the table, while Dex started juggling sparks to amuse Mum and Elise as I crossed the room to Greyson's side.

"No," I said. "It's perfect."

ABOUT THE AUTHOR

Emma is the New York Times and USA Today Bestselling author of the Changeling Chronicles urban fantasy series.

Emma spent her childhood creating imaginary worlds to compensate for a disappointingly average reality, so it was probably inevitable that she ended up writing fantasy novels. When she's not immersed in her own fictional universes, Emma can be found with her head in a book or wandering around the world in search of adventure.

Find out more about Emma's books at
www.emmaladams.com.